THE CHICAGO WAY

MICHAEL HARVEY
THE CHICAGO WAY

Quercus

First published in Great Britain in 2007 by

Quercus
21 Bloomsbury Square
London
WC1A 2NS

A CIP catalogue reference for this book is available
from the British Library

ISBN-10 (HB): 1 84724 172 7
ISBN-13 (HB): 978 1 84724 172 6
ISBN-10 (TPB): 1 84724 173 5
ISBN-13 (TPB): 978 1 84724 173 3

This book is a work of fiction. Names, characters,
businesses, organizations, places and events are
either the product of the author's imagination
or are used fictitiously. Any resemblance to
actual persons, living or dead, events or
locales is entirely coincidental.

10 9 8 7 6 5 4 3 2 1

Printed and bound in Great Britain by Clays Ltd, St Ives plc.

In memory of:

Michael Marchetti
2002–2005

Fallon O'Toole McIntyre
2002–2004

Matthew Christian Larkin
1958–1999

It is hard to contend against anger. For whatever it craves, it buys with its life.

— HERACLITUS

You wanna get Capone? Here's how you get him. He pulls a knife, you pull a gun. He sends one of yours to the hospital, you send one of his to the morgue. That's the Chicago way. . . .

— SEAN CONNERY AS OFFICER JIM MALONE,
THE UNTOUCHABLES

THE CHICAGO WAY

CHAPTER 1

I was on the second floor of a three-story walk-up on Chicago's North Side. Outside the Hawk blew hard off the lake and flattened itself against the bay windows. I didn't care. I had my feet up, a cup of Earl Grey, and my own list of the ten greatest moments in Cubs history.

For the first half hour I was stuck on number one. Then I realized the greatest moments at Clark and Addison are always about to be. With that I settled in and mapped out the starting rotation for next year's world champions. That's when I saw him.

Actually, I sensed John Gibbons before I saw him. But that's just how it was with Gibbons. From waist to shoulders he was of one dimension, that being massive. His head sat on a bulldog neck, with short ears and gray hair clipped close. His nose showed the back rooms of Chicago's alleys. His eyes were still clear, cool, and blue. He cornered me with a look and smiled.

"Hello, Michael."

Gibbons had been retired from the force five years now. I hadn't seen him in four, but it didn't matter. We had some history. He shook off the rain and threw a chair toward my desk. He sat down as if he belonged there and always had. I put the Cubs away, pulled open the bottom drawer, and found a bottle of Powers Irish. John took it straight. Just to be sociable, I gave Sir Earl a jolt.

"What's up, John?"

He hesitated. For the first time I noticed his suit, uncomfortably cheap, and his tie, a clip-on. In his hands he twisted a soft felt hat.

"Got a case for you, Michael."

He always called me Michael, which was okay since that was my name. I didn't want to derail him, but my curiosity held sway.

"Jesus, John, who's dressing you these days?"

The big man reddened a bit and looked down at the outfit.

"Pretty bad, huh? The wife. Did you know the wife, Michael?"

I shook my head. I didn't know anything about John that wasn't three years old. His personal file at that time read WIDOWER. His first wife, an Irishwoman from Donegal, got a message from her doctor one day about an X-ray. Two weeks later, she was gone. I had sent a card and given John a call.

"The wife, the second wife that is, she left about a year ago," Gibbons said. "She was a younger type, you know."

John always had a weakness for them. Women, that is. It's been my experience if you have that sort of weakness, the younger ones tend only to aggravate the situation.

"So you been dressing yourself?" I said.

"For some time."

"And you get all dressed up to come here?"

A nod.

"To see me?"

Another nod.

"I got a case, Michael."

"So I gather."

I freshened his drink and poured a bit more hot water into my mug.

"You remember 1997."

"Before my time," I said.

"Not by much. Anyway, it was Christmas Eve. I had the windows rolled down. You remember I used to keep the windows down. Even when it was cold. Well, I'm driving the squad by myself. Down in South Chicago."

I knew South Chicago. A collection of warehouses and whorehouses. Dry docks and rough trade. A nasty bit of Chicago, crumbling at the edges and blending into Indiana gray.

"I hear a shot," John said. "Roll around a corner and see this girl running down the middle of the street. Head-to-toe blood. The guy is right behind her. He's got a .38 in one hand and a knife in the other. Sticking her as they run."

John closed his eyes for a moment and left the room. When he opened them, he was back. I didn't feel so comfortable anymore.

"Couple decades on the job, Michael. Never saw anything close to it. I get out of the car, she's coming right at me. I just catch the both of them. He's on top and I can still hear that knife. Made like a suction noise. I reach around with my piece and put it to his head. For the first time he registers me and stops."

"None of this is ringing a bell, John."

"It should ring a bell, huh?"

I nodded.

"Well, let me finish. So we are all three on the ground. Me with the gun to his head and the girl in between us. Her face was about six inches from mine. I could smell the death on her, you know?"

I knew.

"So we untangle. I put the guy on the ground and cuff him. He says nothing. I slap him around a bit. Still nothing. I look at the girl. She's cut up pretty good, stabbed more than once in the chest. I get a pulse and call for the medics."

John got up and walked across to the window.

"Hot in here, isn't it?"

John cracked the window.

"It's thirty-five outside with freezing rain and gusts," I said.

"Gusts?" His shoulders turned my way and the rest followed.

"That's what they called them," I said. "Gusts. Gusts ain't good."

John left the window open and walked back to the chair.

"So we get this girl into an ambulance. She was a looker, Michael. Did I tell you that?"

I was waiting for that part. "Let me guess. You fell for her."

"Jesus, Michael. She was covered in blood and half-dead. Besides, she was just a kid."

"Go on."

"Anyway, I find out she was running from his car. It's a shit-box Chevy idling in the middle of the street. I pop the trunk and what do I find?"

"Tell me."

"Sheets of plastic. Rolls of the stuff. And rope. Lots of rope. I open the driver's door. There's plenty of blood. Under both seats, I find custom-made carriers. In one, he's got a bulldog shotgun. In the other, he's got a machete strapped up there. Over both visors, two more leather fittings. One for the gun he had. The other for the knife."

"Not the guy's first dance?"

"No sir," John said. "So I take him downtown and throw him in the slam. It's past midnight, I figure I can sort him out tomorrow."

"And?"

"I come in the next day. He's gone."

"Gone?"

"The chief then. You didn't know him. Dave Belmont."

"Heard the name," I said.

"Nice guy, career cop. Dead now. Didn't ever want any beefs. Just keep your mouth shut and put your time in. That kind of guy. Anyway, he takes me into the office. Says forget about it. Says the guy is gone and it's over. Never happened. Then he gives me this."

From his pocket John Gibbons took out a piece of green velvet. Clipped inside was a silver Police Medal. The highest award a Chicago cop can get. Score one and your career is made.

"Those are hard to come by, John."

"Part of the deal. I get the medal, a pay raise, and promotion. In return . . . "

"You forget about it."

"That's right. So I did."

"And nine years later you want to do what?"

"Well, I really don't want to do anything. But then I got this."

From his other pocket John Gibbons pulled a letter.

"And what is that?"

"It's a letter."

"I can see that."

"From the girl. The girl from that night."

"From nine years ago?"

"Yeah."

"She didn't die, I take it."

"We need to help her, Michael."

"We . . . "

"I poked around a bit." Gibbons shrugged. "Didn't really get anywhere."

As a detective, my old partner was a good piece of muscle. Someone to break down doors, even if he had no idea what might be on the other side.

"You're the best I ever worked with," Gibbons continued. "You know it. I know it. Everyone on the force knew it. If you can help out, I'd be grateful."

The Irishman threw an envelope across the table. I opened it up and enjoyed the warm feeling money can sometimes give a person. Then I looked up and across the desk.

"Tell me about the girl," I said.

Gibbons began to talk. I picked up the letter and, reluctantly, began to read.

CHAPTER 2

The phone rang at three-thirty the next morning. I didn't want the phone to be ringing at three-thirty. But there it was.

I reached for the receiver and knocked the whole thing onto the floor. Then I got up to turn on the light and hit my toe on the steel footing of the nightstand. I cursed appropriately and picked up the receiver. The voice at the other end was breathy, but one I didn't recognize.

"Mr. Kelly?"

"Yes," I said.

"Is this Mr. Kelly?"

I answered who else would it be, and wondered about the face attached to the voice.

"Mr. Kelly, this is Lisa Bange calling from Channel 6 Action News."

Three questions buzzed through the early morning fog I call my brain: What kind of woman has a last name of Bange? Why was Channel 6 Action News calling me at three-thirty in the morning? And what kind of woman has a last name of Bange?

"Hi, Lisa Bange," I said. "What can I do for you?"

"We are calling to get a comment—"

Lisa stopped and I heard some voices argue at the other end of the line.

"Mr. Kelly?"

"Still here," I said.

A bated Bange breath.

"Sorry," she said.

"So, Lisa. Here we are. Just you, me, and three-thirty in the morning."

"Yes, Mr. Kelly. I'm calling to see if you have any comment on the shooting death of a Mr. John Gibbons."

I keep a copy of the *Iliad* in the original Greek on the dresser next to my bed. Beside it is Richmond Lattimore's translation. The only translation worth owning as far as I can see. Behind these volumes sits a nine-millimeter Beretta in a holster. Lattimore might not appreciate the subtlety; Odysseus certainly would.

I checked the clip on the Beretta, then the safety. Lisa kept talking.

"He was shot twice. In the stomach, I think. Down by Navy Pier. But not in the water. Mr. Kelly?"

"Yes, Lisa."

"Well, your business card was found on his person. And so we just thought . . . "

"Where you located, Lisa?"

She seemed surprised. Like everyone in the city of Chicago knew where Channel 6 Action News was.

"Three hundred North McClurg Court."

"Do you have footage of the crime scene?" I said.

"B-roll? Sure."

"I'll give you a statement, and you let me look at what you have. Deal?"

Lisa was in over her head. But I knew the voices were there. After a moment she came back on the line.

"Deal."

"See you, Lisa."

I hung up the phone and got dressed.

CHAPTER 3

The first thing I noticed about Channel 6 was the slant. Not an editorial slant. Channel 6 was built on a landfill and in the process of sliding into Lake Michigan. The smart guys among us would deem both landfill and the notion of sliding into an abyss appropriate analogies for Chicago's local news. Not being a smart guy, I was there for Lisa Bange.

Not that I didn't care about John Gibbons. I did. But he was dead, and nothing I could do would change that. On the other hand, I was out of my bed at four o'clock in the morning, walking down a sideways plastic hallway, on my way toward a newsroom full of people I would either hate or despise. I would view the tape and try to get a line on Gibbons' killer before the cops dumped the whole mess. I figured that was more than enough for someone I hadn't seen in four years before yesterday. I was doing my best. And if Lisa Bange happened along the way, so be it.

She was sitting in a cubicle at the end of the hall, drinking what looked like coffee and smoking what looked like a cigarette.

She was five feet eight and great-looking in that newsroom sort of way. Picture long sweaters and jeans that hang pretty well. Long-limbed and athletic, with loose brown hair and Irish skin the color of cream. She was worth getting out of bed for. She also wasn't Lisa Bange.

"Down there," she pointed.

"You're not Lisa Bange, are you?"

"Down there." She spoke without taking her eyes off the newspaper. *Tribune* crossword.

"Seven down," I said. "Five-letter word for *nonsense*. Try *hooey*."

She lifted her blues from the accursed ink. "*Hooey*, huh?"

I nodded. She scribbled.

"It fits."

"What can I say? I'm good with words."

She pointed again. "See how good you are down the hall." At least this time she smiled.

Down the hall was the Channel 6 newsroom. For four o'clock on a Sunday morning, it had the action thing down pretty well. I was directed to a long row of gray cubicles. Inside the last one I found a thin set of shoulders, hunched over a TV monitor, stop-watch in hand.

"Lisa Bange," I said.

A large pair of 1950s cat-eye glasses appeared over the top of the TV. Directly underneath said glasses was a pallid face twisted into a silent shriek, masquerading as a smile. How pleasant it all sometimes seems. Until you get out of bed, that is.

"Yes," she breathed.

I introduced myself. With a pencil Lisa vaguely pointed to a corner set of cubicles. They were green. I assumed that set them apart.

"Over there. Diane wants to speak to you."

I guess I was supposed to know who Diane was. Not being an avid fan of Channel 6 Action News, I was at a loss. Still, I figured she was the star of this little drama. And she had to be a sight better than Lisa.

"Diane?" I said.

Three heads huddled around a desk turned in perfect sync. They fixed me with a single look, one of practiced disdain. Inside the newsroom Cerberus sat the fatted calf. The pot of gold, if you will, at the end of the *Action 6 News* rainbow. Also known as the anchorwoman.

"You mean Ms. Lindsay," said one of the heads.

"I guess so," I replied.

Quick, like the detective I am, I reached in and spun Her Highness around by the chair. Diane Lindsay gave a bit of a gasp. She had headphones plugged into a small TV set and had not heard a word we said. Across the screen rolled a stretcher. I noted a soft felt hat at the end of the gurney. Two EMTs loaded John Gibbons into an ambulance. Then the tape cut to a single shell casing, cold in the Chicago night.

Ms. Lindsay removed the headset, looked at me, and back at the tape. Then she shut the machine down.

"Mr. Kelly."

She was good-looking. In a redheaded, cold, clinical sort of way. The kind of person you'd think was attractive if you were into guilt and relentless remorse. I didn't have a hankering for either. And Ms. Lindsay didn't seem to take a liking to me anyway. Still, it was four in the morning and I didn't much give a damn.

"You called me down here," I said. "I'd like to see the rest of the tape."

Diane's acolytes had moved around me in a loose sort of triangle. Two took notes. The other sized me up for the boneyard.

"I believe Ms. Bange told you we could talk about that," Diane said.

"Yeah, okay. Listen, we don't talk about anything until we get rid of the audience."

Diane gave the trio a look, and they loped off to a solitary corner of the newsroom.

"Now, Mr. Kelly. Let's chat."

I unclipped the Beretta I'd snuck past the receptionist who, if there was a God in heaven, would have been Lisa Bange. I put the piece on the desk and sat down. Diane took a fresh pencil from the red hive atop her head. Her eyes fastened on the gun as she rammed the wooden end of her number two into an electric sharpener. She brandished the polished lead and pointed to a stack of legal documents that had surfaced at my elbow.

"You'll have to sign all of these before we can let you view any tape shot by Channel 6."

"You mean Channel 6 Action News," I said.

She smiled. I signed.

"There you go. Channel 6 Action News wants to sue me, they get into that long line heading down the Action News corridor."

I pointed toward the hall. Diane just looked at me.

"Now, Mr. Kelly, how do you know Mr. Gibbons?"

"You mean how *did* I know Mr. Gibbons? I mean he's dead, right?"

Diane confirmed with the slightest of nods. John Gibbons was now officially dead.

"He was my partner a while back. On the force."

"Any idea what he was doing down by the pier?"

"None."

"He had your card in his pocket."

"He was a friend."

"He was shot with a nine-millimeter semiautomatic." Diane looked across the desk at my piece. I shrugged.

"You're a private investigator now," she said.

I gave her a nod. This was getting boring.

"Let me see if I can speed this up for you, Diane. No, we were not working together. And yes, Diane, I might be lying. If we were working together on something, I sure as hell wouldn't tell you. Not without getting something in return. Now are you going to roll that tape or do I get to take it home with me?"

"Why do you want the video?" she said.

"The cops tipped you to me, right?"

Now it was her turn to demur.

"Either they think I'm good for the murder," I said, "which is insane, and therefore probably what you suspect. Or they want to know what Gibbons was working on and they think I might know."

"What was he working on?"

I studied a piece of green cubicle just above Diane's head and to the left.

"Look, Kelly," she said. "You're right. The cops did tip me. They do want to talk to you."

The slightest of pauses, and then she continued.

"Now, why would that be?"

I shrugged.

"Here's the deal," I said. "I get anything I think you can use, I'll let you know. If I can, I'll do it before I go to the cops. But it's a two-way street. You screw me and . . . "

I shrugged again.

"Just don't screw me."

"Deal." Diane stuck out her hand. I held it longer than I wanted.

"Now, how about the tape," I said.

She pulled a VHS cassette off the desk.

"This is a dub of the footage we shot tonight. You can take it home. With one additional condition."

"And what might that be?" I said.

"That you take me with you."

Approximately three and a half minutes later, we were in a cab, heading south on Michigan Avenue.

CHAPTER 4

So you're thinking you're going to turn the page and find me in flagrante delicto with Red. Right? Wrong. Diane was just joking. Some strange brand of anchorwoman humor, no doubt.

She did, however, buy me a drink. In Chicago, at a few minutes before five in the morning, the choices are limited but endlessly interesting. We went to the Inkwell, a local hangout for news types, tucked into the shadow of the Michigan Avenue bridge.

"So, Mr. Kelly." Diane drank her whiskey neat with a water chaser. I had a Lite beer from Miller. I figured we were both putting on airs.

"So, Ms. Lindsay."

"Here's to your friend."

"Associate," I said and cracked my tooth on a peanut shell that felt like it was filled with cement. When I opened it, petrified peanuts turned to dust and fell to the floor.

"I hadn't seen John Gibbons in four years before yesterday afternoon."

"That's how he got your card?" Diane said.

"He wanted some help on a case. A woman was assaulted. Long time ago."

I motioned to the bartender. He was asleep, so I threw a peanut at him. It nearly knocked him into the beer cooler. He came out with another Lite.

"And less than ten hours later, Gibbons winds up shot," Diane said. "Shot as in dead."

"The worst kind," I said.

Diane drained her glass. A fresh one appeared at her elbow.

"You know what we call that in the news business, Mr. Kelly?"

"A coincidence?"

"No, Mr. Kelly. In the news business, that's a story."

"I don't know much about news stories. But I do know a little bit about murder. Gibbons wasn't the type to go into anything blind. He could handle himself and knew it."

My little speech gave Diane pause.

"Your friend was shot at a range of one to two feet," she said and passed over a copy of the initial police report. "He wasn't carrying a gun and there were no signs of a struggle."

I glanced through the report and laid it down by my elbow.

"That's interesting, Ms. Lindsay. But let me ask you a question. How much do you make for a living?"

The anchorwoman shot her glass back to the bar and got up to go. I stopped her in an easy sort of way.

"Now don't go off getting offended. Let's say it's a half million."

She started to get up again.

"Okay, okay. Let's say it's a million. Why does someone who gets paid a million dollars go to her TV station in the middle of the night to cover a story about a retired Chicago cop who gets stiffed?"

Diane smiled. Maybe a little too quick for her own good. Then she turned back to the bartender. I shrugged, walked to a window, and looked out. It was the gray just before morning. Buildings blurred and crowded close together. Wisps of fog slid across the surface of the Chicago River, running fast and steady from the locks and Lake Michigan beyond.

Diane sidled close and offered a fresh drink. This time it was whiskey, like hers. She laid her forehead against the window. The last whispers of night pushed gently against the glass. We stayed that way and watched for a while, until the first cold fingers of dawn brushed the top of the Wrigley Building, moved down the white lady, and pretended to warm the city below.

"What's your deal, Kelly?"

"Huh?"

She turned and gave me a look only single women over thirty can manage.

"You're what, thirty-two, thirty-three?"

I took a sip of whiskey and nodded. I was really thirty-five, but what the hell.

"Ever been married?"

I shook my head.

"Engaged?"

Another shake.

"Afraid?"

I shrugged.

She shrugged.

"With these kinds of conversation skills, you should be."

"I love it when you're charming," I said.

"What do you know about the TV business in Chicago?"

"I turn on the TV and there it is."

"Chicago's the third-largest market in the country," she said. "Far and away, the biggest snake pit. I'm in the last year of my contract with a news director who likes blondes and bodies. I have neither."

I was about to disagree but thought better.

"I need a big story or six months from now I'm shooting consumer pieces in Flint, Michigan. After five years in Chicago, Flint doesn't work for me. In fact, Flint never worked for me. Bottom line, I just don't have a lot of time here, Kelly. Then again, if the police are any indication, neither do you."

At least she smiled when she said it.

THE SKY WAS TINGED a smoky sort of pink as we exited the Inkwell. I held the door open for a couple of cops I knew, out-of-uniform guys. They ducked their heads when they saw Diane, but she didn't seem to notice. She was quiet. Maybe she was thinking about the murder. Maybe she was thinking about going to bed with me. Maybe she was just drunk.

"Tell you what," she said. "Why don't you read through the police report and look at the tapes. Then we can touch base."

A taxi pulled to the curb. She stepped into the back and rolled down the window.

"Nice meeting you, Mr. Kelly."

"Bye, Diane."

The cab began to pull away, then paused.

"Oh, and Mr. Kelly . . . "

I leaned forward. She did the same. Our faces hovered at the precipice, inches apart.

"Yes, Diane."

"Whoever killed your friend fired from close range. Makes me think Gibbons must have known his attacker. Probably trusted him."

I nodded.

"And well, Mr. Kelly, doesn't that make you a legitimate suspect?"

She blinked once and waited.

"Talk to you, Diane."

I gave the cab a rap and off it went. She was right, of course. John Gibbons had to have known his killer. And trusted him. Unless the killer was a woman. Then all bets were off.

CHAPTER 5

The cabbie dropped me a half block from my flat. His rig belched white smoke as it drifted around a corner, and I tasted the grit at the back of my throat. My apartment was one of three in a walk-up graystone. Not a bad place, but better in the summer when Wrigley Field was only two blocks away.

I fully expected to find Chicago's finest camped on my stoop. Instead, I found the Sunday morning paper and a Saturday evening blonde. Not necessarily in that order.

She scattered a smile around the corners of my doorstep. I stepped forward to inhale as much as I could. I figured she hadn't opened her mouth yet and this might be as good as it got. I was right.

"Hi, Mr. Kelly," she said. "My name is Elaine Remington. I'm the woman from John Gibbons' letter. The one who almost got killed."

From her bag Ms. Remington pulled a more than capable-looking nine millimeter and pointed it in the general direction of my left eye.

"I'd like to talk to you," she said.

"Sure," I said.

My keys came out of a pocket but had trouble fitting in the lock. Capable-looking nine millimeters will do that to a set of keys.

"If you see any cops inside, yell and I'll shoot them," I said.

She wasn't smiling anymore.

"Better yet, why don't you just shoot them yourself?"

She motioned with the gun and I went inside.

I sat her down on the best chair in the best corner of my flat. I figured it was the gentlemanly thing to do. Besides, she had the gun and would take it anyway.

"Want some coffee?" I said. She shook her head and pulled my piece off my hip.

"Thanks," I said. "How about some orange juice?"

"Sure," she replied. "Orange juice is a good source of potassium. Women need that, you know."

I didn't know and didn't argue.

She unloaded my gun and checked the pipe. I rustled through my fridge looking for another suitable weapon. Nothing came to mind. She had already figured this out and kept talking.

"Sorry about the gun, Mr. Kelly. It's just a precaution. Girl needs to be able to protect herself."

I placed the orange nectar squarely before her and took a less-than-comfortable perch on the sofa.

"How do I know you're the woman from the letter?" I said.

She got up from the chair. With one hand, she began to undo the first few buttons of her top. To my credit, I kept my eye on the nine. It didn't waver.

"Here," she said.

The scar was purple, thick, jagged, and heading south from just under her collarbone.

"It goes to just about here." She pointed halfway to her waist.

"You know how many pints of blood the human body holds, Mr. Kelly?"

I didn't.

"Eight. I lost six. They basically reinflated my body. With blood, I mean."

The gun faltered just a bit. Then found its focus.

"He raped me, too, Mr. Kelly. Did Gibbons tell you that? Probably not. Tied me up like a hog. Laughed about that for a while. Then he raped me."

She flicked her hair back, and the skin under her right eye twitched once.

"Listen, Ms. Remington," I said. "Why don't we put the gun down and talk about it."

"Gibbons was supposed to help," she said. "Now he's dead."

"How do you know that?"

"I saw him last night. A bar called the Hidden Shamrock over on Halsted and Diversey. Gibbons liked to hang out there. You know the place?"

I did.

"I met him there," she continued. "He told me about you maybe helping us and said he had a lead. Said he had to meet a guy down at Navy Pier."

"And you followed him?"

Now her eyes slid away.

"He was supposed to come back to my place close to midnight. When he didn't show, I went down to the pier. I found him there and called the police."

"Did the police talk to you?"

"Until about a half hour ago. They asked me about you."

"How wonderful of them."

"Why do you think they did that?"

"I have no idea, Ms. Remington."

Her smile was tight now. The tic under her eye was constant. Like a heartbeat. I judged the distance from my hand to the gun. Not good enough.

"You think I killed Gibbons," I said. "Hell, he was shot with a nine. Take that one down to the station and have your friends test it."

Her eyes flicked to my weapon lying on the coffee table.

"But tell me first," I said. "Why did I kill him?"

"I don't know that you did, Mr. Kelly. What did John tell you?"

"He showed me your letter."

I reached for a cigarette. She raised the gun and I showed her the pack. Marlboros.

"Okay," she said.

I crossed my legs. She did the same. But better.

"Gibbons asked me to help you," I said. "Then he gave me a retainer. May I?"

I pulled the envelope with cash from my coat pocket and threw it toward her. She didn't bother to look at it. I lit my cigarette and continued.

"So technically, I guess, you're my client. Although I don't see as you need a whole lot of protecting. At least for the moment."

I drew deep and let out some smoke. She coughed a little. I enjoyed that. Sometimes one must live for life's smaller triumphs. Then she finished coughing and started talking again.

"What about the rest of it, Mr. Kelly?"

It's the kind of question you want to have some sort of answer to, at least when someone is pointing the business end of a gun your way. I did the best I could.

"The rest of what?"

"Don't play fuck-fuck with me, Mr. Kelly. What else did Gibbons tell you?"

The possibilities for postmodern witty repartee, not to mention a close, meaningful relationship, seemed plentiful. Or she could just shoot me in the head and be done with it. Then the doorbell rang and the moment shifted.

"Expecting someone?" Elaine said.

"Not so you would notice."

"I'll be just down the hall."

She grabbed her orange juice, tucked her gun neatly into her handbag, and headed toward my bedroom. The bell rang a second time.

"Yeah, yeah."

I opened the door to a gold detective shield.

"Michael Kelly?" said the voice from behind the shield.

"Where the hell you guys been?" I said.

CHAPTER 6

One detective stood at attention. The other was loose-jointed and kicked at a rock on the pavement. I was on the top step, my back to the front door. They both squinted up at me through the morning glare. So much the better. I thought about Elaine Remington, alone in the apartment, rummaging through my various belongings. So much the worse. Loose-jointed flashed his badge again. In case I had any doubts. I caught a glimpse of the gold but no name.

"Dan Masters. This is my partner, Joe Ringles."

Ringles gave a bit of a salute. He looked lost without a swagger stick.

"You been waiting for us, huh?" said Masters. "Why exactly is that, I wonder?"

Masters was the older of the two. Gray buzz cut gave way to a shiny forehead and sharp ears set close. His eyebrows were crisscrossed with scars. The rest of his face was a bag of skin with red holes where eyes should have been and a slash that moved when he spoke. Booze and twenty years on the job will do that to you.

"John Gibbons," I said. "Friend of mine. Found dead last night."

"You want to tell me how you know that, sir?"

That was Ringles. The younger of the two, his buzz cut was still brown and shaved high on the sides. He had no eyebrows to speak of, and the skin was tight over thin cheekbones. His chin was soft enough to make him a target. I gave him the shoulder. Ringles didn't like it.

"I asked you a question, sir."

Ringles stepped forward. He was probably in my space, if I thought about it. I didn't. I just hit him. It doesn't take much if you know how. Just three inches to the solar plexus. I don't think Masters even noticed. Ringles did. He fell backward over a convenient piece of shrubbery. The landing area was just a bit muddy.

"Watch it there," I said.

Ringles came up out of the mud with his piece out. He even looked stupid enough to use it. Fortunately, Masters came around.

"Park it, Joe."

Ringles glared at me over the sight. I stood my ground and tried to ignore the hammer in my chest. Slowly he eased back on the trigger and pulled out the cuffs. I turned back to the older cop.

"Am I under arrest?"

Masters looked at a point in space somewhere between Ringles and myself. Then he shook his head. The cuffs went away.

"I'll drive down," I said. "If it's all right with you guys."

Masters was already heading back to his car. "Town Hall," he said. "You got an hour."

I went back into the house. Ringles was left alone, wiping off the back of his pants. I stopped just inside the door and listened. Nothing. I started down the hall.

"Honey, I'm home."

The back door to my flat was open. Elaine Remington was gone. She had rifled my bedroom drawers but left my value pack of ultra-thin, just-like-nothing-at-all condoms. I was slightly disappointed.

On the mirror, over my dresser, she had scrawled a phone number in lipstick. Just like in the movies. I recognized the number but scribbled it down anyway. Then I filled my pockets with cash. I'd been inside a Chicago cop shop before. It was best to go prepared.

CHAPTER 7

At the corner of Halsted and Addison sits Town Hall, the oldest operating police station in Chicago and looking very much the part. I counted seven cops working the front desk. None of them, women included, checked in under two hundred and fifty pounds. Most of them used Selectric typewriters with multiple layers of white, pink, and green report sheets tacked underneath. Carbon paper and Wite-Out were big items, too. One computer, a Sanyo circa 1982, lurked in a dark and forlorn corner. It was covered in the morning remnants of bear claw and held up a chunk of green plaster leaking off the wall.

"Let's go."

Ringles was gone. Masters had replaced him with a larger version of large.

"This is Bubbles," Masters said and pointed in the general direction of Bubbles' belt buckle.

"And what do you call the rest of him?"

Masters smiled and jerked his head toward the bowels of the station. Bubbles grabbed my elbow and the rest of me followed.

The room was white walls with a cracked Formica table and plastic molded chairs bolted to the floor. A mirror spanned one side.

"Is the mayor joining us?" I said.

Masters slammed me a shot in the kidneys. I cracked my head on the opposite wall, tasted copper, and turned just in time to catch Bubbles' size 15½ up the left side of the head. I watched my reflection bounce off the mirror and fall to the floor. Feet shifted to the left and right. I hung my head and moaned, low and soft. A set of feet moved a bit closer. I came off the ground with a right hand. It connected but not enough. Bubbles had his nightstick out, and he was good with it. I heard my knee pop before I felt it and sat down hard. Masters stepped in again.

"Kelly?"

I swung around to focus on the detective. The eyes were still red and hollow. Basically, uninterested.

"I don't necessarily like Joe Ringles," Masters said. "But he's a cop and you're not. At least not anymore."

I nodded and tried to get up.

"Fair enough. Now why am I here?"

Masters looked at Bubbles, who shrugged like the fun was over far too soon.

"You know why you're here," Masters said.

"I do?"

The detective sighed and picked up a white phone off the white wall. A uniform brought in a file marked HOMICIDE in large black block letters. Like they were proud of it. Then the uniform and Bubbles left. I spit out some blood and told Bubbles I'd catch up with him later.

Masters took one of the three chairs in the room. I took another. The file was between us. Masters read me my rights.

"You want a lawyer?" he said when he was finished.

"Know any good ones?" I replied.

Masters pulled a piece of paper from the file. It was an eight by ten of John Gibbons. He was lying on a piece of concrete walkway. His mouth was open, and he had a hole in his stomach. The detective slid a second piece of paper in front of me. It was a blowup of a fingerprint.

"This is a latent pulled off a shell casing found at the scene."

Masters put a second print sheet on top of that.

"We ran it through the system and got a partial match."

I looked up.

"You don't say."

"Yeah, computer kicked out your name among the possibles. Private investigator, former cop."

I stared at the ridges and whorls for what was probably too long. Then I looked up at Masters, who was looking at me but pretending not to.

"Partial, huh? How many points match?"

"Four."

"When I was on the force, you needed nine to make it stand up and talk for the DA. Has that changed, Detective?"

"Your card was found in his pocket. A partial on the casing. You explain it to me. Starting with how you know so much."

"You talked to some folks," I said.

"This case hasn't left my sight. No one knows about it except Ringles, myself, and the print lab."

"How about Diane Lindsay? Red hair. Shows up on TV every now and then."

The flesh around Masters' eyes furrowed with a smile that never reached his lips. Whoever Diane's source was, it wasn't this guy.

"And then there's Elaine Remington," I said. "Blond hair. Purple scar running from throat to navel."

Masters flinched at that one. Now I could see him putting things together. And he was doing it pretty quick.

"She headed right over to see you?"

I nodded.

"She was inside your house when we showed up?"

"Down the hall," I said.

"Do yourself a favor and explain how she fits."

I shrugged.

"She was assaulted a long time ago," I said. "Gibbons was helping to track the guy."

"Was he getting anywhere?"

"Why don't you go ask him?"

I thought Masters might call in Bubbles for an encore. He didn't.

"We still got the print."

"You do."

"More than enough to charge you."

"You have my gun," I said. "Run it against the slug that killed Gibbons."

"We will, Kelly. As soon as we dig it out of your friend. But you know what, it's a funny thing about bullets. They can be used in one piece just as easily as another. Some of us might figure you killed Gibbons and then dumped the murder weapon. Problem is, you forgot to use gloves when you loaded the clip. Could you be that stupid, Kelly? I say, 'Why not?' "

"I want a lawyer," I said.

"Fine by me."

Masters reached for the phone.

"We're sending you downtown. DA wants to talk to you. Meantime, I'll make sure Bubbles finds you an extra-friendly bunkmate."

CHAPTER 8

The holding cell downtown was a rectangle pit about twenty feet by ten. It had a bench running down one wall, ending with a hole in the floor that I believed was once a toilet. There were seven other men in the cell. Three of them were cuffed to iron rings bolted into the wall. I took that as a bad sign and gave them some room. The other four spread out across the length of the cell. On my left, a white guy with an iron eagle tattooed on his forehead picked green paint off the wall and ate it. On my right, a black guy in Diana Ross drag explained to no one in particular why eating paint was a bad thing. Then he took out a tube of lipstick and began to reapply. I was thinking about asking for a single cell when three-hundred-plus pounds of correctional officer walked into my life.

"Kelly, come with me."

The guard's badge identified him as Albert Nyack. I preferred to think of him as Al. He opened the cage and led me down a hallway to a small windowless room. A room where cops asked questions and, one way or another, usually got answers. Al undid my cuffs and told me to sit down.

"O'Leary wants to see you."

O'Leary was Gerald O'Leary, a former cop and the reason I no longer carried a shield. For the last quarter century, O'Leary played the part of Cook County district attorney. The consummate Chicago pol, O'Leary could usually be found in one of two places: either in front of the camera for the ten o'clock news or with his head stuck halfway up the ass of the man who ruled all he could see. The honorable mayor of Chicago, John J. Wilson.

"Wait here," Al warned and plodded away, twirling a set of keys in his left paw.

Half a cigarette later, O'Leary walked in. I hadn't seen him in person since the day I signed my agreement. He didn't look any different, mid-sixties with a full white mane, straight teeth, clear eyes, and the kind of large square head and empty smile that were perfect for television. He loved looking you straight on and shaking your hand. A couple of years back he began holding your forearm while he shook. It was an old Bill Clinton trick, put to good use in the mirrored hallways of Chicago politics.

"Michael Kelly. Been a while. Let's take you upstairs and have a little chat."

In a matter of moments I was cuffed again, out, and walking with my newest and bestest buddy. We took an elevator up, a carpeted hallway down, and into a conference room. I said nothing. O'Leary hummed a tune I couldn't quite make out. We sat down. An officer undid my shackles. O'Leary read a file and continued to hum.

" 'War Pigs' by Black Sabbath, right?"

The district attorney looked up at me.

"What's that, Michael?"

"You're humming 'War Pigs' by Black Sabbath. Ozzy Osbourne. Am I right?"

O'Leary smiled. He also stopped humming.

"We have a problem here."

"Do we?"

"I knew John Gibbons. Good officer. Good man."

O'Leary's voice had taken on the somber, heavy cadence he used at only the best sorts of press conferences.

"I appreciate the intonation," I said. "I really do. I mean, that sort of intonation takes a lot of effort. It's an art, really. Something you typically save for Irish funerals and executions. Am I wrong?"

The DA just kept on keeping on.

"Michael. We have a former officer murdered and another up to his neck in it. Not a happy day for anyone."

I shifted in my chair. It was padded and more comfortable than the plastic one at Town Hall. Still, I would have preferred the white room and Masters across the table. A kick in the head aside, the waters here felt deeper, the current swift, with a big fish in the water.

"I already asked for a lawyer once," I said. "You want to talk charges, let's at least make it official."

"I was hoping we could avoid that."

"You were?"

"Yes. I don't believe this print to be a legitimate piece of evidence."

"You mean it might not be an admissible piece of evidence, don't you, Counselor?"

O'Leary gave one of those nods I always expected from Charles Dickens and the Old Bailey.

"Bear with me, Michael. If it's a frame, and I'm not saying it is, the question is, why?"

Two years ago, the man across the table had planted a bag of cocaine in my car, charged me with possession, and dropped the case only when I agreed to leave the force. Now we were old friends, discussing yet another frame with my picture inside. I proceeded with all due caution.

"If it's a frame, it's a pretty poor one. Even you can see that.

In fact, especially you, Mr. District Attorney. As to the why, I intend to find out."

O'Leary smiled and gave me the dead eye. I could see a bit of hunger at the corners of his mouth, and the cold chill of yesterday crawled up my back. Then it was gone, replaced by an even more depressing prospect called tomorrow.

"For the moment we'll hold off on any formal charges," he said.

"Until a bigger headline comes along?"

The district attorney shrugged. As if he had done all he could and some people just couldn't be helped.

"You didn't work with me last time, Michael. Look what happened. This time, you might want to think about it. Have a good day."

O'Leary exited stage left. A moment later, the door opened again. My only friend in the Cook County DA's office floated through, wrapped in a cloud of smoke. In his left hand, Bennett Davis carried a cigar that smelled good enough to eat.

"I thought you couldn't smoke those things in government buildings," I said.

The assistant DA sat down in the chair his boss had just vacated, crossed his legs, glanced at the Macanudo, and gave me his most patronizing look.

"Wrong. *You* can't smoke them in government buildings. I, on the other hand, constitute another matter entirely."

Bennett Davis was a different kind of guy. Short and round, balding since he was twelve, and perpetually in love with women he could never have, Bennett went to the DA's office right out of Northwestern and never looked back. He was O'Leary's major hitter, taking all the big cases out of Chicago and rarely coming up short. My friend could go private any time he wanted, jump into a mid–six figures salary with any Chicago firm. Instead he made $65K a year and bachelored it in an $1,000-a-month flat in Lincoln Square. All for the rush of deciding, as Bennett once put it, who goes to jail and who walks. Like I said, a different kind of guy.

"So, Kelly, what the hell are we doing here?"

"Ask your boss," I said.

"What's that supposed to mean?"

Bennett had been kept out of the loop when O'Leary decided to go after me. To this day, the assistant DA carried a measure of guilt he didn't deserve.

"Nothing," I said. "It's just that I know who I've killed and, as luck would have it, John Gibbons doesn't happen to be among that number."

Bennett dropped his cigar into a cut-glass ashtray he had brought with him. Then he tapped his index finger lightly against the conference table. I noticed a brown leather watch on his right wrist. A cheap Timex. Bennett caught my glance, shot his cuffs, and the Timex disappeared.

"How did you know Gibbons?" Bennett said.

"My partner on the force a while back. He showed up yesterday, out of the blue. Asked for some help on an old case. Never got any further than that."

"Gibbons testified at a couple of my trials," Bennett said. "Good cop. The evidence is shit, Michael. Print could be any one of a thousand guys."

"No kidding."

Bennett shrugged, picked up his cold cigar, examined, then relit it.

"O'Leary is just feeling his oats. Looking to make a splash. You know how it is."

The assistant DA smiled, the one they teach you in law school just before they explain the concept of treble damages.

"Here's my advice. Lay low for a couple of weeks. Let the office get you off its radar. Maybe we make an arrest, this whole thing goes away. *Capisce?*"

I understood and told my friend as much. Bennett Davis headed for the door, stopped halfway, turned, and pointed at me.

"By the way, how is she?"

I was waiting for it.

"Nicole is fine."

"Tell her I said hello."

"You tell her yourself," I said.

"That's not how it works. She ask for me?"

"No, Bennett, she doesn't ask for you. At least when I see her, which is, on average, once a year."

Bennett frowned a bit at that.

"You see her once a year and she doesn't ask for me?"

"No."

"I better give her a call."

"Do that, Bennett. But don't hope too hard."

"No?"

"No. She's not your type."

"You're probably right."

Bennett Davis shook his head from side to side, as if to get that fact in its proper place. Then he continued.

"They're probably going to want a statement before we let you go."

I shrugged.

"You should have an attorney for that, Michael."

I gave him the number of a guy. Davis went to give him a call. After one lawyer, the day is ruined anyway.

CHAPTER 9

I lied to Bennett. I see Nicole more like once a month.
Usually it's for coffee at a local shop on Broadway called
Intelligentsia. For my money it's the best joe in the city.

I got there at a little after six that evening. Typical Intelligentsia crowd. Up front, a couple of old men drinking large coffees, doing the neighborhood gossip with Gemma, a pink-haired
barista and queen of the double-shot macchiato. In the back, a
table of DePaul students huddled for warmth around major skim
lattes and tapped away on their PowerBooks. In between, a smat-
tering of NPR types, downing double shots of espresso and talking aloud to anyone who would listen about how much they
hated George W. Bush.

At a counter along the front window was a stunning sort of
woman. She had skin the color of cocoa brushed with crimson,
fine-boned cheeks, and delicate, strong lines for nose, mouth,
and chin. Her subtle smile took you in, filled you up, and left you
contented, at peace with yourself and still thirsting for more. Her
name was Nicole Andrews. She was lead DNA analyst for the
Illinois state crime lab and my best friend.

"Sorry I'm late," I said.

Nicole was drinking a large cappuccino and leafing through

The New York Times. She drew her finger down the side of a page and spoke without looking up.

"How long have we known each other, Michael?"

The answer to that was simple. A lifetime. I grew up in a hard sort of Irish way. On the city's West Side. My mother drank tea, ironed a lot of clothes, and tried to stay out of the way. My father worked three jobs and dragged home $8,500 a year, kicking and screaming. He drank enough to hover between black silence and pure rage. The former was bad, but it was the latter that kept you up at night.

My brother, Phillip, and I slept on a pullout couch in the living room. Phillip was a year older, ten years tougher, and a world wiser. At sixteen, he was caught breaking into a McDonald's. Actually, the cops found him stuck in a venting duct on the roof. A cook heard the screams after he fired up the grill and started making Egg McMuffins. Once Phillip got inside the joint, he stuck a guy with a knife and drew down ten more years. I never saw him a lot after that. Mostly because he hung himself with his bedsheet. They cut him down from the bars of his cell on April 23, 1989.

I didn't have any sisters, didn't need any. I had Nicole. I met her when I was nine. She was seven. It was a hot, heavy afternoon. Late August in the city. We were playing football in the street when she made the mistake of walking by. There was an older kid there named Maxie. He was big and round, Polish and plenty tough. He'd blow his heart out with a speedball on his sixteenth birthday. I didn't cry. Don't know anyone who did.

Maxie hooked Nicole by the back of the shirt. Just for fun. Kicked her to the ground. As Nicole got up, he caught her flush, a hard, flat hand across the face. I remember the sound of her head bouncing off a chunk of pavement. Nicole didn't cry, didn't run. Just picked herself up again, tried to get away. Maxie screwed himself close, screamed in her face. It wasn't the first time I heard the word *nigger*. Nor the last. But it's the one I remember. Then Maxie reached back again, a closed fist. Nicole went straight down. This time she didn't get up.

There was a group now, all white, all watching. I heard some snickers and felt the circle tighten as Nicole lay on the ground. They were excited. Waiting. Predatory.

I don't really remember considering, reflecting, or even moving. I was just there, inside the circle, reaching out my hand and helping the black girl stand up. There was blood at her temple and more dripping from her nose. She seemed oblivious to it. Instead, she just looked at me, curious. More like she wanted to sit down and talk, help me with problems I couldn't yet understand. She seemed to hold this wisdom in a child's look, and dropped it on me like a bomb.

That's what I remember. Me and Nicole, middle of the circle, surrounded by so much hatred and feeling none of it. That is, until Maxie crashed the party. He clubbed me with a forearm from behind and told me to fuck off. Apparently, I was ruining his fun. Even better, I was two years younger and a hell of a lot smaller.

Twenty-six years later, I know for a fact that I can fight. I've boxed in a ring, not as an amateur, but for money. Not a lot of money, but enough to handle most anything that might come down the street. At nine years old, however, I didn't realize what latent talent lay in my fists. That was, until I closed them and laid into Maxie. I blackened an eye, cracked a tooth, and busted his face pretty good. Then I slipped my hands underneath his chin and felt the give, the softness of his windpipe. Once I got there, Maxie stopped struggling and started worrying. I saw the whites of his eyes, oversized in their sockets, and felt the violence and the power within. Just a little more pressure, a bit more, and it would be over. For Maxie. And for me. So easy. So simple. So right.

Seconds before I would have fractured Maxie's windpipe, Phillip came down the street at a run and caught me with a boot across the head. I hit the ground, rolled, and got up. Smiling. It was the first time the blackness had ever thickened behind my eyes, ever misted them over. Not the last time. But the first. I was nine years old and I liked it. In time, I would learn to love it. Now, I only fear it.

After Maxie, no one in the neighborhood messed with me very much. Or Nicole. No one ever played with us too much either, but that was okay. Nicole understood me, understood the world in a way that seemed beyond time. Two and a half decades later, we were here. In a coffee shop. Talking about a murder.

"Known you a lifetime," I said.

"Best friends?" Nicole said.

"Yes."

"Then why does my best friend get pulled in on a homicide beef, spend half the day in jail, and not pick up the phone to call me?"

The DA's office had finally kicked me loose at a little after noon. Such news apparently traveled well.

"You heard about that?" I said.

"Yes, Michael, I heard about that. I also knew John Gibbons. Now would you like to explain to me why the DA thinks you killed him?"

"It's a little complicated," I said.

"No kidding. You can start whenever."

Nicole leaned back on her stool, took a sip of her cap, and waited for a response. She could wait a long time. I knew that from experience. I took a deep breath. A cell phone buzzed in her handbag. Nicole held up a finger and checked the caller ID.

"Hang on. I have to take this."

My friend walked away. I stirred my coffee. After a few minutes she returned.

"Sorry about that. Listen, I know this is important, and believe me, I want to hear the story. Whatever it is. But right now I gotta run."

"No problem. What's up?"

Nicole pulled on her coat as she talked.

"Did I tell you about the task force I'm on?"

I shook my head.

"Come on. I'll give you a lift home. It's on the way."

Nicole headed north on Broadway and took a left on Addison. She talked rapidly as she drove.

"Last month the state formed its first rape task force."

"Never heard of it."

"I'm telling you about it. It's a SWAT team of specially trained nurses, detectives, forensic staff, and counselors. We get called in to deal with sexual assaults in the city."

"Why sexual assaults?"

"Lot of reasons. Mostly, though, because evidence is not being collected properly. You know how it is. The victim is traumatized. The nurse is trying to comfort and take the rape kit."

"The cops are trying to get a statement. . . . "

"Exactly. Bad stuff happens."

Nicole cruised past Wrigley Field and took a left on Lakewood.

"The SWAT team is different," she continued. "Each person has a job he or she is trained for and nothing else."

"So the nurse does her rape kit. . . . "

"And that's it. Doesn't communicate with the victim in any way. That is left to the detective and counselors."

"Less for the defense to attack at trial," I said.

"You got it. Everything is controlled and documented. A clean record from the time we get on scene."

"Nice."

Nicole pulled up in front of my building and turned to face me.

"I oversee collection of the forensic evidence. Start a chain of custody for our lab. Pretty easy stuff. The point is, though, we're at the scene and create a record."

"You headed there now?"

"Yeah. A break-in and assault on the Northwest Side. The victim's still at her house."

Nicole checked her watch.

"We're meeting there in forty-five minutes."

"How about I tag along?"

My friend cocked her head and pushed a look of curiosity across the car.

"Tag along. Why?"

"Sounds interesting. Besides, this murder thing I'm involved in . . . "

"I remember the murder thing."

"There might be a rape connection."

Nicole exhaled softly and looked out into the newly born night. The quiet was suddenly heavy between us and I felt the weight of years take hold. Not the careless intimacy of a lover. Much more than simply a friend. It was a connection that could only be forged between children. A connection you got maybe once in your life. More often, more likely, never. Then Nicole turned back my way and spoke.

"I hear you, Michael. And I'd love to help. Thing is, I can't just take you along."

"How about I follow?"

Nicole shook her head once and shifted into drive.

"Can't stop you from doing that. But I won't make it easy. And you won't get into the crime scene. Now get out."

She pulled away almost as soon as I slid out the door. My car, however, was parked at the corner. I got behind the wheel and was on her bumper within a block. I flicked my headlights. She looked up at her rearview mirror. I still had my coffee, took a sip, and followed.

CHAPTER 10

The house was just south of Montrose and east of Cicero, at the wrong end of a street called Pensacola. It was a standard split-level, except gone to seed with green garbage bags stuffed in the windows and ruts of mud where a lawn should have been. A double set of railroad tracks ran past the back of the house. A single cruiser, flasher turning sadly, was parked in front. I caught up to Nicole as she popped open her trunk.

"Just can't help yourself, Michael. Here, take this."

She hefted a black leather case my way.

"Don't give your name to anyone and stay out of the way."

"No problem."

"And wear gloves. Double gloves and booties. You leave any DNA here and I'll kill you." Nicole slammed the trunk shut and we walked toward the house.

A RAPE SCENE is a lot like a homicide except the victim is still alive. You might figure that to be a good thing. A lot of times, though, you'd be figuring wrong. The house on Pensacola was one of those times.

A couple of uniforms stood on the front stoop, trying to stay warm and looking for a chance to get back in the cruiser. They waved at Nicole and didn't take a second look at me.

Inside, a couple of print guys worked on a small pane of window broken out of the kitchen door. Point of entry. A good bit of breeze blew through the hole but the house still smelled. Small and poor. Not an auspicious sort of up-and-coming poor. Poor with a desperate edge. A lifetime kind of poor. One handed down to kids as a coming-out-of-the-womb sort of prize.

The refrigerator had a flyer for a singles night at the Wells Street Social Club affixed to it. Beside that were a few pictures. School photos of young kids and a couple of wedding snaps. Up high on the fridge was a high school prom shot, circa 1987. An overweight girl stuffed into a dress with plastic red roses on it. Her date was cut out of the picture. Beside that, a magazine shot of Brad Pitt and Angelina Jolie on the beach, except Angelina's head was gone and the overweight high school girl, now an overweight woman, had taken her place. Someone had written STUD with an arrow pointing to Brad's smiling face. I took it all in as we walked by and decided I didn't miss being a cop.

"Down here."

Nicole pointed. Smears of what looked like blood led down a short, cheap hallway to a single room jammed into the end. We already had booties and gloves on. Nicole skirted the blood and led the way into the room.

"Hi, Vince."

Vince was everything today's cop should be. Hispanic, thirty to thirty-five, curly black hair cut close, white shirt and blue suit that hung lean and long off a well-tapered build. He had a laptop open on a nightstand and a PDA clipped to his belt, right in front of his gun and shield.

"Nicole."

Vince took a look at me and back to Nicole. We all stepped back down the hallway and into the living room.

"This is?"

"Michael Kelly. An old friend and former cop."

I held out a hand.

"Nice to meet you."

Vince reflexively stuck out a gloved hand. I figured he would.

"Vince Rodriguez."

"Michael is just along to observe. He has a strong interest in the program."

"I'm sure he has a lot of interest, Nicole, but this is a crime scene."

My friend reached out and brushed the sleeve of Vince's suit. I could see him flinch, then relent. Nicole caught my eye and then the two moved a few feet away. I waited as they whispered, tried not to watch, and made a mental note to ask Nicole about her personal relationship with one Vince the Cop. A few minutes later, both came back happy. Or at least relatively so. Vince took the lead.

"You can come on in. But just observe. No talking, no touching, nothing. And if the victim has a problem . . . "

"I'm gone."

"Right. Okay, Nicole, let me catch you up real quick. Point of entry was the kitchen. Victim's name is Miriam Hope. Had a brother visiting from Indiana. They were watching TV in the living room, didn't hear a thing. Guy used a knife to subdue. Tied the brother up and threw him in the second bedroom. Then our guy went into the kitchen and got some dishes."

"Dishes?"

"He puts the brother on the floor and lays the dishes on his legs and body. Says if he hears the dishes move, the sister is dead. Brother is next."

"That's a new one."

"Yeah. Then he goes back into the living room where he has Miriam tied up. Rapes her repeatedly."

"How long?"

"Maybe a half hour in the living room. Then he took her into the laundry room. Made her jump up on the washer."

"Raped her there?"

"Yep. Vaginal in the living room, anal and oral in the laundry room. Then back to the living room. Kept running the knife up and down her body. Then he cut her throat. 'Just enough to scare her,' he said."

"That's it?" Nicole said.

"Yeah, she says he wore a mask and gloves the entire time."

Vince's PDA beeped. He stepped away to make a call as Nicole opened up her laptop and began to tap away. After a minute or so, Vince returned. Nicole spoke without looking up from her screen.

"Did he use a condom?"

"She says he did."

"We'll find out pretty quick when we do the kit. Did she struggle with him when he cut her?"

"A little," Vince said. "You're thinking he might have cut himself?"

"Yeah."

"I already asked her. She doesn't think so."

"Where's the brother?"

"Sent him downtown. He never moved a muscle until the police showed up. Dishes still in place. They got him medicated."

"Who's handling the rape kit?"

"Christine Sullivan is your nurse."

"She here?"

"Just arrived. She wants to do the examination back at the hospital."

"I'll need a few minutes with the victim first."

"That's fine. I was just finishing up her statement."

Vince led us back into the room. The woman from the refrigerator was half sitting on the bed, talking quietly to a counselor who was holding the woman's hand. I could see red and purple welts on the woman's wrists where the rope had cut her skin. She was wearing a long nightshirt that said NORTH SIDE CHICAGO GIRL on the front. It was ripped up the side and stained with blood. She had fuzzy slippers on. One foot was tucked up under her. The other dangled and shook lightly. A bandage covered her neck. The wound didn't seem serious. Then again, it wasn't my neck. Vince crouched down so he was eye-level with the victim before he spoke.

"Miriam, these people need to collect some forensic evidence. I'm not going to introduce you because I don't want you talking to them. As I explained before, I want you only to talk to me or the counselor here. Makes it a lot easier when we catch this guy. Okay?"

I could see why Vince was on the team. His voice was soft, smooth, and reassuring. Miriam's eyes rolled around a bit in their sockets and settled back on the detective.

Nicole opened up her case and set out some small envelopes and tweezers. She began with the victim herself, collecting small bits of evidence off her clothes and bedding. Meanwhile, Vince and Miriam continued to talk.

"Let's go back to the attack, Miriam. Why do you think he

used the knife? Was there something you said, maybe, that got him angry?"

"I don't know."

"You remember what he was saying at the time?"

"No. Like I told you, I think he felt like he was losing control."

"Why?"

"I don't know. I just think he needed to scare me, to show me he could use the knife. I think he could have killed me."

"Why didn't he?"

"I talked him out of it."

Miriam's voice firmed up a bit. She looked around the room and returned to Vince.

"I read about it in *People* magazine. If you're being raped, the best way to survive is to talk to your rapist. Make him see you as a person. So that's what I did. Told him about my life. About my brother's visit. About T-Kat. Where is T-Kat?"

"I don't know, Miriam. We have an officer looking around the neighborhood."

"Oh no, T-Kat is here. He never leaves the house. Neither one of us likes to leave the house very much. Anyway, I told him about T-Kat and about my job. About the shows I watch at night. *American Idol.* Anything I could think of. After a while he put down the knife and just listened. Then he took me down the hall and into the bedroom."

"What did he do then?"

"Well, he didn't rape me anymore. He just lay down beside me."

Nicole touched Vince's arm.

"Hold on a second, Miriam."

Nicole and Vince conferred for a moment, then Vince returned to the victim.

"Can you show me exactly where he was lying?"

"Sure. Right here on the left side. I think he might have been crying at one point. That's when I knew he wouldn't kill me."

Vince's PDA beeped again.

"That's the ambulance, Miriam. We're going to take you to the hospital for the examination I told you about."

"Will I spend the night at the hospital?"

"Probably."

"Where's my brother?"

"He'll be at the hospital, too."

"Okay. But you guys have to find my cat. His food is in the kitchen."

"You got it, Miriam."

The ambulance rolled out five minutes later. Vince came back into the bedroom. Nicole was just finishing up.

"I called in a couple more techs," she said. "They're going to process both bedrooms, living room, kitchen, and laundry room. They're also going to take that carpet up."

"What do you think?" Vince said.

"I think he probably used a condom. If he was wearing gloves, he probably didn't cut himself. But it's worth a shot."

"Yeah."

Nicole pointed to a set of rolled-up bedsheets.

"The victim thinks he was crying. If so, we might have some tears."

Vince smiled.

"And some DNA?"

"Maybe. I'll let you know. Okay, I gotta run. I'll call you."

"Thanks, Nicole."

The two shook hands. Very proper and professional. Too much so. Vince turned my way.

"Thanks for staying out of the way. Find it interesting?"

"Very much. For what it's worth, your guy's a killer."

Nicole glanced up at that. Vince cocked his head and gave me a funny look.

"What makes you say that?"

"The way she described him. The guy was on his way. Almost there."

"You think he was going to kill her?" Nicole said.

I looked at Vince.

"I think it was a close thing. Not sure why he stopped, but you can bet it had nothing to do with Miriam or her stories."

"Or *People* magazine," Vince said. "Come on out here for a second."

Rodriguez led us through the kitchen and into a small back-yard. It was dark now. Pieces of light from the kitchen window cast the scene into silhouette. A clothesline ran off the back of the house. A cop stood nearby. As we got close, I could see why. Miriam Hope's cat was hanging from the line, stiff in the cold, a length of panty hose cinched tight around its neck. Vince shone his flashlight on the animal, then to the ground.

"We think he took the cat as he left the house. Found it like this. Didn't want to tell the victim until I got a statement."

Rodriguez snapped off the light and ordered the officer to cut the animal down. The highway was nearby, and traffic rolled into the night. Some chatter floated in from the open door of a tavern down the street. Otherwise, it was quiet.

"Call me when you work up the evidence, Nicole. Nice meeting you, Kelly. How long you been off the force?"

"Been a couple of years."

"Well, you still got the instincts. Thanks for the input."

Then Rodriguez was gone and it was just me and Nicole.

"No, I'm not sleeping with him, Michael. Not yet. And consider it your good fortune he doesn't have a personal life. First year in Homicide. Probably the only detective in the city that doesn't know you just got pulled in for some face time with the DA. Now buy me a beer and you can tell me just how much trouble you're really in."

CHAPTER 11

We sat under the El tracks on Webster at an ancient DePaul bar called Kelly's. I had a can of Bud and a burger. Nicole had a Diet Coke.

"What made you take this gig?" I said.

"The task force?"

"Yeah."

"That's not what we're talking about."

"I know, but the other stuff will wait. Talk to me about this."

I tried to hold Nicole's gaze, but she broke off. I took a sip of beer and waited.

"I went back again," she said. "Just last week."

"Why?"

"Why not? It's where we grew up."

"You don't want to forget, do you?"

"What I want doesn't really matter. Some things just don't go away. Probably be the last thing I think of when I pass over. First thing I remember on the other side. And that's all right. I've learned to live with it. Learned how to grow strong from it. You should, too."

"I'm good," I said. "You know that. I just worry about a scene like tonight."

Nicole smiled and held out her hand. I took it.

"Michael, you're always good. Always fine. At least that's the part we all get to see. Sometimes, though, I wonder."

I didn't say anything, didn't move very much.

"The SWAT team's a good thing for me," she continued. "Lets me do something."

"The empowerment thing?"

"Yeah, the empowerment thing."

My friend looked empowered, almost too much so.

"You sure?" I said.

"Yes. Besides, it gets too rough, I got you around."

"Whether you like it or not."

"Absolutely. But let me ask you a question?"

"Shoot."

Nicole lifted her glass and talked around the side.

"How exactly you going to save this poor black girl if you're sitting in a prison cell?"

"I guess it's time for my story."

"It is."

And so I told her. About Gibbons and Elaine Remington, the print and Diane Lindsay.

"You sleeping with her?"

"No."

Nicole rolled her eyes.

"Matter of time. I know Diane. She does some work at the Rape Volunteer Association."

"And?"

"You're in over your head."

"Never stopped me before."

"Really? When was the last time you slept with a woman?"

I shrugged. Nicole cut right to it.

"I'm going to guess there's been no one since Annie. And that's been . . . "

She counted on her fingertips and looked toward the ceiling.

". . . over a year."

There had actually been plenty of women since Annie, but it was all playacting, dipping a toe in the water. I had a feeling Diane Lindsay would take me to the deep end and that, as my friend hammered home, might be a problem.

"Simple fact of life, Michael. What's done is done. You gotta move on. Hard as it is, everyone else already has."

"Let's try one thing at a time," I said. "Right now, she's a journalist and I'm a potential story. As in 'murder suspect' sort of story."

Nicole sat back, dragged a straw idly through her drink, and looked into its caramel-colored depths. I took another sip of beer and studied the nearest EXIT sign. Sometimes friendship can be hard. Especially with me on the other side. After a while Nicole shrugged and let it go.

"Have you talked to Bennett?"

"Yeah. He says to just lay low. Whole thing will blow over."

"Bennett is usually right," Nicole said.

"True. By the way, he asked for you."

"Bennett's a sweet guy."

"Yeah. And still a little obsessed."

"I told you we talked. Straightened that all out. Long time ago."

"The boy is only human, Nicole. Just another face in the fawning crowd."

"Whatever. Now get yourself another beer and give me the dirt on Diane Lindsay."

I didn't have any dirt, or anything else to offer, on our local news celeb. So I made up a few things, which seemed to make Nicole happy and, of course, is the American way.

CHAPTER 12

I left Kelly's at a little after ten p.m. and parked on Addison, just around the corner from my flat. I needed a smoke, shrugged into the night, and walked north along Southport Avenue. A half block from the Music Box Theatre, I brushed shoulders with the past. Annie was walking out of the old-time movie house and she was with someone, a tall, probably good-looking someone. He leaned over to speak at a crosswalk. She laughed into his chest, slipping a hand around his waist in a way I preferred not to remember.

The light changed and the couple approached, arms now linked, strides matching perfectly. A friend once told me that was a sure sign a couple was having sex. I leaned back, into the shadows of a convenient Chicago alley. They floated past. I caught a glimpse of her hair, maybe a cheekbone washed over in the pale reflection of neon. Then they were gone.

I moved into the slipstream and followed for another block or five. Her scent was there. Or maybe it was just me. Anyway, I followed, feeling more than I wanted. Nicole was dead-on. It shouldn't be that way. But it was.

After a while, I had my fix and dropped off the pace. Nearby, an

Irish bar named Cullen's beckoned. I wandered in and ordered a pint. Then five more.

Four hours later, they announced last call. A half hour after that, a more than nice waitress offered me a lift home. I took it. We made time for a bit in her car, but she had to get up early. I said okay, went inside, and fixed a cup of tea. I thought about taking a look at the report on Gibbons' homicide but knew I was drunk. Instead, I watched late-night Chicago flow past my window. After a while, I finished my tea and lay down, promising myself to fall asleep before the memories arrived.

CHAPTER 13

The next morning was Chicago cool, a slippery slope in late fall that could quickly deteriorate to cold, freezing cold, arctic cold, and why-the-fuck-would-anyone-live-here cold.

I made myself a cup of coffee and listened as the weather banged against my windows. Then I did what most runners do. Ignored the elements, got my running stuff on, and headed to the lakefront. A mile later, I felt loose and warm. The wind was steady and in my face. I kept my head down and plowed through. At four miles, I turned away from the lake, felt the breezes shift at my back, and let them chase me home. When I was done, I sat on my stoop as the sweat dried and the endorphins flowed. I'd be a little sore later on, but it was worth it. And would be worth it again. Tomorrow.

After the run, I showered, dressed, and found my car on the street. I headed west, through a light dusting of local traffic and into a dowager of a Chicago neighborhood near Humboldt Park. I parked in front of a Ukrainian church with a Madonna icon that used to cry but now just looks at you. Still, the people come. Still, the people leave money.

I got out of my car and stretched my eyes down the street. To my left a row of graystones marched into the distance. To my right a car parked at an angle to the curb. Two figures sat in the front seat. One drummed his fingers along the dashboard. A bass line growled from a pair of speakers in the back. I stepped close to a two-flat to read its number and stepped back. A stone gargoyle, face rubbed and smooth with age, smiled from its rooftop perch.

Halfway down the block I found the address I was looking for. In the last months of his life, John Gibbons had taken a room here. At least that's what he'd told me. Like the rest of the street, it wasn't much. For a man in the supposed prime of life, it was even less. For me, it was a place to start.

I walked across a shabby lawn to an even shabbier porch. As I walked, I felt, then heard something. A scattering of Kibbles 'n Bits crunched underfoot. I should have taken it as an omen. I didn't.

The door cracked open a couple of inches, then maybe four more. The pointed face of a woman peeked across the threshold.

"Hello there," I said.

The woman shifted and pale light washed over us both. Her face carried a bit more oval that I'd first thought, with high cheekbones and deep shadows underneath. The hair was thin, diluted by time and a lack of sun. Thick glasses sealed up small brown eyes pinpricked with black. They crawled over me and then beyond.

I thought maybe she hadn't heard me and was about to speak again when the woman gave forth with a noise, somewhere between a squeak, a grunt, and a snicker. Then I heard the shifting of feet inside.

"I'm a friend of John's," I said. "John Gibbons, that is."

I moved one foot onto the threshold, just inside the doorjamb. The heavy maple door crushed my big toe.

"Keep your foot back there," she said through the now-closed portal.

I hopped lightly and pretended it didn't hurt.

"You caught my foot there, Ms. . . . "

I looked at the mailbox name above GIBBONS.

"Ms. Mulberry."

I swore I heard a cackle although I'd be hard pressed to say I knew exactly what a cackle sounded like.

"Serves you right there, Mr. John Gibbons' friend. What do you want?"

"Nothing, Ms. Mulberry. Just some back rent I know John was owing. I wanted to make up the difference. . . . "

The big door suddenly swung open, and an interior light clicked on. Through the screen I could see a woman, ageless in the worst way possible. Maybe sixty, maybe eighty, she was too dusty and out of focus to get a handle on. Perched on each shoulder was a calico cat, entwined around her legs four or five others. Kittens and cats lounged on the stairs behind her. Some of them wore miniature ice bags strapped to their little cat heads. Mulberry must have caught me staring.

"They have migraines. From the heat, you know."

"But it's October."

She flashed me a look, magnified by the Harry Caray glasses.

"Never mind," I said.

I was inside the house now, inside a sitting room stuffed with felines and their respective droppings. I managed to get a handkerchief close to my face and found a spot on the sofa. To my left was a small alcove. Inside it, a desk littered with cuttings from newspapers, plates of half-eaten food, and an ashtray filled to overflowing. On the wall was a bulletin board with Post-it notes and index cards skewered with thumbtacks. Mulberry pulled a ledger out of a gray filing cabinet she kept next to the desk and laid it flat between us. The entries were handwritten in ball-point, and immaculate. The landlady admired her handiwork for a moment, then looked up.

"Bring a check?" she said.

Her eyes fastened on my hand as I reached inside a coat pocket.

"Actually, Ms. Mulberry, I have something better than that." I flashed my investigator's license.

"I'm here because John Gibbons is dead."

The ledger flew shut. She glanced at the name on the license, then threw the look back my way.

"The police have already been here. Been and gone, Mr. Kelly. I wish you'd go, too."

Little cat faces gleamed at me from various corners of the room. Something drifted by my ankles, but I didn't jump.

"I need your help, Ms. Mulberry."

"He was murdered, wasn't he?" Her smile revealed a set of teeth that were better left undisturbed.

"Yes, he was, ma'am."

"The police didn't tell me that. But I knew all the same. Just like *Law & Order*. Was it brutal?"

"Shot in the stomach and left to die down at Navy Pier. That's no picnic."

Now the landlady leaned forward and touched my arm.

"Was he in the lake? They're supposed to be blue when they're pulled from the lake."

I shook my head.

"No, his body was found just past the pier."

Her eyes had widened and glowed a warm copper. An angora moved to the couch and settled close by her cheek. The other cats drifted away.

"This is Oskar. Spelled with a *k*. He's my alter ego."

I nodded and looked from purring angora to fruitcake landlady.

"I put Sun-In in Oskar's hair. Now it matches mine."

I had to admit the resemblance was uncanny.

"You want to go upstairs and see John's room?"

I nodded again, and she pointed to a set of darkened stairs.

CHAPTER 14

I went up the stairs, down a brown hall, and into an even browner room. A bed with gray sheets tilted in one corner. A torn shade covered the only window. A slice of sunlight backed through it and onto an opposite wall.

I turned to find Mulberry at my shoulder. Her angora wrapped itself around my ankle.

"Can you give me a little room?" I said.

The landlady took a half step back. I guess she called that room. Her nose flared a bit as she spoke.

"The police went through the drawers."

She pointed to a crooked dresser that sat by the window.

"They didn't take anything, though. I told them if they did, I'd make them sign. Want to see the form? I typed it up with a Gateway computer."

I drifted toward the dresser and opened a few drawers. Nothing much. A couple of pairs of pants, some shirts.

"No wallet here or nothing, Ms. Mulberry?"

"No. He only had the one suit he was wearing. A simple man." I nodded.

"Nice enough man," she said. As if I didn't believe her.

"Any other personal stuff?" I said. "Papers, books, that sort of thing?"

Mulberry held her chin with one hand and shook her head. Then she picked up the angora and began to stroke it. The cat looked at me and I found it difficult to look away.

"She asked about that, too," Mulberry said.

"The detective?" I said.

"Not the detective. The woman that called later."

"What woman would that be?"

"The one on television. You know. The bitch with the red hair."

"On Channel 6?"

"That's the one. She came yesterday afternoon and looked through this stuff. Just like you."

"Just like me, huh?"

"Yep. She didn't get anything either. Told me not to talk to anyone else."

I sat down on the bed.

"Son of a bitch," I said.

The angora hissed and Mulberry arched her back. Or maybe it was the other way around.

"Don't swear in front of Oskar. He doesn't like it from strangers."

The old woman laid out Gibbons' clothes, put what looked like a shaving kit on top of them, and got the whole thing ready to bundle into a bag. My old partner had died alone and already found his hole in the ground. The rest of his life was here, in a dirty brown room and a Dominick's shopping bag.

"It's not so bad."

Mulberry spoke softly and kept one eye closed. The other loomed large through the thick corrective lens.

"What's not so bad?" I said.

"Dying alone. Once you lose your choices, it's not so bad."

"You think so?"

"I do. You should leave it be now and go."

I shrugged, took a twenty out of my clip, and dropped it on the bed. For Kibbles 'n Bits, I told the woman. I told her if she ran across any of Gibbons' personal papers or books to call me.

"What about the police?" she said.

I dropped her another twenty.

"What about the redhead?"

Two more twenties.

"Give the bitch nothing," I said.

Mulberry smiled. Bubbles of green saliva kicked up between her front teeth. I left the house quickly, promising myself to brush and floss. Regularly and with determination.

CHAPTER 15

I returned to my office and sat in the quiet of midmorning, waiting for the new women in my life to fall into place.

The landlady was lying to me. Why, I had no idea.

My paying client liked to threaten me with guns and wanted me to solve a murder for which I was already a suspect.

Then there was the third female, one who sometimes bought me drinks and was undoubtedly using me to get herself a story. All of which was all right if there was even a remote possibility she would sleep with me. At least, that's what I told myself.

I sighed and put my feet up. A paperback copy of *The Odyssey* sat on a corner of my desk, right next to a bucket of nine-millimeter slugs. I opened it up and read about Odysseus, who was bewitched by Circe and spent a year on her island, not to mention in her bed. Didn't seem like the worst thing in the world, except when Circe tried to turn Odysseus into a pig. Life can be a tricky thing. Especially where women were involved.

I put down Homer and picked up the here and now. I needed an education, quick and dirty, about an old rape that might be spawning fresh murder. And I thought I knew just where to get it.

CHAPTER 16

Cook County's evidence warehouse sits at the corner of Twenty-third and Rockwell on the city's South Side. A pile of red and white bricks, surrounded by barbed wire and flat, vacant pavement, the warehouse holds the bones of Chicago's crimes. Eight stories high and chock-full.

Ray Goshen was six feet two and had to run around in the shower to get wet. His shoulders were as wide as my fist, and his neck didn't support his head, which tended to tilt to the left—although sometimes, when he got angry, I swore it tilted right. Whichever way he tilted, I always felt myself looking sideways at Ray and never really able to get a handle on what he was saying. Not that the head should matter. Tilted or not, the words all come out the same. Or so one would think. Anyway, in the world of Chicago evidence, Ray Goshen held the keys to the kingdom. He met me at the door, head leaning right and, true to form, not a happy man.

"What you doing down here, Kelly?"

"Hey, Ray, nice to see you, too."

"Last time you were here was not a good thing."

Last time I was here was almost a year ago. I'd gotten a tip on some home movies a killer named Alan Lake had covertly made from his jail cell in Stateville prison. He and his buddies smoking some weed and just having a hell of a good time. A client asked me if I couldn't track the tapes down. Goshen let me take a look through some of the evidence in the warehouse, and I found Lake's wallet. In it was a phone number. Twenty-three years later and it still worked. Someone still answered. She was Alan Lake's half sister. She had a copy of the tape in question and was more than willing to barter. A few dollars later, I had the tapes. A week after that, my client put them on the ten o'clock news. I didn't know about that part of the bargain. If I had, I'm not sure it would have made a difference. It did to Ray.

"They traced it back here, you know," Goshen said.

I knew that but pretended I didn't.

"Asked all kinds of questions. Nearly lost my job."

I knew that, too. Fact is, I'd watched the whole thing. From a distance. Fortunately, my client had a conscience, at least when pushed. They all tended to when pushed. She made a call and Ray Goshen kept his job. Otherwise, my client would have lost hers. That's what I told her, anyway. Goshen had just chalked it up to his good luck, which was fair enough.

"You owe me nothing, Ray. I know that."

"Fucking Kelly. This is about Gibbons, right?"

I nodded. Goshen knew Gibbons, worked the evidence locker at Gibbons' old district.

"I didn't kill him, Ray."

"No shit, Kelly. That doesn't mean you won't go to jail for it."

"Not likely."

Ray gave me a look like he half didn't believe me. I half didn't believe myself. Still, Goshen could never resist playing God with his evidence. Besides, he loved the gore. I knew that and counted on it.

"What do you want?" he said.

"It's an old file," I said. "Maybe it ties in. Probably not."

"You got a case number?"

"No. I got the name of the victim and a date."

I shoved a piece of paper in front of Goshen, who clicked his flashlight on it and then tilted the beam up.

"Rape or murder?"

Goshen's smile was missing a few parts. Coupled with the flashlight it was like talking to a human jack-o'-lantern. One with a broken neck. Still, he was the man with the keys. Keeper of the kingdom.

"Rape," I said.

Goshen scratched his private parts and started to laugh.

"How old was she?"

"Nineteen, twenty, maybe."

That tickled him even further.

"Come on."

We walked through the first floor, past rows of shelving stretching thirty feet to the ceiling, jammed with the various and sundry. Knives and pliers, machetes and cudgels. Two-by-fours and bedposts, metal shanks and flex cuffs. Toilet-seat covers, window frames, lengths of rope, twine, piano wire, and bed-sheets. The tools of murder, rape, and plain old mayhem, some of them sealed in plastic, some jammed into cardboard boxes, others just lying about with a tag and a piece of illegible scrawl attached thereto.

Goshen turned a corner and found his way to a small office. I could see the light inside. Beside the office was a black metal door. Goshen fished out a key and fit it into the door's lock.

"Bit of history in here, Kelly."

Goshen opened the door and clicked on a light. The room

looked like it used to be a supply closet. Now it was filled up with brown boxes on one side and a row of wooden shelves on the other. I took a step inside and sneezed. Everything was covered in dust.

"See the boxes," Goshen said.

I did.

"See the shelves."

I did.

"This is Grime. Not all of it, mind you. We have three other rooms for that boy. But this is some good stuff."

Goshen pulled out a stack of Girl Scout magazines once owned by John William Grime, Chicago's very own street mime and serial killer. They looked like normal magazines, except all the Girl Scouts were naked.

"Found cartons of this stuff inside his house. Sick fuck."

The warehouse man fingered one of the magazines, put it back down and picked up a plastic evidence bag. Inside it was a girl's school ring.

"See this? Suzanne Carson's ring. They found this in the attic. You remember Carson?"

I remembered Carson. Anyone who knew anything about Chicago crime would. She was Grime's last victim. The Girl Next Door. The case that led police to the house on Hutchinson and the fifteen bodies buried underneath. Through the plastic evidence bag, Goshen played his hands across the ring.

"You come in here a lot, Ray?"

For a moment there was a touch of hunger about his lips and eyes. Then Goshen subsided and dropped Suzanne's ring.

"My job is to keep this stuff straight. Let's go."

We locked up Grime's broom closet and walked next door. Goshen's office was small and jammed with more boxes of evidence. In one corner was a shipping cart full of handguns and rifles.

"They're getting melted next week," Goshen said. As if the guns needed an explanation. Which they didn't.

The office walls were covered with a brand of grit only true despair can create. The only decoration was a pinup calendar from August 1983. The girl on the calendar looked like she was about thirteen, and she was naked. Not coquettishly naked. Disturbingly naked.

"You like her?" Goshen said. He was behind me now, chin nearly on my shoulder.

"She's a little young, Ray."

He shrugged, moved back around the desk, and sat down.

"Have a seat."

From a drawer, Goshen produced an enormous green book with a red binding. He opened it and began to turn the pages, slowly and with care.

"Your girl. How old did you say she was?"

"About twenty."

"Raped, you say?"

"I did."

Goshen stopped turning pages.

"Did she fight?"

"Is she in the book, Ray?"

Goshen looked at me like I should be happy I wasn't stuffed underneath Grime's house and left there for a good while.

"How the fuck do I know? Let me take a look."

He returned to the ledger.

"You get a lot of people coming in here?" I said.

"Sure," Goshen said. "People like police officers. You know, the guys who actually belong here."

I snuck a look at the pages as Goshen turned. The entries were all handwritten. The first page I saw was dated January 1, 1934. Goshen stopped turning again.

"Yeah, yeah, I know. Fucking ancient. But you know what? Handwriting makes people think about what they put in. And besides, it's pretty damn hard to disguise your scrawl, in case you ever tried. So we say, fuck the computers. Let everyone write it all out. We just keep adding pages to the ledger. And there it is."

Goshen was flipping pages now. Each was large and took two hands to turn.

"Is this the only copy?" I said.

"Fucking pessimist. Yeah, it's the only copy and been the only copy for most of the last century. Fucking pessimists."

He stopped the turning.

"Here we go. The crime happened in 1997, right?"

"Right."

"We search by file number. Page by page. Here. This covers 1980 through the nineties."

Goshen unclipped the ledger and split up the hundred or so pages cataloging two decades of Chicago crime.

"Don't fuck these up," he said.

"I got it."

Fifteen minutes later Goshen found an entry.

"Goddamn it, Kelly."

"Yeah?"

"Elaine Remington, December twenty-fourth, 1997?"

"Yeah."

"Next time come in with a goddamn case number. I ran a search for this evidence just the other day."

"For who?"

Goshen slammed the ledger closed, blew his nose into a barrel under his desk, and crossed one knee over the other.

"Couple of pukes from the DA's office."

"Shit."

"Yeah." Goshen smiled. "Thing is, I hate the DA even more than your sorry ass."

"Lucky for me."

"Got that right. Told the two of them everything was numbered; go ahead and search the place."

"How long did they last?"

"First guy. About an hour. Second guy was a go-getter. Went the full day. Never made it off the first floor."

"Think he ever got close?"

"I know he didn't. The first floor only carries cases through 1975."

"Didn't tell that to the DA's men, huh?"

Goshen gave me the blank gaze of a city bureaucrat, willing to stand there until I figured it out for myself. Or at least until quitting time.

"You have a map of this place?" I said.

Goshen tapped his forehead.

"Right here. But you have to ask the right question. Let's go."

The elevator was a birdcage job with one of those old cranks you have to hold down until you get to your floor. Goshen turned it on with a skeleton-looking key, and we started up. The warehouse man kept his eyes fixed on the crank. Not because he didn't know how to work it, but because his alternative was to look at me. Didn't exactly make me feel warm inside. Still, we were moving.

"Fifth floor," Goshen said. "Nineteen ninety through '99."

He cracked the elevator door and we walked out. Rows of iron shelving stretched upward and ran off into the darkness. Bits of light from what might have been bulbs filtered down from the rafters. Useless except as a reminder to go back downstairs and get a flashlight. Fortunately, Goshen was ahead of the game. He jumped into a forklift and pulled a flash from his pocket.

"Let's go," he said, and powered up the lift. I got in and we drove.

"Kind of a big place, this fifth floor, Ray."

"Lot of sick fucks, Kelly. Lot of sick fucks. This is it. The late nineties."

Goshen played a light over lumps of black, coffin boxes of evidence covered in dust. Forgotten by everyone. Cataloged by Ray.

"Here, put these on."

Goshen handed me a set of latex gloves and a white breather. I started at one end of an aisle. He started at the other. The work was slow, box by box. Pull one off the shelf, open it up, and pick through the pieces of old crimes.

Some of the material was strictly forensic: small plastic bags of hair, blood smears, or nails clipped off a corpse.

Then there was the echo of what was once a life.

In one box, coloring books, the pictures half finished, a child's name in crayon, smeared with blood.

In another, a CD of Pearl Jam's *Ten*, AMANDA scrawled on the cover with a flower. Underneath the CD, a calendar from 1996. Filled with dates that never mattered. People never met. A life never lived and now forgotten.

Two hours into the process, I picked up a small box with 12/24/97 scrawled across the side. My heart tightened for two reasons. That was the day of Elaine Remington's attack. Even better, the signature on the box belonged to John Gibbons.

Goshen was around the corner working on another aisle. I sliced open the box and found a single manila envelope inside. It appeared to be intact, with Gibbons' initials and the date written across the red evidence seal. I sliced through the seal and slid out a single item, a green women's polo gashed in several places and crusted with blood, now the color of rust. I felt a presence at my elbow.

"What you got?" Goshen said.

I showed him the evidence box.

"The date is right and it's got Gibbons' name," I said. "But there's no case number."

Goshen picked up the envelope and turned it over. His fingers were thin, nails long and ragged.

"Nothing on the envelope, either." The warehouse man winked. "Almost like someone wanted it to be lost."

"I'm thinking this is the shirt my victim was wearing."

"I'm thinking you might be half-ass right for once. Let's go back to the office."

We sat down with two cans of Old Style and the shirt between us. It was almost winter in Chicago but mid-July in Goshen's cubbyhole. A fan chugged away in one corner. Goshen popped open his beer and pushed half the can past an impossibly large Adam's apple, never taking his eyes off the shirt. And never touching it.

"Officially," he said, "this piece of evidence doesn't really exist. No case number, no log-in report, no other identifying marks."

Goshen craned his neck, rolled his eyes, and pushed at the shirt with a pencil.

"I got to go out and clean up that fucking mess you made out there. When I come back, I have a lot of work to do. I don't want you here, and I don't want any more distractions lying around. You got it?"

I got it.

"You really don't like the DA, do you?" I said.

Goshen gave me a look of pure nothing and left. Like any good civil servant, he cherished institutional hatred, nurtured the otherwise forgotten slight, and polished a grudge like it was gold. Whatever the DA's office had done to Goshen, it wasn't good for them. For me, however, it was a different story entirely. I picked up the shirt carefully, folded it into its envelope, and slipped out of the warehouse. As quickly and as quietly as I could.

CHAPTER 17

I returned to my office and slid the green polo into one of those secret hiding places they teach you in private-investigator school. Also known as my bottom left-hand drawer. Then I turned on the radio. ESPN was doing a hot-stove report on the Cubbies. Be still my heart.

I listened intently, pondering deep thoughts, such as what manner of men might pay Alfonso Soriano $136 million to play baseball and where, pray tell, I might get such a gig. Then I noticed a piece of paper slipped under my door. I walked over and picked it up. Eat-A-Pita was having a special on char-grilled shrimp pitas layered with onions and wasabi sauce. I turned off the hot stove and was about to head out when the phone rang. I didn't recognize the number but picked up anyway.

"Kelly, it's Vince Rodriguez."

The detective's voice seemed a little stretched. Whatever he needed to talk about, Rodriguez had given it some thought and was uneasy.

"You eat yet?" he said.

I told Rodriguez about the special at Eat-A-Pita. He seemed properly impressed.

"How about I meet you there," he said. "Half hour."

. . .

I FOUND RODRIGUEZ in a booth by the window. I figured the detective wanted one of two things. Help with a case. Or help with Nicole. I had barely sat down before I got my answer.

"You and Nicole," Rodriguez said.

"Yeah."

"Friends since you were kids."

"Nicole told you all that, huh?"

"A little bit."

"She grew up a couple houses down the street. Over on the West Side. I looked out for her growing up. Now I think she looks out for me."

I took a cursory look at the menu and kept talking.

"Why the interest, Detective?"

I tried to keep the grin out of my voice. Across the table, the Unflappable One squirmed.

"She probably told you. We got a bit of a thing."

"A thing?"

I took a sip of water and waited.

"You know how it is. On the job and stuff."

A waitress drifted over. We both ordered the special. Rodriguez added an iced tea.

"If she likes you, don't try to figure it out," I said. "Just take it as a blessing. Pray she doesn't wake up one day and change her mind. At least that's what I'd do. Is that all you wanted to ask me, Detective?"

"Pretty much. I just wanted to see, you know."

"Whether we were more than friends?"

"Yeah."

I shrugged.

"Never have been. Just not like that."

I thought Rodriguez would let it lie. I was wrong.

"Is there something else going on with her?"

"How so?" I said.

"I don't know. Just seems like there's some kind of hurt. When you were around the other night, it got a little easier. At least, it seemed that way."

"How much does she mean to you, Detective?"

"You think I like making a fool of myself in front of an ex-cop I barely know?"

"You give it time. You let her figure it out. Let her figure you out."

"I'm thinking maybe we shouldn't work together. Maybe that would make it better."

"Can't answer that for you."

Rodriguez emptied a packet of sugar into his tea and watched it dissolve.

"I'm not a guy who's been married before," he said. "No divorce or any of that stuff. You were a cop. You know what I mean."

I did.

"Give it some time," I said. "She's worth it."

Our orders came, and we ate in silence for a bit.

"Any progress on the rape?"

"Still waiting for Nicole's lab work," the detective said. "If she can get DNA off those bedsheets, we might be in business. By the way, what exactly makes you think this guy is a killer?"

I shrugged.

"Your victim says he had finished raping her. Done. But he continues with the knife play. Runs it along her ribs, tears up the side of her shirt. Small cuts to the throat. Why?"

Rodriguez waited.

"He was playing with her," I said. "Like a cat plays with a

mouse. See if he can get a rise out of her. A little more excite-ment. Guy like that, he's building to something. A release."

"He kills her," Rodriguez said.

"That's what the cat does with the mouse."

Our waitress drifted over. Rodriguez took a refill on his tea.

"I asked around about you," he said. "Heard you were pretty good with a case file."

The detective was right. In 2003 Chicago had six hundred fresh homicides. I cleared twenty-five of them in eight months, working alone. The next guy had half that and he was working most of the time with a partner. I didn't share any of that with Rodriguez. Still, it was nice someone downtown remembered.

"That was a while back," I said.

"How are you with it?"

"If you mean do I see the faces at night, the answer is yes. But it gets better."

Rodriguez picked at the last of his shrimp and pondered night-mares not yet born. I reflected on the dead that lived just under-neath my eyelids.

"Why didn't it happen with Miriam?" he said.

"If I had to guess, I'd say she got to him somehow. In a sense."

"Not sure I buy that, Kelly."

"I'm not saying he felt pity for her. No. Guys like that, they feel sorry for themselves. Something in the way she talked, what she said, how she acted. Triggered his self-pity."

"And saved her life," Rodriguez said.

"It's a theory."

"Yeah. Next girl might not be so lucky."

Vince's PDA buzzed. He flipped it open, read the message, and typed in a response. Then he was out of his seat, a few bills on the table, moving through the restaurant. I was on his shoulder.

"You got the gift, Kelly. We just got another possible sexual assault. Couple of blocks from here. In progress. You up for it?"

"You sure?"

"They tell me you used to be good. Why not? Just don't shoot anybody unless they shoot first."

We got in his car and peeled north on Clark. Rodriguez radioed Dispatch.

"This is Rodriguez. I'm two blocks east, heading to the eight-oh-seven in progress. Copy."

Dispatch crackled back.

"Affirmative. Two squads on scene. Officers searching building for the suspect."

We rolled up to a center-entrance Chicago three-flat, an older building called the Belmont Arms near the corner of Belmont and Sheffield.

Two uniforms, one short, one tall, stood at the entrance to an alley on the building's east side. The shorter one stepped forward. Rodriguez flashed his badge just as the cop's shoulder mic barked. He hit the MUTE button and took a quick look at the detective's shield.

"Yes, sir, Detective. Attack occurred in the alley. Then the suspect ran into the building. We have two units inside. Hold on a second."

The officer turned away, mumbled into his shoulder, then turned back.

"They're on the first landing. If you want to go in, they'll wait there."

Rodriguez took a radio from the uniform and walked toward the building. The cop walked with us and kept talking.

"The suspect's a white male, five feet nine, one hundred and seventy pounds, wearing a black bomber jacket and blue jeans.

According to the victim, he covered his face up and is armed with a knife."

Rodriguez drew his gun and entered the building. I followed. We climbed the stairs and found two cops waiting. The stairwell was dimly lit, the walls gray with streaks of dirty sunlight from a pair of windows cut high into the landing. The older of the two uniforms got us up to speed.

"The other team is securing the back exits. Hallways run in both directions from the top of the stairs."

"How many apartments on each floor?" Rodriguez said.

"Three. No telling who's home."

"So he could be inside any of these units?"

"Yes, sir. Three floors' worth."

"Okay. First thing we do is sweep the entire building, from the top down. Look for any sign of forced entry. If not, then we go unit by unit. Knock on the door, ID yourself, and ask to come in."

We walked to the top floor together. The uniforms stacked on the left side of the hallway, crept around the corner, and disappeared. Rodriguez and I slipped around the other corner, guns drawn. Twenty feet down a door was ajar, light spilling into the hall. Rodriguez cruised up close, quiet. No sign of forced entry. Rodriguez eased the door in, three inches, half a foot. Over his shoulder, I could see a piece of hallway. Beyond that, a living room.

The detective gave me a short nod, then moved, low and fast, across the threshold. I followed, breathing slow and scanning. To my left was a couch that folded out to a bed, a nineteen-inch TV tuned to *Judge Judy*, and a set of windows that looked out over Belmont. Rodriguez eased across the living room, down another hallway, and stopped. He motioned for me to stack behind him.

"Blood," he whispered and pointed to a smear along a baseboard. Then he moved around the corner and into the kitchen. More slashes of blood crisscrossed the walls toward what looked like a pantry. That is where we found the old man. In the final crook, in the final cranny of his studio apartment. At the very end of his life.

The wallet in his pocket would tell us his name was William Conlan. He wore one of those old-fashioned sweaters with patches on the elbows and had a pair of reading glasses knocked askew but still on his face. William's eyes were open, his lips were parted, and the fingers on his right hand pointed our way, seemed to beckon. In his neck he had a black-handled knife, plunged to the hilt. Blood was pooled on the floor and spreading rapidly around us. Rodriguez radioed for backup, slid to his knees, and felt for a pulse. Nothing.

Paramedics arrived and began to work on the body. I moved around the blood to get a better look at the knife. The handle was old and cracked. I walked into the kitchen and pulled open the drawers.

"What do you see?"

It was Rodriguez, hands and forearms stained crimson.

"You should have worn some gloves."

Rodriguez turned on the faucet and washed the blood down the drain.

"I don't worry about getting AIDS from eighty-year-old men. You find the knife?"

I showed him the drawer, full of odds and ends, including three black-handled knives identical to the one in the other room.

"Must have started out here," I said.

"The assault victim says the guy had a knife in the alley," Rodriguez said. "Why not use that one?"

I shrugged.

"Who knows? He grabs this one out of the old man's hand and

just hits him. Anyway, they struggle down the hallway a bit and into the pantry."

"Guy can't be too far away," Rodriguez said and walked over to a small window at the back of the kitchen. It was open and looked out over a row of rooftops running south alongside the El tracks.

"What do you think?" he said.

"I think it's worth a look."

Rodriguez climbed through the window. I followed.

CHAPTER 18

I stepped out the window and onto a fire escape. Night was dropping over the city, and the iron underneath us creaked in the breeze.

The roofs in Chicago are mostly flat and covered with either gray tar paper or hard black rubber. That is, unless the rooftop happens to be on the 3600 block of North Sheffield or the 1000 block of West Waveland. Then, of course, it is covered with bleachers, beer, and drunk baseball fans paying $200 a pop to watch the Cubs find new ways to lose baseball games. But I digress.

Rodriguez flicked on a flashlight and dropped his head over the side of the fire escape. The adjacent roof was slightly below us. The span across looked to be maybe five feet. Not a lot if you're standing on terra firma. Quite a bit more when it's three stories down to the blacktop.

"Looks doable," the detective said. Seemed like more of a query than a statement.

I nodded and swung my leg out over the side. Before Rodriguez could stop me and especially before I could think too much, I braced myself against the railing and pushed off. I cleared the expanse easily. I also caught my foot on the stone parapet that guarded the adjacent building's edge and ended up face-first on the deck. I heard a thump beside me and a light step moving away.

"Let's go, Kelly. This guy isn't waiting on us."

I offered up the best curse I could think of and followed the detective's flashlight. The roof was deserted except for a single air conditioner shut down for the coming winter. The only entrance was a metal door locked from the inside. Rodriguez played his light across the alley to the next building. The span across was at least thirty feet.

"Unless our suspect is Carl Lewis," I said, "I'm guessing he took a pass."

Rodriguez shined his light down to the pavement. Just in case our guy thought he could fly. No body crumpled in a heap below.

"Shit," the detective muttered.

I pointed to the El tracks crouched alongside the building.

"What do you think?"

Rodriguez's flashlight found a service ladder bolted to the side of the tracks and within arm's length of the roof's edge.

"Let's go," he said.

We swung up the ladder and onto the tracks for Chicago's Brown Line. Rodriguez shined his light on a thick piece of metal running alongside the main set of tracks.

"Third rail, Kelly. Not good."

The third rail powers Chicago's El, offering six hundred volts of heavy-duty current and instant death to anyone who touches it. I gave the rail a wide berth.

"If he came up here, he probably headed south," I said. "Away from the crime scene."

Rodriguez nodded and we started out at a jog. The next El stop was Diversey, maybe a half mile distant. The flashlight gave us two or three feet worth of yellow space. Otherwise our vision was limited to ribbons of streetlight cutting across steel. I felt a vibration under my feet, then the rumble of a train, still in the distance. We stopped and listened.

"Which way is it headed?"

"Not sure," Rodriguez said. "We should be all right if it's on our side. Plenty of room for it to get by."

I was glad he thought so but didn't say anything. The rumble stopped. The train was probably picking up passengers. In the ensuing quiet, I heard a stumble, maybe a curse, then a footfall.

"He's out there," I said.

Rodriguez began to move forward again. Twenty yards later we made out the first outlines of a person, just a black smudge slipping along the far side of the tracks. In the distance the rumble began again and picked up steam.

"Can we catch him?" Rodriguez said.

I was a miler in high school. With a strong wind, on a good track, I can still clip off a six-minute mile. On train tracks, in the black of night, with six hundred volts humming two feet to my right, maybe not quite that fast.

"Give me the flash," I said.

It was probably a quarter mile now to the next platform. I guessed our guy was maybe two hundred yards ahead. The only good news: I had a light and he didn't. I settled into a run that was more of a lope. Behind me, the rumble had died again as the El train stopped at Belmont. I dodged a rat that scurried across the tracks and picked up my pace. I had a good sweat going now and could see a jumble of yellow up ahead. Diversey. I stopped just short of the platform, looked, and listened. The elevated was surrounded by taller buildings here, commercial stuff, cutting off any light from the street. There was no creeping, no scratching, no sound of movement. Then the rumble started up again. Much closer. I looked back as a flash of white came around a sudden corner. The 7:05 Brown Line express was right on time.

I sprinted the last twenty yards and scrambled up onto the platform. Ten people were passing the time in various stages of waiting. One couple made out on a bench in a corner. Three people had headphones on, eyes closed, tapping away to their internal rhythms. Two people read the *Trib*; one, the *Sun-Times*. Another typed away furiously on his BlackBerry, waited, laughed furiously to himself, and typed away some more. Finally, there was one woman, alone on an island, talking to herself, never waiting for a response. None of the ten struck me as a desperate killer. Even worse, none took the slightest notice of yours truly, emerging from the soup of a Chicago night with a gun in one hand and flashlight in the other.

Thirty seconds after I arrived, the train roared through the station without slowing an inch. Twenty seconds after that, Rodriguez climbed up from the depths.

"That was fun," he said.

"Had to check it out."

The detective nodded. "I'll get some uniforms to ask this crowd what they saw."

"Hell, he could have walked down those tracks bare-ass naked and no one in this crowd would have noticed."

Rodriguez shrugged and walked away, radio in hand. I headed down to the street. The detective caught up with me on the sidewalk.

"I have to get back to Belmont and help process the body. They need someone to sit with the assault victim until Nicole's team gets there. Can you help us out?"

"Sure."

"Should only be about ten minutes. Don't ask her anything. Don't touch her. Just sit."

"Where is she?"

"In a cruiser at the back of the alley. I already cleared you. Her name is Jennifer Cole. And Kelly . . ."

"Yeah?"

"She's twelve."

"Great."

"Like I said, babysit. If she talks, just listen."

We walked north on Sheffield Avenue. Rodriguez to an old man who had been knifed in his own home. Me to a twelve-year-old who had been attacked in her own city. I couldn't figure out which was worse.

CHAPTER 19

I found the cruiser right where it was supposed to be. Jennifer was sitting in the backseat. I sat up front. There was a layer of Plexiglas between us.

"Hi, Jennifer. My name is Michael."

The girl was folded up in a blanket. I could see the silver and red of her school uniform underneath. She looked out the window, chin on knees, at the underbelly of the El. After a moment she shifted position, then answered.

"Hey."

That was it. Just hey.

"I'm not a cop," I said. "So you don't have to answer a whole bunch of questions."

She had light red hair, wide-spaced green eyes, and a sprinkling of freckles in between. She had bruises on her neck, her upper arms, and underneath her jaw. They were yellowed and looked like they might have come from a man's grip. A man's fist.

"If you're not a cop, why are you here?"

"I used to be a cop. Now I'm a private investigator. Sometimes I help out."

"Oh. Some guy attacked me."

"I know, Jennifer."

"That's good."

She laid her head down against the fold of her knees and sighed.

"They're finding my parents right now. They're going to be pissed."

"I wouldn't worry about that, Jennifer."

"You don't know. They'll be pissed."

"You're twelve years old?"

She nodded.

"I was headed home from school."

"But you took a detour?"

"I was going to take the El downtown. Walk over to the Apple store."

"Cool store."

"It's open 'til nine. But that's why they'll be mad."

"They won't be mad."

"You don't know my dad."

I thought about Rodriguez's instructions. About not talking to the girl. Then I took another look at the girl. Then I forgot about Rodriguez's instructions.

"Tell me about it," I said.

"I don't think so."

Silence. Then she continued.

"He got me with the basketball."

"The basketball?"

"I was walking across the alley, blocked off from the street by those."

She pointed toward two large green dumpsters. Between us and the illusion of safety on Belmont.

"He came up out of nowhere. Dribbled the ball off his foot or his leg. Something like that. Right into the alley."

I looked outside. A red, white, and blue ABA ball had rolled up against one of the iron girders that held up the El.

"You followed the ball," I said.

"I took a step."

"Anyone would. It's instinct. He knew that."

"You think so?" she said.

"Yeah, Jennifer. I think so."

"He was behind, pushing me. With the knife. Put a hand over my mouth and started dragging me."

I noticed a short set of stone steps cut into the side of the Belmont Arms. At the bottom of the steps was a wooden door. Looked like it had been kicked open a long time ago. My guess was that was where Jennifer Cole was supposed to wind up. Inside the cellar of the Belmont Arms, where assault would have ripened into rape and perhaps worse.

"How did you get away?"

"Scratched him. Bit him. He let go and I screamed. Then he ran."

Jennifer's voice was brittle to the point of dust. She showed me her teeth as if to prove she could bite. Then she started to cry. Quietly. Reluctantly. As if she needed permission. I waited. No idea what was next, what should be next.

"You get a look at him?"

She shook her head.

"I'm so fucking stupid."

"It's not your fault, Jennifer."

I didn't know how else to comfort the girl behind the Plexi. She was evidence, waiting to be processed. Another case waiting to be worked. A burst from the squad's police radio kicked the conversation forward.

"I think your parents are here," I said. "I'm going to go up and find out. But first I need to ask you one more question. The bruises on your neck and arms. You didn't get them today, did you?"

Jennifer looked down at her arms and shook her head.

"Who did that to you, Jennifer?"

She shrugged her shoulders and wiped her nose.

"My dad gets mad sometimes."

"How mad, Jennifer?"

"Pretty mad, mister. Pretty fucking mad."

I laid a business card flat against the Plexi.

"Jennifer."

She looked up.

"You see this number?"

She nodded.

"Remember it. Call it anytime you have a problem. You understand what I mean?"

She nodded.

"You got the number memorized?"

She nodded again.

"Say it back to me."

She did.

"Good. Remember the number and get through today. Tomorrow gets better."

I left the girl the way I found her and walked to the front of the building. Nicole had just arrived.

"Your vic's in the cruiser," I said.

"Thanks. They told me you were here. That's two assaults in two days. How did that happen?"

"Luck, I guess. You think they're related?"

Nicole shrugged.

"Probably not. Both attackers used a knife to subdue. But this one was bold. Broad daylight on a busy street. Besides, this one killed."

"Assault victim's a kid, Nicole."

"I know. We'll get her some help. Where's Vince?"

"Upstairs with the body. Victim says she scratched the guy and bit him on the hand. Might want to look for blood."

Nicole shook her head.

"No blood yet. But we did find this."

An evidence tech handed her a Baggie. Inside was a used condom.

"Where?"

"Back of the alley."

"Doesn't make sense," I said. "The kid says she fought him off."

"You mean she wasn't penetrated."

"That's what I mean."

Nicole handed the evidence back to her assistant.

"Happens a lot. These guys put on the condom before they attack. Then they get excited during the struggle. Lose control."

"You think that's what happened?"

Nicole shrugged.

"Could be. Good news is we get a profile to run through our database. See what comes back. Sounds like our victim's a tough kid."

"Don't think she has much choice," I said. "Check out the bruises on her face and neck."

"From the assault?"

"From her old man. Sounds like he's using the kid as a punching bag. Anyway, she's scared of him."

"We'll look into it."

"What does that mean?"

Nicole lifted her chin and folded her arms across her chest.

"It means Family Services will talk to her parents and do what they can. That's all we can ask for, Michael."

I didn't see the point in pursuing it so I didn't.

"Okay, I gotta run."

Nicole wanted to say something more, but I was already out of the alley and across the street. They had strung out some crime-scene tape, and a small crowd was beginning to form behind it. Just inside the tape, a female cop was talking to a man in a cash-mere overcoat.

"Yes, sir," the cop said. "Your daughter is fine. She's being examined right now and then you can see her."

He was early forties, receding hairline, well on his way to a comb-over. A big guy but soft. Middle-class soft. Too many nachos, too much time on the couch. The coat, however, looked nice.

"You listen here," he said. "My kid is back there. They tell me she was attacked. I want to see her, and I want to see her now."

As he spoke, the man jabbed a fistful of fingers into the cop's protective vest. The officer caught his hand and turned it in on itself. The man's knees gave a bit. The cop spoke quietly and quickly.

"I understand you're upset, sir. I understand that's your daughter. But you're going to play by the rules here. Rule number one. You touch me or any other officer again and we put the cuffs on you. Put you in the back of a cruiser. Are we clear?"

The cop didn't wait for a response, didn't need to. I moved up as she walked away. Jennifer's father was still shaking his hand and mumbling to himself.

"Fucking bitch."

"Excuse me, sir."

I flashed what might have been a badge but wasn't.

"What do you want?"

"You're the victim's father?"

"You going to let me see her?"

The arrogance was gone. In its place, the instinctive wariness of a coward.

"Take a walk over here, sir."

I moved him away from the crowd, back under the elevated tracks. In just a few feet we were alone, at least alone enough.

"What do you want?"

Up close, his face was as soft as the rest of him. A part of me felt sorry for the man, for what he was about to endure with his child. That part of me, however, wasn't part of this conversation.

"Your daughter, sir. She seems more scared of you than she does the man who just attacked her. By my way of thinking, that makes you one of two things. A pedophile or just another asshole who likes to punch up his kid. I'm voting for the latter, but what really matters is . . . what do you think?"

The guy could go one of two ways. Fear followed by denial. Or rage followed by denial. I wasn't entirely surprised when he swore and made a lunge for the collar of my coat. He missed and fell to the pavement. I followed him down, slipping my left hand up under his neck, pulling him to his feet, and pinning him to the side of the building. With my right hand I flipped open the snap on my holster and took out my gun. I held it close between us. His eyes widened when he felt steel pressed against his body. I could smell urine and took a step back.

"Glad we got your attention," I said. "I'll make this real simple. They are going to put you in a room with some people from

Family Services, DCFS, all that bullshit. Tell you how you need to control your temper around Jennifer, especially after all this trauma. You listen, don't listen. I don't give a damn."

I tightened my grip a bit. His breath shortened to a wheeze, his eyes fastened on the black end of a nine millimeter. From the corner of my eye, I could see a part of the crowd, outside the tape, peeking at us through the girders. I moved my body between him and any potential audience.

"You hearing me?" I said. "Don't speak, just nod."

He popped his head once.

"I'm going to check up on Jennifer from time to time. See how she's doing with school. You got any problems with that?"

A shake of the head.

"Good. I hear anything from her. Tomorrow, next week, next month, five years from now. Anything from Jennifer and I come find you. We talk again. Except this time, you eat a bullet. Tragic suicide. Chicago-style. You think it doesn't happen in this city? Think again. Now get the fuck out of here and go make your daughter feel better."

I dropped the guy where we stood. He fell to the ground and tried to cover up the suit he had already soiled. Then I walked back through the girders, down the alley, and under the crime scene tape.

Most people would say it was just a couple of bruises. I was out of line, overreacted, did more harm than good with the rough stuff. Most people, however, have never walked in a cop's shoes. Never seen a ten-year-old sold by her pimp on a street corner, then stripped naked and beaten with a hot hanger. Or an eleven-year-old boy, chained to a radiator by his mom and fed dog food for kicks. Or a girl, all of thirteen, handcuffed to a mattress and forced to service men until she is so torn up inside, she dies on the way to the hospital. Most people don't see any of that.

Even a little bit of what adults can do to kids. So most people don't overreact.

I found my way inside the El station, slipped through a turnstile and onto the platform. A couple of girls stood nearby, teenagers, listening to their iPods and talking at the same time. It was empty talk: school, boys, clothes, boys, movies, boys. I sat and listened. Never had anything so stupid sounded so good.

CHAPTER 20

The next morning Jennifer was big news. Page one of the *Chicago Sun-Times.* Twelve-year-old assault victims, especially white ones, will do that to a newspaper.

William Conlan was in there, too. Three sentences, five paragraphs into the story. Apparently old guys who live alone don't rate so high.

I shrugged and sipped my coffee. By week's end, both would be forgotten, swept away by the clutter of fresh crime, fresh bodies, fresh story lines.

Just after eight o'clock, I got in my car and headed south on Racine. I took a right at Fullerton and worked my way west toward Humboldt Park. The sun was out, bright and hard. Still not too cold, but there was a bite in the air. Snow by nightfall.

I parked a block from John Gibbons' apartment, popped the trunk on my car, and pulled out a soft leather duffel. If Gibbons was looking at Elaine Remington's rape, he should have had a working file in his room. Maybe the landlady knew where it was. Maybe not. Either way, it was probably somewhere in the house. Hence, the duffel bag.

Inside were two pairs of latex gloves, a flashlight, some rope, and a set of picks. I had noticed an index card tacked to the bul-

letin board in Mulberry's office. It was for an appointment with a
doctor. This morning at eight-thirty. I put on the gloves, zipped
up my coat, and checked my watch. Eight forty-five. Time to go.

The front door was a lot easier the second time around. In less
than a minute, both locks slipped free and I was inside. Morning
light filtered through trees and threw patterns across the walls. I
flicked on a flashlight and moved through the sitting room,
toward the alcove where the old lady kept her records. The door
to the alcove was closed. I pushed it open.

Mulberry was sitting in an old-fashioned swivel chair behind
her desk. She was wearing a blue dress with a green brooch. Her
hair was pinned up, and high heels hung off her feet. Mulberry
was dressed for her appointment. The landlady, however, had no
need for a doctor. Now or ever again.

I took a closer look at the face. Her eyes had bulged a bit. The
mouth was slack. There was blood crusted under each nostril, on
her lips, and chin. I nudged the body an inch or so with my foot.
One leg crumpled against the other, revealing a mass of white
flesh, spider veins, and just a hint of lividity underneath. The
landlady had been dead awhile.

I moved away from the body and cast my light around the
room. The filing cabinet was open, contents pulled out and
strewn about the floor. I didn't see anything worth touching or
taking. I eased around and nudged open the desk drawers. Nothing there, either. I pulled back, felt a tingle, and looked behind
me. A pair of eyes gleamed in the darkness. Oskar moved softly
onto the landlady's shoulder. Mulberry's body shifted again. The
cat jumped lightly to the floor. I noticed, for the first time, two
puncture marks surrounded by a bruise high up on the landlady's
arm. I played my light on the sleeve of the old woman's dress and
saw two corresponding holes. The typical Taser delivers fifty
thousand volts of electricity in five-second intervals. Enough to

knock you to the ground but not kill you. Apparently, someone forgot to tell Mulberry. I turned off the light and decided to take a look upstairs.

Gibbons' old room was to my left. A floorboard creak, however, pushed me to the right. At the end of the hallway were two doors. I turned the doorknob on the first and inched it open. No light on the other side. I reached in and felt the floor. Cold. Probably a bathroom. I moved across the threshold, maybe half a foot. I heard a ping, felt a sting in my left shoulder. Almost immediately, I knew what it was, knew what was coming, and then felt it.

The first jolt did its job as I went to my knees. I was halfway up when the second blast hit. I felt my chest tighten and my heart accelerate. Another blast and I was on my back, unable to breathe with a Volkswagen on my chest. My final thought before I blacked out was that a heart attack was one hell of a way to die.

CHAPTER 21

I woke up on the floor. The lights were still out, the house quiet. I could hear a truck grinding its gears down the block, felt a breeze from an open window, and saw a sliver of sunlight bouncing off a vanity mirror. I got up slowly and took inventory. Some burns for sure, and my shoulder was tender from the Taser. I was alive, however, and that put me one step ahead of the corpse cooling a floor below. I threw some water on my face and took a walk over to the window.

This is where my guy had gone out, probably along the roofline and then dropped down into the yard. Why he didn't kill me, I didn't know. Maybe he thought he had. What he was after was an even better question.

I went back downstairs. A clock on the wall told me it was late afternoon. I'd been out more than a while. I tiptoed through a half-dozen cats and back into the dining room. Mulberry was still sitting in the alcove, still very much dead. Oskar glided past me again and jumped up on the desk. He stared at his owner for a moment, then started to lick at the blood on her face. I figured it was time to go.

Two blocks later I pulled into a White Hen and bought some

aspirin, water, and coffee. Then I drove another couple of blocks, found a pay phone, and called in the body.

As I drove home I thought about the landlady, the touch of greed behind her eyes, and wondered if she didn't invite death across her threshold. Then I pulled a phone number from my pocket. My head hurt, but not too bad. It had already been a long day, and no one was waiting at home to cook me dinner or bandage my wounds. I figured a drink could only help. And I knew just the place.

CHAPTER 22

The bar was warm with wood and light that drifted softly into corners. A woman in a Burberry tweed and a man in a peacoat huddled close by a fire, seasoned with just a touch of peat. On the other side, an old man in a watch cap pulled on a pint while his pal produced a bodhran from its case. A third joined him with the squeeze box. The pint drinker held a fiddle across his lap. Now he took it in one hand and a bow in the other. It appeared a session was in order.

"Can I help you?"

The accent was West Coast. More like Galway. The face was sharp Irish, with a high forehead, brown hair in wisps, and ears sculpted close to her head. The eyes were blue and moving.

"Guinness," I said.

I sat back to enjoy the ritual. The glass was fresh and held tight against the brass fitting. The pour was clean. She drew it three quarters full and placed it on a wooden box atop the pump. While the pint settled she wiped an ashtray, took an order for an Irish breakfast, and drew off a Smithwick's. Then she pulled again on the Guinness and topped the pint with a froth slick and sweet as morning cream.

"Brilliant," I said.

"Ah, fuck off with the brilliant. You're a Yank and that's all there is to it."

I winked and Megan curled a smile my way. She was the best the Hidden Shamrock had to offer and one of my favorites. I hadn't been through the door in over a year, but it didn't matter. The Guinness was still the finest in the city. John Gibbons knew that and made the Shamrock his local. I caught Megan's attention and asked about my former partner.

"Indeed, John was in," she said. "Last Thursday night, it was. Sat just a bit down from where you're at now."

Megan sipped at a cup of Barry's tea. She drank it strong with milk and two sugars.

"Was there a blonde with him?" I said.

"There was. She's been coming in most nights. Nothing but fucking trouble."

I pulled a phone number from my pocket, the one Elaine Remington had scrawled on my bedroom mirror.

"This still the bar's number?"

"It is."

"The pay phone?"

A shake of the head. Megan pointed to a phone behind the bar.

"We don't have pay phones anymore what with the cell phones and that load of crap. Like a fucking switchboard in here on a Friday night."

"I bet," I said. "How well did you know John?"

"As well as I know any customer. No more. He in trouble?"

"He was found dead Sunday morning. Down by Navy Pier."

Megan stared at the dregs in her mug for a moment. Then I followed her gaze up and across the bar. Elaine Remington stood in the doorway.

"That would be her, Michael."

"Yes, it would."

I got up from my stool. Elaine met me halfway across the bar. She didn't have a gun this time. At least not one pointed my way.

"About time you got here," she said.

"Expecting me?"

"I'm in here most nights. Figured sooner or later you'd show up. How about buying me a drink?"

Megan was waiting at the bar, bottle of Jameson in hand.

"The usual?" she said.

Elaine nodded. Megan set up two whiskeys, neat. My client took the first in one go. Then she leaned up against me. I guess in case I was cold.

"I drink seven of these every night," she said.

"Whether you need it or not."

She called for number three, knocked back two, and giggled.

"You're cute," she said.

"You talk too much."

"You're still cute."

I had heard this conversation, between a blonde and a detective, somewhere before. Elaine lit up a cigarette, blew smoke in my direction, and continued.

"Gibbons was more like a father figure. You know, that whole thing. Want one?"

I moved back a bit and watched her work. Just the slightest tremor in her hand as the shot glass went up and back down. It didn't look easy.

"Why do you do that?"

She wiped her mouth, then at a trace of moisture at the corner of one eye.

"Keeps me straight. You know some peeps have their latte. Me, I have seven lattes. After that I look for some company."

The bar was quiet now. Not really, but it seemed that way. She filled my eye, and I shaped my mind around it. I didn't want to but still felt the heat. Some women were just that way with men. The crazy talk continued.

"Let me ask you something, Mr. Detective. How much do you know about rape?"

I shrugged.

"You ever know a girl who'd been raped?"

"Plenty," I said.

"I mean really know, as in romantic."

I shrugged again. She whetted the knife.

"Think you could, you know, be with her after something like that? No, let me rephrase, after someone had her like that?"

I took a look down the bar. Mostly because I didn't know where else to look.

"Thought so," she said and drained number four.

I jumped in and tried to make it better.

"You were brutalized and almost murdered, Elaine. That's an act of violence, plain and simple."

"Textbook answer, Mr. Kelly. They teach you that at the police academy?"

Her voice was a bit louder but still controlled. She was drunk. Just not as much as I expected.

"I know you were a cop. Gibbons told me."

She nodded with the smallest of smiles. Looking sly for no apparent reason. Then she picked up her cigarette, almost guttered in the ashtray and drew down. I blinked and saw her at fifty-three. Alone, in a hotel bar. Still able to catch the occasional eye. Still on the hustle. She exhaled and the smoke filtered through a shaft of light coming in from the street. Now the face was relaxed repose. At fifty-three, she was pure class. On the beach, brown and healthy, she had a car with a driver, freshly cut flowers in all her rooms, and lunch on a patio with drinks. Two paths. Her future in the balance. Like everyone else, she'd make her choice. Some small decision would set the events in motion, lead her down one path or the other. Lung cancer in a trailer park or a home in La Jolla. The choice was there. Like everyone else she'd make it and never even know it.

"Your friend was trying to help me," she said. "At least that's what he told me. Now he's dead."

"You're thinking it might be the guy who attacked you?"

"Thought about it."

I sipped at my pint and stared at a sign that said GOOD DAY FOR A GUINNESS with a black toucan underneath.

"Makes you wonder," I said.

She smiled again, in a way that was neither warm nor tender.

"Makes me lock the door at night."

Megan came by. Elaine seemed better now and asked for a glass of water. I took out a notebook and a soft black pencil.

"Going to write me a letter?" she said and shook her hair free.

"Just trying to organize some thoughts here."

"You should get a laptop."

"You should be on a leash."

"What's the matter, Kelly? We're on the same team here. You need to find the killer. If I'm right, the killer needs to find me. It works."

"Using you as bait is a bad idea."

"Because?"

"For one thing, dead clients tend not to pay their bills."

"I still have a gun."

I was delighted to hear my client was still packing and told her as much. She chewed at the corner of a fingernail and looked at herself in the bar mirror. It took her a while to get sick of that. Then she finished off numbers six and seven. Not a bother.

"Point is, Mr. Kelly, I can handle that end of it."

For what it was worth, across a drift of smoke and chatter, she fit the part. At least on this night, in a warm bar, where talk was talk and not a matter of consequence.

I looked over my client's shoulder, across the Shamrock, and through the front window. A dusting of snow fell quickly and softly, covering up the gray of Halsted Street. Lake-effect snow, Chicagoans called it. Beyond the white was the glare of neon, a tangle of traffic and people. A gust of wind blew the weather clear, a gap appeared between cars, and a single figure scooted across the street. Her head was covered with a newspaper. She leaped across a flow of ice and slush half congealed in the gutter and landed on the sidewalk. I was about to look back into the bar when the woman pulled her head up. For a moment, it seemed like Diane Lindsay knew exactly where I was and why I was there. For just a moment. Then surprise flooded her features. She waved, slipped toward the door, and into the Shamrock.

"Excuse me a second."

I got up from my chair and intercepted the journalist before she got too close to my client. I wasn't sure if I wanted them to meet. And was even less certain why I wasn't sure. No matter, Diane was past me, Elaine already out of her chair and rearranging herself in a single movement.

"Hi, I'm Diane Lindsay."

The two shook hands as if they had been expecting to all along. Diane sat down. Elaine sat with her. Diane talked to me, but kept her eyes on Elaine.

"The new client, Michael?"

"Something like that," I said.

"Aren't you on television?" Elaine said.

Diane pulled off a pair of leather gloves, leaned back in her chair, and considered my client like she might a warm glass of milk on a hot summer day. Only when she was done did she speak.

"Yes, I'm on television. And your name is?"

"Elaine. Elaine Remington."

"Nice to meet you, Elaine."

Diane stuck a thumb my way.

"If you don't mind me asking, what do you need this guy for?"

"I don't mind at all. I was raped when I was still pretty much a kid. Mr. Kelly is helping me find the bastard."

"May I ask why?"

"Mostly so I can look him in the eye, show him the scars, and let him know I made it."

Elaine took a sip of water.

"After that, of course, I'll say a small prayer, pull out my gun, and blow him straight to Judgment Day. Amen."

Elaine laughed so hard water came out her nose and she nearly choked. I glanced at Diane, who shrugged. My client continued.

"Just kidding. I was born country Baptist. Love that righteous vengeance sort of thing. You brought up religious, Miss Lindsay?"

"Not so you'd notice."

"Well, I was. Me and all my sisters. We stay close even today. Religion will do that to a family."

"I bet," Diane said. "Let me ask you something, Elaine. You remember details of the attack?"

"Some. Why?"

"Just seems funny. After all these years, you show up here, looking for the bad guy. Even find yourself a hero."

Diane leaned forward. Elaine leaned with her.

"Seems like maybe it's a lot of bullshit, Elaine. If you know what I mean."

Diane smiled. Elaine smiled back and slipped the shirt off her shoulder, just enough to catch a corner of her scar, still purple, still angry.

"Gotcha, Diane. Except they don't give these out in 'Let's pretend we got fucked by a pervert' class."

Diane leaned back, pressed her lips together, then managed a sip of her pint.

"I'm sorry. Sometimes reporters need to test a little bit."

"No problem, Miss Lindsay."

The two women touched glass. Then Elaine stood up. Diane followed suit.

"I'd actually love to hear the whole story someday," she said. "So would my viewers."

Elaine shrugged on her coat, slipped on a set of earphones, and powered up an iPod she had in her pocket.

"Maybe," she said. "Let's see how things shake out. Here's a number where you can reach me."

Elaine scribbled out the information for Diane. Then did the same for me.

"Don't forget about me, Mr. Kelly."

"I won't," I said.

My client reached out and hugged me. It was awkward but brief. Then she was gone. Diane held up a finger.

"I need a second with her," she said and followed Elaine Remington into the snow.

CHAPTER 23

I sipped at my pint and watched through a funnel of wind and white. Diane Lindsay stood at the corner of Halsted and Diversey, her back to the lakefront, taking the brunt of the storm off her head and shoulders. Elaine huddled close, shifted her weight from side to side, and stamped her feet in the night. Now Diane leaned forward as she spoke, filling the gap between them with a tangible sense of energy. Elaine moved away, subtle but certain, her back foot taking the weight of her body. She didn't seem to be saying much, mostly listening as Diane gestured. I wondered what was taking so long. I wondered how the reporter was doing. It looked like hard work.

Ten minutes later Diane returned to the bar. I had moved to a booth in the back and was working through a plate of bangers and mash. To my left was the notebook and pencil. On the pages were assorted thoughts, such as they were.

"What's in the notebook?" she said.

"You're in my light."

Diane sat down. Megan took her drink order.

"This is my booth, you know."

"Would you like me to move?" she said.

"No, you can stay."

"So what's in the notebook?"

I turned it around so she could read my scrawl.

"I'm just trying to figure out how many people have hired me in the past two days and for what. Best I can figure, I have at least two new clients."

"One of whom is dead."

"Exactly. And then there is you."

"Am I in there?"

She pulled the notebook closer. I pulled it back. Her finger-nails were painted a dark red and scratched across the page. It was a small sound but violent in its own way.

"Get your own notebook," I said. "How did it go with her?"

Diane shrugged.

"Not bad. There are a couple of different things I could do with her story. I just wanted to let her know what some of the options were. Get her thinking about it."

Megan put a hot whiskey in front of Diane. From across the booth I could smell the Jameson, scented with cloves. Nice drink on a cold night.

"What did you think of her?" I said.

"Your client?"

I nodded.

"She has some issues."

"You think so?"

"I do."

"Why did you go after her so hard?"

"Why not? Sometimes it catches them off guard. Brings out the truth whether they like it or not."

"And this time?" I said.

"She was raped."

"Yeah, she was. Feels it like it was yesterday."

"That can be a dangerous thing."

"I know," I said. "Gibbons was working her case when he was killed."

"How did you inherit his client list?"

I moved my shoulders. Up, then down. Maybe half an inch. Diane let it sit for a moment, then shifted the conversation.

"I heard the DA's office had you in for a chat."

"You heard that?"

"I did."

Diane checked her watch.

"I also heard they no longer consider you a suspect."

"Does that kill your big story?"

"You tell me."

"Still got a murder," I said. "Still got an old rape to solve. If you want to tag along, might be kind of fun."

"Is that all you got?" she said.

"What else is there?"

"Right before I left the newsroom, a call came across the police scanner. They found a woman's body at Gibbons' old place."

"And?"

"I made a call. It was his landlady. A woman named Edna Mulberry."

Diane took a sip of her whiskey, pulled her coat tight against her body, and looked out the window. On Halsted Street the snow fell, thicker now, wet and heavy.

"Hard when death gets so close," I said.

"I talked to her two days ago, Kelly."

"I saw her myself yesterday."

"She didn't help much."

"I know."

I wasn't sure if I was playing poker or consoling a friend. I figured it was safer to assume the former. At least until further notice.

"Are you being straight with me, Kelly?"

"Maybe. How about you?"

"I'm a little shaken."

"It's called death. Used to get me right in the spine. Turn me cold all over."

"You ever get over it?"

"Unfortunately, yes. Take it from me, you're better off feeling sick to your stomach. Shows you're human."

Diane pushed her drink away and put on her gloves.

"You live near here, Kelly?"

"About a mile."

"Is it warm?"

"I can try," I said.

"Let's go."

We headed out of the Shamrock and into some sort of relationship. Short term, I was looking forward to things. Long term, maybe not so much.

CHAPTER 24

I fell asleep with a woman beside me, yet woke up alone. The phone rang and I picked up the receiver, expecting to hear Diane Lindsay explain why. Not quite.

"I'm twenty minutes from your house. Might be a good idea if I come up for a chat."

His voice was flat. It reminded me of long afternoons in a dark saloon. The patrons drink in cheap liquor and recycled smoke. Each stares straight ahead into his respective past. In other words, it didn't sound good. At nine in the a.m., especially so.

"And a good morning to you, Detective Masters."

"Yeah. You got coffee?"

"There's a Dunkin' Donuts on Clark and Belmont. Pick up a couple. I take mine Boston-style."

The detective hung up before I got to tell him that was with cream and sugar. Maybe he already knew.

I rubbed my face in the glass of the bathroom mirror, took a minute, and put away the night before. She had asked why I kept my shirt on. I told her I was modest. She thought that was cute. The truth, however, stared at me in the mirror. Two bruises, small punctures where a killer had used me for a pincushion.

By the time I showered and dressed, Masters was leaning on

the doorbell. He wasn't exactly smiling, but he did have the coffees and a bag that looked full of what I suspected were doughnuts. We sat down at the kitchen table, split up a half-dozen honey-dipped, adjusted the coffees, and got down to business.

"Let me ask you something, Kelly. Do you work at being a fucking jag-off? Or is it something genetic?"

I took a sip of my coffee and contemplated the moment. It's important to contemplate the moment when it's a good one. Once I opened my mouth, the moment would change into something else. Maybe better, but probably worse.

"Exactly what's the problem, Detective?"

"You know what the problem is. What the hell you doing over at the evidence warehouse?"

"Working a case."

"That's all you have to say?"

I dunked a doughnut but kept it in the coffee too long and lost half of it.

"Goddamn it," I said. "Hate when that happens."

"Jesus H. Christ." Masters made a move to go. I stopped him.

"You want a shot of something in that coffee?" I said.

"You want to quit fucking around?"

I nodded. The detective drained his cup and held it my way.

"Keep the coffee and just pour the shot."

I rustled up a bottle and poured him a dose.

"I went over and talked to Goshen about Elaine Remington's rape. Just nosing around."

"What did you find?"

"Nothing," I said. That was a lie. It happens sometimes.

"The DA no longer considers you a suspect in the Gibbons thing," Masters said.

"I know. It helps to have evidence."

"Some things just need to play out, Kelly. You know how that goes."

An image of Gerald O'Leary came before my mind and I nodded.

"No hard feelings?" the detective said.

I shrugged.

"Good. Let's talk about Mulberry," Masters said.

I raised an eyebrow and hid the rest of my face behind a doughnut.

"Look, Kelly, I know you talked to the landlady. I have a feeling you might have even found her body. So let's talk."

"Mulberry's dead?"

Masters shifted in his seat, took a deep breath in, then out. He was fishing and we both knew it.

"Yeah, she's dead. Whoever killed her tore the place up pretty good. We figure robbery. If you figure otherwise, now would be a good time."

The detective sat back, sipped at his Jameson, and waited. I took a minute I didn't really need. Then I spoke.

"I think Gibbons gave her something or left something behind in his room. Whatever it was, it got them both killed."

"Let me guess," Masters said. "You also think it has something to do with the Remington thing?"

"I do."

"The one you went to the evidence warehouse on."

"It's a theory."

"Why?"

"Gibbons worked that case as a patrolman," I said. "Remington tracked him down and asked for his help in clearing it. Then he got himself dead."

"That's it?"

"So far."

Masters looked at me like he'd rather not. He siphoned off the last of his whiskey and stood up.

"I'm going down to the autopsy. You want to come along?"

"No thanks."

"What are you going to do?"

I plucked a volume of Cicero off the corner of the kitchen table and held it up in the morning light.

"Read," I said. Masters took a look at the title, shook his head, and left.

I let Cicero drop back onto the table and pulled up an old homicide file I had stashed by my feet. The El rumbled nearby, a horn honked, and a hint of thunder echoed in the distance. I didn't notice. Instead, I turned the pages and read.

CHAPTER 25

The package had arrived via FedEx just before Masters did. I knew Mulberry wasn't what you'd call generous by nature. If she'd sprung for special delivery, it was probably worth a look. And not with a Chicago cop looking over my shoulder.

The landlady didn't include a note or any explanation. Just an old police file. Back in the day it would have been called a street file. Chicago cops were famous for them. A duplicate copy of everything in the official file, and a few things maybe the defense didn't really need to know about.

Got a print that doesn't make sense? Open up a street file.

Blood work you don't want to see in court? Throw it in the file.

A potential witness that's going to mess up your case? Bury him in the street file.

Keeps things moving along once you get to trial. Of course, it's illegal, immoral, and causes innocent men to go to jail. But hey, in the big city, that's just the way it goes sometimes.

This one consisted of ten pages of material: pink carbon copies, typed undoubtedly on one of the Selectrics I saw at Town Hall. Elaine Remington's name was on the first page, an incident report filled out by none other than Patrol Officer John Gibbons. The rest didn't seem like much. A report from the medic who worked on Elaine at the scene, the ER nurse, and a follow-up from a second cop, cosigned by Gibbons' commanding officer, Dave Belmont.

I flipped to the last page, this time a green carbon, from the prosecutor's office. Again, routine stuff: "Unknown assailant attacks white female. No usable forensics. No known suspects. Will monitor. Signed Bennett Davis, Assistant District Attorney."

Bennett was three years into the job in 1997. Already a star. The name Elaine Remington probably meant nothing to him, but I made a note to ask.

I went back to the top of the file and began to read. Across the better part of a legal pad I scratched out every piece of potential information in the street file, reorganized it all, and tried to see the connections. Besides Davis, there were at least four names on my list, people I needed to talk to. I picked up the phone and began to dial.

An hour and a half later, I knew more and understood less. I had started with a phone call to a friend in the Illinois secretary of state's office. For ten dollars you can get a copy of anyone's driver's license, which happens to include their home address. The process usually takes two weeks by mail. My friend does it over the phone and under the radar.

The first name I got back was Gibbons' old boss, Dave Belmont. He stopped renewing his license in 2004 when he died of a massive heart attack. Made sense to me.

Next were Joe Jeffries and Carol Gleason. Jeffries was the EMT who worked on Elaine. Gleason was the ER nurse. According to the Department of Motor Vehicles, both moved out of state: Jeffries to California, Gleason to Arizona.

I jumped on the Internet and Googled their names. Nothing. Ran a few variations with different search engines. Still nothing. Then I dove into Nexis' database of newspaper clips.

In 2003 the *San Francisco Chronicle* ran two hundred words on a local named Joe Jeffries who took first place in a halibut tournament. The picture was of a ten-year-old holding a fish bigger than he was. Wrong guy. In 2004 a Carol Gleason wolfed down thirteen hot dogs in three minutes to win Tucson's Labor Day Dog Wars. Sounded like it could be my gal. I pulled up a little bio and discovered Carol was a homemaker and lifelong resident of the desert. Scratch the hot dog queen.

Then I accessed a part of the paper where everyone gets a turn: the local obits. Jeffries took about an hour. The EMT died in 2000 in a hotel room near Fisherman's Wharf. Paper said suspicious circumstances and let it lie. I printed out the notice and got to work on Gleason. She took a bit longer, but I finally found her in a clip from *The Arizona Republic*. One paragraph. Retired nurse, former Chicago native. Age forty-three. Shot dead during a home invasion in 2002. There was a picture of her in surgical scrubs, smiling. The copy said she left a husband, four children, and would be missed by all. End of tragedy. Move on to the next.

The only other name on my list was Tony Salvucci, a desk jockey who processed Gibbons' John Doe suspect. He was easy to find because he was still on the force, made it all the way to lieutenant before he was shot. Twice in the head in 2004. In an alley on Chicago's South Side. I knew the area. Not a great place to die. Not that I ever found a spot I'd consider good.

I looked up the number for Phoenix's murder squad and put a call out to the desert. I told a woman I had information about an old murder, gave her Carol Gleason's name, and waited ten minutes.

"Detective Reynolds, how can I help you?"

He sounded old and weary, a cop with neither kith nor kin, ridden hard, put away wet, and not happy about any of it. In other words, exactly what I was looking for.

"Michael Kelly. Private investigator out of Chicago."

"We're all happy for you, Kelly. What can I do for you?"

"I'd like to get some information on a cold homicide. Victim's name is Carol Gleason."

Reynolds didn't miss a beat.

"We got these new phones, Kelly. Took me a week and a half to figure out how to answer the goddamn thing. Anyway, they have this big screen that comes with the phone. Tells me who I'm talking to. I guess in case I was some kind of asshole who would forget that. Also tells me who's on hold and why they want to talk to me. So I'm looking at my screen and it says 'Kelly, Michael. Claims he has information on Carol Gleason murder.' The operative phrase there is 'has information.' Not 'wants information.' Has it. Because if it said 'wants information,' you can be damn sure I'd have never picked up the call. So what is it, exactly, I can do for you?"

"Sorry, Detective. Must have been a computer error."

"Uh-huh. Fuck the computer."

"Exactly," I said. "Listen, if you give me just ten minutes. . . ."

"You have half that."

"You remember the case?"

"I worked the original crime scene. Must be four, five years ago. Shot once in the chest. Never solved. Tell you the truth, it was a little strange."

"Strange how?"

"Well, we put it out to the press as a break-in, robbery-gone-wrong sort of thing. For me, it never really played that way."

"Why not?"

"You know what, Mr. Kelly. Would you mind telling me your interest here? Before I get too far down the road, that is."

I explained to him who Carol Gleason was, in another life, in another time.

"So she was the attending nurse in this sexual assault?"

"Correct."

"And her name is in your old file?"

"Right."

"I still don't see how her death connects up."

"I'm not sure it does," I said.

"But you want to make sure?"

"Something like that."

There was a pause over the line. Heavy. Then Reynolds made a decision.

"It looked like a break-in at first. Front door forced. Evidence of a scuffle in the living room. Problem is, there was nothing missing. Jewelry and cash upstairs, untouched."

"Rape?"

"Nothing."

I could hear some shuffling over the phone as Reynolds searched for the file.

"Then there were the autopsy photos," the detective said. "Something we never released to the media. Gleason was tied up before she was shot. Struggled with it. Significant bruising on the arms and wrists."

"Sounds like an execution to me."

"Exactly. Now you show up with her name in an old case file. I think to myself, maybe this is the connection. Maybe this is where she got herself dead."

"Maybe we're chasing the same ghosts."

"Could be. I tell you what, Kelly. Why don't we exchange files. You get yourself access to Carol's homicide book and I get a look at your street file. See if something clicks."

I agreed. Reynolds promised to copy the Gleason file and FedEx it to me.

"Probably take a week or so, the way they move around here," the Phoenix detective said.

"I'll get you a copy of my stuff by week's end," I said.

"Fair enough, Kelly. Let me know if you turn up anything."

I clicked off with Reynolds, circled Carol Gleason's name on my list, and punched up Masters' cell.

"Yeah."

"It's Kelly again."

"I knew that."

"How was the morgue?"

"Hopping. Gibbons' landlady sends her best."

"How'd she die?" I said.

"None of your fucking business."

I waited. Sometimes, that's all it takes.

"Massive electrical shock," Masters said.

"Accidental?"

"She was Tasered. ME says the device must have been rigged, delivered double the normal dose. At least a hundred thousand volts. Blew out her heart."

I swallowed and took a quick read on the old pulse. A hundred thousand volts and still ticking.

"Kelly, you there?"

"You know a cop named Tony Salvucci?"

The detective's voice came back. This time with an edge.

"I knew him. Killed in a shooting a couple years back. What of it?"

"He's tied in to the Remington rape."

I could hear the hum of traffic over the line and then the blast of a truck's air horn.

"How so?"

"He took the report from Gibbons. Handled the paperwork."

"How did you turn up his name?"

I knew that was coming but just moved on through.

"Look, Masters, I don't know how this all fits but that doesn't mean it won't. I'd like to get a look at the file on Salvucci's death."

"Cop shooting? Never going to happen."

I figured that and had a backup request ready.

"How about the file on Remington? Everything you have."

"What do you know about cold cases?" Masters said.

"I watch the blonde on CBS."

A bit of a wheeze came blowing through the line. It seemed an effort, but Masters didn't disconnect.

"We got something now called a cold case squad. They specialize in clearing old crimes. Use a lot of DNA and all that happy horseshit."

"Impressed, huh?"

"Who knows. You ever watch Bill Kurtis on A&E."

"The guy with the voice?" I said.

"Chicago guy. Good buddy of the mayor. Anyway, he has a show. Not the one with the blonde. These guys do real cases."

"*Cold Case Files.*"

"You watched it?"

"I saw it once," I said.

"Lays out these old investigations, all the forensics."

"Real-life *CSI.*"

"Whatever. Anyway, Kurtis buttonholes the mayor with this stuff. How cops across the country are clearing these old files and Chicago is doing squat. Now we got a cold case squad. They have all these old files stacked away somewhere."

"So I go talk to them about Remington?" I said.

"Don't bother. I ran the case number after we talked this morning. The cold squad doesn't have the file."

"Should they?"

"Yeah, they should probably have something. Which leads me to wonder how you can pull names out of a file that the Chicago PD says doesn't exist."

I knew Masters wanted to help. I also knew I needed someone on my side.

"I have a street file on this case."

"You took it from the landlady's house."

"Mulberry FedExed it to me. Got here this morning. Just before you did. Got the receipt to prove it."

"Maybe. But you were still at the house."

I wondered how he knew. With a veteran cop like Masters, sometimes it's just a feeling.

"Okay, I was there. Didn't touch a thing. Just called it in."
Nothing.

"Want to see the file?" I said.

More nothing. Then, something.

"You know Mr. Beef down in River North?"

I didn't know a man in Chicago worth knowing who didn't know of "The Great Beef" on Orleans Street.

"Tomorrow afternoon, twelve-thirty," the detective said. "Bring the file or don't bother coming at all."

Masters hung up. I leafed through the old file again, looking for something worth a person's life and not finding it. Then I thought about the polo shirt I'd pulled from Goshen's warehouse. I picked up the phone and made a final call.

After I hung up, the guilt held on. For just a bit. Then it dissipated. Like it always did. The friend was an old one. Too old not to help. And I knew it.

CHAPTER 26

The State of Illinois Forensic Science Center is located in the 1900 block of West Roosevelt Road, a mile or so from where O'Leary's cow kicked over the lantern that burned down a city. I got there at just after six o'clock. The lab was large and empty. Nicole sat at her workstation.

"Let's see it, Michael."

I put the street file on her desk. She turned her nose up. I wasn't sure if it was at me, the file, or both. Then she slipped on a pair of latex gloves and began to turn pages.

"You didn't pull the file from this woman's house?"

"She sent it to me."

"Gibbons' landlady?"

"Yes."

"And now she's dead?"

"Electrocuted."

"An accident?"

I shook my head.

"Not likely. By the way, the DA's giving me a clean bill of health on Gibbons."

"Just like Bennett promised."

"He's rarely wrong," I said.

"I'll be happy for you tomorrow," Nicole said. "What do you want today?"

I plucked a one-page hospital report from the file and handed it to her.

"This is from the ER nurse in '97. Says my client was taken straight to surgery after admission."

"Elaine Remington?"

"Yeah. I called the hospital but they won't give me any more information."

"This was almost ten years ago. They might not have anything on her. Even if they did, I'm not sure it would be a lot of help."

"How about a rape kit?"

"If the hospital did one, it would be with the police."

"That's what I'm hoping."

Nicole closed the file and pushed it across the table.

"Get rid of that. I never saw it."

I pushed the file back into the fold of my jacket and waited. Nicole sighed and walked to a window.

"How much do you really know about rape, Michael?"

"That's the second time I've been asked that in as many days."

Nicole offered a thin look at her reflection in a contoured pane of glass. Then she turned back my way.

"I don't mean the act itself. What I'm talking about is perhaps worse. In the lab we call it the politics of rape. Can be a tricky thing. Not like murder. I mean, in a murder the victim is dead. There's that certainty. Rape—not so much."

She walked across the room, held her ID against a scanner, and opened a large gray door.

"Come on."

We entered a walk-in cooler filled with rows of steel shelving stacked to the ceiling with evidence kits.

"These are Cook County's old rapes."

"How many do you have?"

"There are almost seven hundred kits in this room. All of them contain semen or some other bodily fluid that needs DNA testing."

I whistled.

"That's nothing," Nicole said. "On the South Side, we have an old slaughterhouse converted into cold storage. Probably another thousand kits stored there."

"All waiting to be tested?" I said.

"Hard to say. A lot of the evidence is old and degraded. Not much left to test. Still, we get hits."

"How many?"

"I've tested about a hundred kits myself and gotten ten cold hits."

"Convictions?"

"In eight of the ten. Even better, three of the offenders were eventually linked to other assaults. One of the guys raped twenty women. Killed two of them."

Nicole led me out of the evidence locker and slammed the door shut.

"Problem is, there's only one of me."

"And thousands of kits."

"You got it. Plus, each test costs money. At least five thousand a pop for STR-DNA testing. And that's where it gets complicated."

"You have to decide who gets tested and who doesn't."

"Actually, the DA decides."

"Who gets buried?" I said.

"Who do you think?"

"I'm gonna guess you're not testing a lot of kits from ladies of the evening."

"Hookers don't get raped, didn't you know that? And if you're black? Well, the next priority request I get for a black woman's kit to be tested will be the first."

"I have a reporter you need to talk to."

"Diane Lindsay? Not as easy as that, Michael. Not if I want to stay in the game."

"Think about it."

"Let's talk about your girl. She's not a hooker, and, good for her, she's white. Problem is, she's a nobody. A very cold case everyone has forgotten about."

Nicole sat down at a computer terminal and typed in Elaine's information.

"Let me see what I've got. May take a minute."

I sat down at an adjacent workstation and picked through a stack of rape kits, still sealed and waiting to be processed. Each bore the name of the victim and date of the attack. After the victims' names were a series of dates and letters, circled and initialed. I asked Nicole a question but already knew the answer.

"The *D* stands for deceased," Nicole said. "The *A* means there was a violent assault attached to the crime. I told my boss I thought all sexual assaults were violent."

"And you were wrong?"

"Date rape. The girl who drinks too much at the party. They go to the bottom of the pile as far as testing is concerned. We call it the 'she asked for it' syndrome."

Nicole looked up from her terminal and then continued typing.

"I got your girl. It appears all her physical evidence, including a rape kit, was destroyed in 2004."

I felt the padded envelope in my pocket. Inside it, a woman's shirt covered in blood. For the moment, I figured it was better to play dumb. Besides, I was very good at it.

"Why would they do that?"

"Statute of limitations had run. Technically, the DA could still prosecute if they got a DNA match. In cases where there is no identified suspect, however, the evidence usually gets destroyed."

"Doesn't make much sense, does it?"

"Not these days. I can extract DNA from a sample that's fifty years old."

My friend shrugged.

"Like I said, you don't really understand rape until you understand the politics around it."

"But you can run tests on evidence that old?"

"I just said that, Michael. What is it you need?"

"Maybe a little DNA testing. Just between friends."

"Are we talking about this woman here?"

I nodded, slid the envelope out and across the desk. Nicole looked at it but didn't touch.

"So you do have something."

"Evidence warehouse. No name, no case number, and conveniently misplaced."

Nicole slid on a second pair of gloves, picked up the envelope, and examined the seal.

"You cut this open?"

"Couple of days ago. Prior to that it was dated and initialed. Those are Gibbons' initials, by the way."

"And the date?"

"The day Elaine Remington was attacked. Nine years ago."

She pulled at the open end of the envelope, shook out the shirt and played her fingers through the knife holes.

"How many times was this woman stabbed?"

"Not sure, but I make it to be about fifteen."

"And you say she survived?"

"Sort of. She drinks seven shots of whiskey a day. But she's pretty good at it."

"Girl has got some major problems."

"Probably. Right now she's a client, and this is her best shot at getting some answers."

Nicole put the shirt back in its envelope but didn't seal it.

"Follow me."

We walked through another set of doors, down a white corridor, and into yet another white lab.

"This is our prep area for DNA extraction. First thing I need to do is examine the garment and figure out what kinds of tests to run."

"You all right with this?" I said.

Nicole stretched the shirt onto an examining table and handed me a pair of goggles.

"Let's try not to talk about it. Put these on."

She pulled a wand from a holster bolted to the examining table and flicked off the overhead lights.

"This is an ultraviolet laser. We use it to search for bodily fluids the human eye cannot see."

As she spoke, an intense green light arrowed through the darkness and found a piece of the torn shirt. Nicole continued talking as she played the light across the garment.

"Different wavelengths of light react with different fluids, causing them to glow. Depending on how I set the laser, I can pick up bloodstains, saliva, and, of course, everyone's favorite, semen."

"What color is semen?"

"Yellow's the lucky color. Sort of like that right there."

Nicole pointed a gloved finger to the lower right side of the garment. I saw a spray of yellow, translucent against the lasered green, just below a large bloodstain. Nicole carefully marked the location with pins and photographed the site. Then she examined the rest of the garment, finding three other possible hits. After an hour she turned off the laser and flicked on the lights.

"We got something."

"You think so?"

Nicole took a pair of scissors and carefully began to cut at the areas she had marked with pins.

"I'll run a presumptive chemical test, but you can take it on credit. Someone left semen on that shirt."

Each piece of shirt was placed into an evidence bag and tagged. Nicole shut down the inspection area and led me back to her workstation.

"I can start DNA extraction tonight."

"How long will that take?"

"Usually we're talking six weeks. If I drop everything, I can have preliminary results back in twenty-four hours."

"What are you thinking?"

"Two things. First, I want this piece of evidence out of my life as soon as possible. Second, I think you need to get your friend in contact with some people I know."

"After this is done, I'll talk to her."

"Do that, Michael."

"Fine. Now, here's a question. Say we get a profile. Then what?"

"Let me guess," Nicole said. "You want a run through CODIS?"

CODIS was the state's genetic databank, home to the DNA of thousands of felons from across the country.

"Is that possible?" I said.

"It might get flagged, but I can probably hide it. The real problem comes if you get a match. You'd have a name and not a thing you could do about it."

"Legally," I said.

"That's right, Michael. Legally. Your evidence is probably tainted, as well as the CODIS search."

"Let's just get the name, Nicole. After that I'll figure out the rest."

My friend was about to respond when voices drifted down the corridor. Nicole packaged up the shirt and slid it into a drawer behind her desk.

"I'll hang on to this and give you a call when I get something."

She pulled one of her cards from a pocket and wrote on the back.

"Unless I miss my guess, you have no discernible social life these days. At least this will get you out of the house."

Nicole pushed the card across the table. On the reverse she had written "Drake Hotel, Friday, 8 p.m."

"It's this Friday. In the main ballroom. Don't be late, and wear something you haven't picked up off the floor. That means black tie."

"What am I attending?"

"A fund-raiser. For the Rape Volunteer Association. All these issues we've been talking about and maybe some help for your girl. There will be a lot of women there."

I smiled.

"Don't be too happy. It's going to cost you five hundred dollars to get in."

"That's okay."

"And most of the women you meet will have been raped. So watch your step. By the way, Ms. Lindsay will be there."

"Really?"

"Yes, indeed. So we can see you two together, out on the town."

I felt my face grow a little warm and dropped my eyes.

"So you two are sleeping together," Nicole said.

"It's not like that."

"It never is. But she'll be there anyway. Now get out of here. I still have a couple hours' worth of work to get through."

"Thanks, Nicole."

"Don't thank me until you see what I can do."

She didn't sound happy. I couldn't blame her. I didn't have the right to ask for her help, but I did anyway. Now we'd all live with the consequences.

CHAPTER 27

I left the lab at a little after nine o'clock. Evening traffic was light, and I drove carelessly toward the lake, dangerously close to Annie's high-rise. At times it seemed my car had a mind of its own. Took the lefts and rights needed to put me on her block. I'd sit for an hour or so in the darkness. Not watching. Not really. Not stalking. Just a chance to be. To think. Essentially, to torture myself.

Tonight, however, the car zigged when it should have zagged. Took a left away from Annie's place and into some sort of future. Diane opened the door before I got up her front stairs. She didn't ask about my day, didn't want to talk about the night before or tomorrow. We just had a drink and enjoyed the quiet. Sometimes that's enough. This was one of those times. Then we went to bed. I fell asleep before my head hit the pillow.

CHAPTER 28

River North is Chicago's answer to Soho on the East Coast and Venice Beach on the West. Not much of an answer, but what the hell, it's the Midwest.

Twenty years ago the area was rife with tumbledown hotels and warehouses. Today the warehouses are art galleries; the flop-houses, million-dollar condos. The sidewalks are wide, clean, and full of admen dressed in Ted Baker and carrying portfolios. The women are nice to look at. Younger, in their twenties and early thirties, they wear low-riders and belly rings. Tattooed and perpetually cell-phoned, they curl themselves around a Cosmo at bars like the Martini Ranch, waiting to be discovered or better yet, find an investment banker who will carry them off to a duplex in Winnetka, 2.5 kids, and an expense account at the North Shore Country Club. If all else fails, women in River North get drunk, dance on the bar at Coyote Ugly, and scout around for some fun. Sometimes known as guys like me.

In the heart of River North sits an unassuming storefront, red-brick with a plate-glass window and whitewashed frame addition. A single-bulb electric sign is hammered in out front. The black block lettering reads MR. BEEF. To the untrained eye, it might seem like just another sandwich joint. Inside, however, is an entirely different matter. Inside, in fact, is an entirely different state of mind.

To the left is the counter, peopled by three or four workers, yelling at one another in a variety of languages. On the other side of the counter are the customers, various and sundry specimens of Midwestern Man, stuffed and on display.

Specimen #1: Large belly hanging over frayed leather belt, Wrangler jeans, Red Wing work boots, and a key ring dangling on the side.

Specimen #2: Large belly hanging over fake leather belt, Men's Warehouse suit, cracked Florsheim shoes, and a cell phone clipped on the side.

Specimen #3: Large belly hanging over money belt, Tommy Bahama silk pants, Cole Haan slip-ons, and a racing form stuffed in a side pocket.

And on it goes.

Each day any and all forms of Midwestern Man line up, single file, amid pictures of Leno, Letterman, Sinatra, and, of course, Da Coach. Midwestern Man, however, ignores all the pretty faces on the wall. He is here to pay homage to the true star of the show: Da Beef.

It is sliced thin off a roasting skewer and slid into a soft Italian roll. The beef is ordered dipped or not, with hot, sweet, or both. Dipped means the entire sandwich is dipped in its own juices before being wrapped up in white paper and shoved across the counter. Hot and sweet refers to peppers, usually.

Order a hot, sweet beef, dipped—you get it with the works. You also get some of the crudest sexual comments known to man as the sandwich is being prepared. They come from the regulars, average age 107. They sit like the peanut gallery they are, stacked on stools along the front window, all day, every day. They sip coffee and talk about sex they haven't had since Christ was a carpenter. Nice guys, funny guys. A lot of fake hair, a lot of chains, a lot of grabbing themselves. There are worse things to be doing when you are 107. Like being dead.

I got to Mr. Beef ten minutes late for my lunch with Masters. I ordered a sweet beef, dipped, and found the detective in a far corner, under a movie poster for *Reservoir Dogs*. He had a toothpick in his mouth, was drinking a Coke, and picking at some fries.

"Sorry, I got hung up," I said.

Masters took one look and grunted.

"Every time I come here, I wonder why I ever eat anywhere else. Hold on while I get another sandwich."

Five minutes later, we were both set up. Me for lunch. The detective for an encore.

"You want to talk about the file," I said.

Masters hoisted his beef with two hands, took a bite, and looked at me through hunched shoulders as he chewed. It wasn't pretty. It wasn't supposed to be. Then he drank down twenty ounces or so worth of Coke and belched.

"Where is it?"

I pulled a sheaf of papers from an inside pocket.

"Like I told you over the phone, she sent them to me by FedEx."

"These copies?"

"Yeah. I kept a set."

Another belch. More subtle this time. Then a sucking sound as Masters hit the bottom of his soda cup.

"Figured that," the detective said.

"There is a copy of the FedEx slip as well."

"No sweat, Kelly. I don't have you killing Mulberry. Just like I don't have you killing Gibbons. I told you, that was the DA's thing."

Masters spread the papers out on the table and gave them a quick scan.

"A police report, medical exam, and follow-up. I don't see anything in here worth much."

I kept quiet. Masters continued.

"Five fresh murders landed on my desk this morning. Triple homicide on the West Side and a mom who fed her two kids a load of Drano."

"Nice."

"Yeah. In other words, I don't have time for this shit."

Masters rolled up his sandwich wrapper and shot it into a barrel a few feet away. Then he folded up the copies I had given him and stuffed them into a back pocket.

"Want to know what I think?" he said.

"Sure."

"Gibbons was in the wrong place at the wrong time down on Navy Pier. Got himself mugged and then shot for good measure."

"His wallet was found on his body."

"Gibbons' landlady got her house broken into."

"How many guys break into a house with a Taser rigged for kill?"

"It happens," Masters said. "Especially to women who live alone."

"No connection between the two?"

"Nothing that I can see."

"You don't believe that."

"Show me a connection and I'll listen."

Masters got up to go.

"You know, I could charge you with about six different offenses, starting with obstruction of justice and tampering with a crime scene."

"But you won't," I said.

"I will if you hold out on me again."

I nodded as if I understood and thought about the package I had given Nicole.

"Next time you find a body," the detective continued, "pick up the phone and give me a call. I told the guys up front you had the tab for lunch. Pay on the way out."

Masters walked out the door. I took a bite of my sandwich and wondered just how much the cop had actually eaten.

CHAPTER 29

I was half a block from the Beef when the Chicago mob stuck its foot into my life. They did it via a note tucked under my windshield wiper: "Come in for a cannoli."

I looked up. At the corner of Superior and Franklin, under the El tracks where they like to film *ER,* sits a shack of a coffee shop called Brett's. In the front window was a guy named Joey Palermo. He lifted an espresso cup my way. I stuffed the note in my pocket and headed over.

"Vinnie needs to speak with you," Joey said.

"What, no hello?"

Palermo was a high-level hitter for Chicago's *capo di capi,* Vinnie DeLuca. I knew Joey from my days as a cop. Big guy. Nice guy. Could crush your larynx like a Dixie cup and offer a sincere apology as you choked to death at his tasseled and loafered feet.

"The boss says it's a matter of some importance. Shouldn't take more than a half hour."

Joey held open the front door to Brett's. I followed him out. The cannolis didn't look all that good anyway.

CHAPTER 30

Just south of Wrigley Field sits its canine counterpart, known to the locals as Wiggley Field. The dog park was empty, save for an old man sitting on a park bench, smoking a cigarette and trying to ignore a standard poodle.

Vinnie DeLuca had lived in the neighborhood for the last decade. Why, no one could figure out, although plenty of people tried. Vinnie started in at nine years old, a runner for Capone's gang on the South Side. Today he was eighty-six, the last living link to Scarface and the undisputed leader of Chicago's outfit for at least the last three decades.

Vinnie was old-school. At his age what else could he be? In the late seventies he conceded the street trade in drugs and guns to Chicago's gangs: first to the Gangster Disciples, then the Latin Kings. Now it seemed they changed names every week. Vinnie still took a cut but never really looked back. Instead, the family took its business downtown, infiltrating Chicago's corporate culture. Wiseguys set up on the Board of Trade and the Merc, on LaSalle Street, inside the lending rooms of banks and boardrooms. Millions of freshly laundered dollars went into real-estate development, strip malls, and shopping centers. Of course, Vinnie never went anywhere without a politician or two in his pocket.

With the money they could throw at a campaign, the family usually had its pick.

The old man was rarely seen in public these days. I watched from the front seat of my car as he finished his cigarette and threw the butt to the ground. The poodle lifted his leg and christened it. Vinnie kicked the dog, took what looked like a racing form from his back pocket, and began to read. I got out of the car and walked toward the park. I could see Joey Palermo get out of a Lincoln halfway down the block. I spotted two other cars. Behind the tinted windows were men with guns, waiting, watching, probably bored but ready to kill me just the same.

Palermo entered the park before I did and sat on a bench some distance from Vinnie. Joey had a cup of Starbucks, but no dog. He pulled one of Brett's cannolis from a bag and ignored me as I walked by.

"You Kelly?"

Vinnie spoke without looking up from his form.

"Yeah."

"Sit down."

Vinnie motioned to a spot beside him. I sat.

"You like dogs?" he said.

"Yeah."

"I started feeding this thing rat poison two months ago. Look at the bastard. Never looked better."

Vinnie reached out to kick the dog again but missed.

"A hunting dog. Take him out, kill some ducks. I could live with that. But this thing. It's embarrassing. My wife loves him, so what are you gonna do?"

"Get a new wife?"

"Now there's an idea."

The old man folded up his racing form and reached out to shake my hand. A lot of thin bones. Loose flesh and veins. The grip of an old man, with neither the time nor the need to impress the world, including yours truly.

"Joey tells me you're a stand-up guy."

I shrugged. Vinnie had a thermos at his feet. He pulled it up and poured a cup of coffee.

"You want some?"

"No thanks."

"Joey's got extra cups, you want any."

"I'm good, Vinnie."

He took a small sip and then smacked his lips together two or three times, as if to knock the idea of taste back into them.

"Fucking coffee. Can you smell that?"

I nodded. The coffee looked strong and rich.

"I got no smell, no taste, nothing. This fucking poison they push into my veins. Chemotherapy, my ass. You ever had that?"

I shook my head. Vinnie crooked a finger my way.

"Forty years from now, remember what I tell you. Do yourself a favor. Find yourself a nice bathroom and swallow a bullet."

Vinnie leaned forward. A gust of wind kicked between us and I caught a whiff of his decay.

"I spend most of my days in the bathroom," he said. "These assholes wait outside, trying to figure out if I'm still breathing. I take two, three hours in there, work on the racing form. Get a little peace and quiet. You want to eat a bullet, bathroom is as good a spot as any."

I was trying to figure out if I should thank Vinnie for the free advice but the old man just kept rolling.

"You're not going to die today, Kelly. Don't tell me the thought hadn't crossed your mind. Anyone who comes to meet me, the thought crosses their mind. You'll go home and you'll live. Fuck your wife, girlfriend, whatever."

The old man pulled a blackened cheroot from an inner pocket

and took a look around, as if daring anyone to stop him. No one did, so Vinnie DeLuca lit up.

"How do you feel about our district attorney, Mr. O'Leary?"

Vinnie angled his face away and into the sun. The change was subtle, but certain. The death mask was gone. Family business at hand.

"We have some history," I said.

DeLuca took another small sip of coffee, nodded, just the lightest bit of movement, and crossed one leg over the other. He was wearing black wool pants, blue socks, and black shoes with thick rubber soles.

"Maybe we have a common interest here. In perhaps seeing him at a disadvantage."

Vinnie motioned to Joey, who had pulled up close. Now he took a seat on the bench.

"You know Joey?" the old man said. "Yes, I know you do. He was approached by a contact from the DA's office a couple of weeks ago. Gentleman wanted to hire some local muscle. Interesting?"

I nodded. Vinnie nodded.

"Yes, I thought so, too. Someone inside wanted information on a case your partner was working on."

"Former partner," I said. "But I'm with you."

"I told Joey to go along."

"See what develops," I said.

"Not a bad thing to know what the DA's office might be interested in. Especially in our line of work. Joseph?"

Vinnie DeLuca drew on his cigar, then dropped his head to his chin, as if the effort of speaking had exhausted him. Joey picked up the thread.

"I met this guy once. At a hot dog stand in Cicero. Didn't know the guy. Seemed pretty nervous. Told me it was a private matter. I pushed a little. He gave me the idea it was someone from the DA's office who was asking."

Palermo offered up a shrug.

"Maybe he was lying. I don't know. I was supposed to find out all I could about the old rape Gibbons was working. See if I could locate the case file."

"And then Gibbons got dead."

Vinnie lifted his eyes a fraction and rejoined the conversation.

"Not our doing, Mr. Kelly. That's important."

"I never even got to Gibbons," Joey said. "If I had, it wasn't going to be like that."

"This district attorney, O'Leary," DeLuca said. "He ruined your career. I know this because we helped him."

Vinnie's eyes shifted across my face but read nothing. He kept talking.

"The matter intrigues me. I think, perhaps, it also intrigues you."

"What do you think is in the file?" I said.

Vinnie got up to go.

"I don't know what's in the file, but I think you have it. Or can get it. Either way, I leave this information with you. If I profit by whatever course of action you take, all the better. If not, so be it."

"Just so you know, chances are I play it straight."

"I can live with that."

"I know, Vinnie. But can I?"

"You'll live to see me in the grave and many days after, Mr. Kelly. Just remember what I told you."

"About the file?"

"About the bathroom and the bullet. Come on, Joey. Pick up the cannolis and let's go."

CHAPTER 31

The Drake is classic Chicago. Wide sidewalks and revolving doors. Doormen in black overcoats, whistling taxis and calling everyone sir and ma'am. A red carpet runs up the stairs, across a wide expanse of lobby, and dead-ends at a reception desk staffed by old men wearing black glasses sliding down long noses. These men understand the secrets of Chicago, how to get a window table at NoMI, tickets to Monet at the Art Institute, and, even better, a ducat on the forty for the Bears-Packers. They are in the know and keep it close to the vest, sliding a note across the concierge table and taking a folded fifty at the proper moment.

"Hey, Eddie."

Back in the day, Eddie Flaherty boxed for money. Like most of the Irish, he could take a punch. Like most of the Irish, one day he took too many. Today Eddie was a prime mover at the Drake, hooking up locals, players, and any celebs that came into town.

"Kelly. What the hell brings you in here?"

"Been a while."

"Four, five years, at least. You were a detective. Then you were in the papers. Then you weren't a detective anymore. Figured it for some tough luck."

I shrugged.

"Like I said, it's been a while."

"So what brings you in?"

I had on a tuxedo, gray tie, and my only pair of cuff links. Still, Eddie couldn't figure it out, so I slid my invitation across the counter. The old fighter pulled out his reading glasses.

"You heard of this group?" I said.

"Rape Volunteer Association. Sure. This is their third year here. Heavy hitters, lawyers, doctors, judges. A lot of women who have been, you know, raped. Bad stuff. But good people."

"You know who runs the show?"

"Nah. They're in and out. Once a year. I think it's set up through a woman judge, but I couldn't tell you much more than that."

"Thanks, Eddie."

"Sure. You going to this thing?"

I fingered the lapel of my monkey suit.

"That's the plan."

"A lot of them hang in the Palm. Get tea and all that stuff before the thing gets started."

I rapped a knuckle on the desk, drifted across the lobby, and into the Drake's Palm Court. Amid the marble statues and harp music, tinkling water fountains and green ferns, I spied groups of women. In twos and threes mostly, they feasted on platters of suspiciously small sandwiches, trays of sinfully large desserts, and cup after cup of brown tea. I found an empty seat, ordered an Earl Grey, closed my eyes, and listened to the harpist. He wasn't playing anything I recognized, so I opened my eyes and took a look around.

A woman, maybe early forties, crossed her legs and caught my eye. She was great-looking in that old-money sort of way, with streaked honey-blond hair, white teeth, and a nut-brown tan that screamed desert in the soon-to-be death grip of a Chicago winter. She had the sculpted mouth and thin nose of aristocracy. Her eyes were wide, deep, and intelligent, with more than a little fun lurking somewhere beneath. She had gone to Northwestern or the University of Chicago, was successful, good-looking, and knew it. She was probably out of my league. When I dove in, however, she didn't seem surprised.

"I love this stuff," I said.

"Stuff?"

"The tea, the music, just the place."

"You come here a lot, do you?"

Apparently, Irish guys with bent noses are not a common sight in the Palm Court. I ignored the jibe and moved forward.

"I wouldn't call myself a regular. But I do like a cup of tea."

I hoisted a cup and saucer in her general direction.

"I'm sure you do, Mr. Kelly. Although rumor has it you litter the stuff with something stronger on occasion."

I halted my cup a scant inch, perhaps two, from my lips and returned it to said saucer.

"I believe I am at a disadvantage, Ms. . . . ."

The woman extended her hand. The grip was firm. The grip was cool. The grip was nice.

"Rachel Swenson. I'm chair of the association and a friend of Nicole Andrews. I told her I was going to hide out here before we got started. She asked me to watch out for you."

"So you staked out the Palm Court?"

"Actually, I started in the Coq d'Or."

She gestured to a large oak door leading to the Drake's main bar.

"I was there fifteen minutes, picked up three phone numbers, two room keys, and a vice cop who asked to see my ID. I figured a cup of tea was in order and you could fend for yourself. Then I sat down and found myself seated across from an Irishman look-ing like a brawl about to happen but with some intelligence around the edges."

"That was how Nicole described me?"

"Something like that. You want to go into the event?"

"Do we have to?"

"I am the host."

Rachel got up in one motion. She had that Grace Kelly in *Rear Window* sort of movement. An immaculate, elegant flow you couldn't learn or even think about. Unless you didn't have it, that is. Then it was all you thought about. I followed along and caught words as they floated back over her shoulder.

"So you want to ask me now or later?"

"Ask what?" I said.

She stopped halfway up a set of stairs leading out of the Drake lobby and turned.

"How and why I became chairperson of this group."

It was an interesting question. Not as interesting as the fact that Ms. Swenson felt she and I shared the possibility of some sort of "later," but that would have to wait.

"It might be because you're a woman and a judge," I said. "I figure there's a bit more to it than that."

"There is. Nicole said you're a private investigator. Used to be a cop."

I nodded.

"Then you know a little bit about rape."

"I know I used to hate working them."

"You ever visit a victim a year after the attack?"

I shook my head.

"Ever think about the range of this crime?"

"The woman who finds a stranger in her apartment to the lit-tle girl who waits for her uncle to knock on the door."

Rachel nodded.

"Exactly. There are so many different strands to sexual assault, and yet we tend to treat them all the same. Like they have the same cause. The same effect on their victims."

"And you're going to change that?"

"Rape is a complex crime and requires a lot more nuance, Mr. Kelly. Not so much in the investigative aspects. But in the treatment of survivors and in prevention. We need to start talking about that."

We walked the rest of the staircase in silence and stepped into the Drake's Grand Ballroom. I saw Nicole, floating in a crowd at the far end of a roomful of cocktail chatter. Vince the Modern Cop was with her. They looked successful, happy, and poised for more.

"It was nice meeting you," Rachel said. "For what it's worth, your friend Nicole was right."

"How so?"

"She told me you had a different take on things."

"You mean for a man?"

"I mean for a person. Believe me, when it comes to sexual assault and Neanderthal thinking, women take a backseat to no one."

"Really?"

"The 'she asked for it' syndrome?" Rachel said. "Fueled by the whispers of countless generations of females. Passing judgment on one another while silently thinking: 'There but for the grace of God go I.' Don't get me started. I have a speech to give. It was nice meeting you."

And then she was gone, engulfed by a gaggle of women apparently wanting a moment of her time. I grabbed a scotch at the bar and pushed my way toward Nicole.

"What did you think of our chairwoman?"

Diane Lindsay had materialized from the left, riding close,

hand resting on my shoulder. If Rachel Swenson looked good—
and she did—Diane looked better. She was wearing some sort of
dress, cream-colored silk and thin enough to be little more than
nothing at all. Her body felt alive, tight, and restless underneath.
I liked the way she leaned in when she spoke, as if we were the
only people in the room. Or at least the only ones who counted. I
especially liked her scent.

"She's a judge?" I said.

"Yes, indeed. Not a bad-looking one, either."

"If you say so."

"You can too, Kelly. Not a sin, you know. By the way, you look
hot in a tux."

"Thanks," I said. "You ever work with this group?"

"Nicole Andrews and you are buddies, right?"

"Yeah."

"She didn't tell you about my project?"

We started to walk, working our way through the room.

"What project?"

"I interview rape victims for the association. Document their
stories. Just me, the subject, and a camera."

"Who gets to see the interviews?"

"Only the subject and whoever else she authorizes. Sometimes it's just a form of catharsis. They want to get the story out
there. Let someone hear it out loud."

"And sometimes?"

"Sometimes they want other women to watch. To see and
hear what happened to them. Seems like it's a good lesson."

"Really. How many subjects have you taped?"

"Over three hundred women. Seven hundred hours of
interviews."

"Interesting?"

"You might say."

"How so?"

Diane stopped and considered me for a moment.

"You really want to know?"

"I asked."

She moved to a spot along a portable bar, waited for a moment until the crowd cleared, and then continued.

"Among other things, I have on tape at least three women describing in detail how they killed the man that raped them. In two of the cases, the man was her husband."

"Seriously?"

"Absolutely. One made it look like a fall down the stairs. The other went down as a home invasion."

I whistled.

"The authorities know about your project?"

"Each time the DA's office stepped in and reviewed the footage. Justifiable homicide. No charges filed."

"Who handled it?"

Diane pointed across the room. Toward a short, bald lawyer, holding an unlit cigar and looking very uncomfortable.

"Speak of the devil," Diane said. "I have to go powder something. Why don't you buy the assistant district attorney a drink?"

Bennett Davis sidled over, took Diane's hand, and reached up to kiss her on the cheek.

"Miss Lindsay. My ten o'clock fix, two hours early."

Diane looked even better when she was being admired by another man. And graciously so.

"Thank you, Mr. Prosecutor. If you could take care of my date here for a moment, I have to find the ladies'."

Diane moved off. Bennett took her spot and motioned for a bartender.

"Her date, Kelly? You didn't tell me about that. Can I get a scotch on the rocks? Thanks."

Bennett got his drink, swirled the ice around with his fingers, and took a sip.

"No smoke?" I said.

"Not allowed. Fucking cretins. But hey, don't change the subject. Diane Lindsay. Come on."

"Nice lady," I said.

"Yeah, nice."

"Listen, Bennett. I don't know if you had anything to do with O'Leary backing off. Nor am I going to ask."

I held up my drink.

"But if thanks are in order, consider it done."

"Forget about it," Bennett said. "They had nothing, and I told them as much. Anyway, it all blew over."

"Just like you said."

"Exactly. You get a new girlfriend, and everyone is happy."

"Everyone but John Gibbons."

"Yeah, everyone but John."

"Where is the investigation at?"

"Don't know," Bennett said. "The police are working it, but right now we're hands off."

I thought about Goshen and his visitors from the DA's office. Then I thought about the street file and my talk with Vinnie DeLuca.

"You sure about that, Bennett? No one is working this?"

A wrinkle flew into the lawyer's brow, and he put his glass back on the bar.

"What are you hearing?"

"Nothing," I said.

Bennett leaned closer and I wondered if he wasn't a bit drunk.

"Then why are you asking?"

"Easy. Retired Irish cop murdered at Navy Pier. Just seems like someone from the DA's office might get involved."

Bennett decompressed a bit.

"Sorry, Michael. Just a little keyed up."

"I can see that," I said.

"Internal stuff. Office politics, you know."

I didn't know and didn't ask. Bennett Davis told me anyway.

"O'Leary loves to keep us at each other's throat. His management style. Keeps anyone from getting too big, going after the top job."

"Someone like you, maybe?"

"Maybe. No one ever knows who is running what in the office. So, of course, everyone tries to get an angle, cook up the next big case. A lot of bullshit."

Bennett leaned his mouth down to his glass and took another hit on his drink. His eyes moved around the room and back to mine. The prosecutor smiled, pulled a handkerchief from his back pocket, and wiped his face.

"I don't do well at these things," he said. "Haven't had hair since high school and didn't look good then."

"You make your living in front of a jury, Bennett."

"Completely different animal. I'm in control there."

A couple cruised by. Bennett Davis smiled a hello and continued talking out of the side of his mouth.

"Out here, I'm working without a script."

"One more business thing, Bennett. Then we put it away."

"Sure."

"I ran across an old rape case you worked. Victim's name was Elaine Remington. Ring a bell?"

"Remington, huh? Can't say that it does. How old is it?"

"Nine years," I said.

Bennett shook his head.

"Goddamn, Michael. Nine years ago. Did we go to trial?"

"No."

"Pled out, huh? Sorry, pal."

"Actually, it wasn't a plea, either. More like the suspect just disappeared."

"Disappeared?"

"Yeah. Forget about it. Just saw your name on a piece of paperwork and thought you might remember."

"Not a problem. Tell you what, I'll look it up on Monday. See if I have anything in the files."

Beyond Bennett, I could see Nicole and caught her eye. She took Rodriguez by the hand and started over.

"Nicole's heading over," I said.

Bennett craned his neck around for a look.

"Where?"

"Right behind you. Walking across the room."

The prosecutor's head snapped forward.

"Shit. She with someone?"

"Bennett."

"Is she with someone?"

"Yes."

"I gotta go."

Bennett Davis finished his drink, slid away from the bar and into the shadows. I'd say one thing. For a portly fellow, the assistant DA could really slither when he had to.

CHAPTER 32

Why the rush?"

Diane had returned from wherever. Just in time to see the back of Bennett Davis' bald spot.

"Long story," I said. "By the way, are we a couple tonight?"

"What do you think? Say hi to Nicole."

A group of chattering men drifted away. Nicole moved into the void and drew close.

"I'm so glad you came," she whispered. Then she hugged Diane, pulled back, and looked at both of us in that "I approve of this coupling" sort of way. Rodriguez loitered to Nicole's left: smooth, chilled, and waiting to be opened.

"Vince," I said and offered a hand.

"Nice to see you again, Kelly."

The handshake was dry, the look sincere. I wanted to hate the guy. He was making it difficult. Nicole introduced the detective to Diane.

"I know this face," Rodriguez said. "Nice to finally meet you, Ms. Lindsay."

"Feeling's mutual, Detective Rodriguez. I certainly have heard the stories."

Everyone laughed at that except me. I wondered what the stories were about Rodriguez, and why I didn't know anything about them. The conversation moved right on past.

"Did you meet Judge Swenson?" Nicole said.

"I saw her on the way in," I said. "Rather, she picked me out of a crowd. Thanks a lot."

Nicole laughed.

"You're not hard to describe, Michael. When we were growing up, his nickname in the neighborhood was Irish. Big ears, crooked smile."

"Isn't that cute," Diane chimed in. "Do tell us more."

Nicole was about to oblige when Rachel Swenson mercifully moved to the podium and adjusted the mic. The crowd grew quiet, and the judge began to speak.

"There are more than one hundred million women in the United States. Almost twenty percent of them, roughly eighteen million, have been raped. The majority of those, more than once.

"You have a daughter getting ready for college. Consider this. One out of every four students can expect to be attacked by the time she graduates. Of that number, eighty percent will know their attacker.

"Overall, this country sees more than eight hundred thousand sexual assaults each year. That's thirteen times higher than Great Britain. Twenty times higher than Japan.

"During the two hours we gather here tonight, more than one hundred and fifty women will be assaulted. During the minute and a half I've been speaking, two women, somewhere in this country, have been violated.

"Do we have a problem, ladies and gentlemen? I think so."

Rachel stepped back from the podium and the crowd simply breathed. No applause, no chatter. Just a lot of quiet. I wasn't sure what the tuxedoes expected, but this wasn't your typical Gold Coast fund-raiser. The judge moved back to the mic.

"Thank you, everyone, for coming. My name is Rachel Swenson. I am the chairperson for the Rape Volunteer Association and your host for the night."

CHAPTER 33

W hat do you think?"

Rachel Swenson was wrapping up her talk when Diane moved close, a cup of ice in hand.

"I think it's powerful."

"You should see some of the interviews I've got."

"I'd like that."

Diane jiggled some ice into her mouth and crunched down.

"I believe you, Michael. I'm just not quite sure if you'd approve."

"Of your interviews?"

"Of the content. The confessions. Woman sits in front of my camera and explains how she gutted her husband like a fish. Man raped her every night for a lifetime. That is, when he wasn't raping her children. Self-defense? Revenge? Most of these women would tell you it doesn't really matter. As long as the guy is dead."

"You're a journalist, Diane. How does it make you feel?"

"At first it bothered me."

"Bennett appears to be giving you some cover."

"That's true. Even so, as I listen, as I get to know the women, I see their point."

"You could pick up the knife yourself?"

"Didn't say that. But I can see it. At least from where they sit."

"Those tapes would make one hell of a story."

"Maybe," Diane said. "But that's not going to happen."

Then she leaned over and kissed me softly.

"Enough of that. It gives me a headache. This is nice tonight. I like it."

"Like what?" I said.

"This. Being here. With you. Your friends. It feels good. Feels a little bit like home."

She spoke the final words reluctantly, with a haunting sort of sadness; delicate, yet indelibly etched in the cast of her features. A sadness that trembled at the precipice of some deep well I could guess at but probably preferred not to. Diane slipped her hand in mine.

"I have to call the station. After that, let's go."

I nodded. She kissed me again, lightly on the forehead, then the cheek. I watched her melt into the crowd. There was something going on in this relationship. I just wished someone would clue me in as to what it might be.

"Hey."

I turned. Nicole drew an arm through mine and we headed across the ballroom floor.

"What did you think of the night?" she said.

"What am I supposed to think?"

We found an empty spot, near a set of floor-to-ceiling windows that looked out over a river of headlights flowing north and south along Lake Shore Drive.

"I wanted you here," Nicole said. "I wanted you to understand."

"You thinking of telling your story, Nicole?"

She moved away from the window. I held out an arm to stop her, but she didn't need it.

"Not to worry, Michael. This girl isn't talking."

"It's all right, you know."

"Is it?"

"Diane told me about her project."

"The interviews?"

"Yeah."

"She asked me a couple of times if I wanted to participate. Just like that. Didn't ask if I'd been assaulted. Just seemed to know and moved right to it."

"Really?"

"Yeah, really. She's a sharp one, Michael. If I were you, I'd keep her."

"Maybe."

"Maybe? Seriously, what exactly could be wrong with that woman? She's smart as hell. Drop-dead gorgeous. Down-to-earth. Funny. Dedicated. Want me to keep going?"

"A little too intense, maybe?"

"The commitment thing, Michael. It's really a problem."

"It's not a commitment thing, Nicole. I like her. Okay. Maybe I'll like her a lot. Let's just wait and see."

"You wait too long, the world moves right on by."

Nicole stepped close and drew both arms around my waist.

"I'm sorry, Michael. I'm being a pain, but I just love you. A lot. I know you hate to hear that, but I do and I always will."

"I don't hate to hear it, Nicole."

"Okay, you like it."

"Didn't say that, either."

"Damn, we have some great talks."

She laughed. I laughed.

"I'm happy, Nicole. Not incredibly happy. Not yet. But that's going to be there. I just want it to be real. To be right. Most of all, I guess I want to deserve it. You understand?"

"No."

"But you trust me."

"Unfathomably and irrationally so."

"Good. Now tell me about our friend Detective Rodriguez."

"What do you think?"

"Truth?"

Nicole stepped back and gave me a single nod.

"I think he's the one," I said.

"How did you know?"

"I just know."

My friend looked away, out over Lake Shore Drive, into the jeweled and beating heart of the world's greatest city. Believe it or not, I actually had a handkerchief to offer.

"Thanks. The makeup is going to run."

"Don't worry about it," I said. "Happy will do that to you."

"Yeah, it's all of that. I never would have believed it. But it's amazing."

I gave her a minute.

"Been a long run, Michael."

"Think it's coming together?"

"I do," she said.

We began to walk. Slow and nice.

"By the way," I said, "Bennett was asking about you. Again."

"I didn't see him."

"Does he know about Rodriguez?"

"He does now." Nicole smiled. "Bennett's sweet."

"Like I said, obsessed. In a good way."

"You jealous, Michael?"

Nicole tried to grab the back of my tux, but I moved away, drifted down toward the lobby. I could see Rodriguez at the bar and Diane just beyond. I felt relaxed, maybe too much so, and a bit disconnected. I wondered how this was really playing for me. It would be interesting to find out.

"What are you guys doing afterward?" Nicole said.

"Not sure. Maybe a late dinner, drinks. You game?"

Nicole shook her head.

"Vince has got early duty tomorrow and I'm swamped. By the way, I haven't forgotten about you. I ran a DNA extraction on that shirt. Should have something soon."

"You have time?"

"It's a little crazy right now, but I can get it done. Got some strange stuff going on in the lab these days."

"How so?"

"Some things I can talk about. Some I just can't."

I turned to face my friend.

"Go for it."

"Right now?"

"Why not."

"Okay. Vince and I did a workup of unsolved sexual assaults over the past five years. We have targeted seven assaults on the North Side, all home invasions, all within two miles of one another."

"Same MO?"

"Pretty close. Attacker keeps his face hidden, so we have no suspect description. The one you rolled on with me the other night . . ."

"Miriam Hope?"

"Right. She's part of the group."

"DNA?"

"None so far. Miriam's our best bet. I'm running her bedsheets right now. If the rapist cried, he may have left some tears. It's a shot."

"This is just you and Vince right now?"

"Yeah."

"All right. Now, what can't you talk about?"

"The twelve-year-old. . . ."

"Jennifer Cole?"

"Yeah. I ran the semen we found in the alley. . . ."

"And?"

"Can't talk about it."

"But you want to."

"I need to."

"How do we do this?" I said.

"I don't know yet. Give me a little time."

I shrugged. Nicole squeezed my hand.

"I gotta run," she said. "Thanks again for coming tonight. Thanks for the talk. Means everything, Michael."

I gave her a final hug just as Diane drifted over. We moved through the Drake's revolving doors and into the October night that was Chicago. I took a final look back and caught my oldest friend's eye. Nicole began to wave, but a couple passed between us. When the path cleared, she was gone.

I searched the lobby and found her a few feet away, turned at an angle, talking to Bennett Davis. Rodriguez was nowhere to be seen. I smiled. As the Irish say, everyone loves a trier.

I moved onto the street and into a cab. Diane and I had a late dinner at Gibson's. It was nice but not quite real. We were eating the meal and drinking the drinks, telling the stories and grinning the grins, feeling the part, but not quite.

I had the cabbie drop Diane off at her apartment. Then I went home alone. An hour later I was fighting to stay awake and failing miserably. In that moment of clarity just before sleep, I thought of Nicole, alone in her lab, working through the night and into the next day's dawn. I wanted to get up, wanted to keep her company. Instead I fell into a cold slumber, a heavy sort of quiet pressing down and stretching toward the darkness.

CHAPTER 34

Fingers of gray light crept through my window and across the bedroom floor. Outside and below I could hear the small voices of morning: a door slamming, then a garbage truck as it moved through an alley. I thought about getting up, maybe a cup of coffee and the paper. The truck shifted gears and moved off, its rumble drifting me back to sleep. Then the phone rang. Caller ID said ILLINOIS STATE POLICE LAB. I picked up on the third ring.

"Hello."

"Michael, it's Nicole. Did I wake you up?"

"Just getting up. Why are you down there so early?"

"I couldn't sleep last night, so I came down to the lab. Thought I'd work on your samples before anyone else got in."

"Probably not a bad idea."

"Definitely not."

"Why?"

"We got a profile."

"From Elaine's shirt?"

"Yes."

I could feel a tingle at the back of my neck and a bit of heat moving up toward my temples.

"Can you identify it?"

"I ran it through CODIS at a little after three this morning. Got a match."

I was already half-dressed and reached for a pen and paper.

"I'm on my way. Give me the name of the guy."

"It's not that simple."

"How do you mean?"

"Remember last night when I told you about Jennifer?"

"You didn't tell me anything about Jennifer."

"Yeah, well, all the stuff I didn't tell you about, it just got a whole lot worse."

"Because of Elaine's shirt?"

"Michael, you better get down here. Right now."

CHAPTER 35

I got to the lab at a little after seven a.m. Parked in a lot that was empty save for Nicole's silver Cherokee. The front doors were locked. The lobby beyond appeared to be empty. I tried Nicole's cell phone but got no answer. Shit. I moved around the side of the building, wondering if there was another entrance. Nothing.

I walked along the back of the building now. The El ran close by. I tried Nicole's cell again. Still nothing.

My heart rate ticked up a bit, and I felt for the gun clipped to my waist. A line of dark red streaked along the cement to my left and up into a rusted set of girders. I knelt down and ran my hand across the stain. Still wet.

In the distance I could hear the rumble of an approaching train. I moved underneath the tracks. Quickly now, the rumble grew. The ground shook, the approaching train threatening to block out any other reality. I swung between a second set of girders.

Nicole was lying on her back, head tilted, mouth open, the only sound the train as it roared overhead. Around her throat was a necklace of bright red, sweating heavily every time she took a breath, soaking the University of Chicago sweatshirt she wore underneath. I knew enough to know it was arterial blood. Probably a straight razor, used from behind. I knew enough to know that no tourniquet, CPR, or first aid would save my friend's life. Instead I just held her close. Her eyes tracked mine. She didn't try to speak, just focused on me, accepted her fate. Within a minute or so, the light began to fade. She squeezed my hand once, then slipped away, quietly, in the early morning, under the El tracks.

I placed her back down on the ground and thought about all the times we never had, all the things I never said, all the things most people probably think of—way too much to contemplate and way too late in the game. Then I pulled out my cell phone and punched in 911. I held Nicole until I heard the first ambulance. Then I put her down for the last time, walked away, and wondered when I was going to cry.

CHAPTER 36

Three hours later I was in my office, door locked, shades drawn. I had my feet up on the desk, looking straight ahead at nothing. My cell phone chirped. I ignored it. The office phone rang once. Again. Ignored that. Then I heard footsteps in the hall and a knock at the door.

"What do you want?" I said.

It was Vince Rodriguez, standing over me, looking like he needed instructions on how to live the rest of his life. Like most cops, however, he was used to putting things away, and that's what he did.

"Tell me what happened?"

"I gave them a statement at the scene," I said. "Tape recorded it, so you can listen along if you want. They took my shirt, photos of my hands and arms. Probably looking for the slash marks that would show how I cut Nicole's throat. You want a drink?"

I pulled the Powers from my desk drawer. Rodriguez took off his coat, hung it on a hook, and sat down.

"You didn't kill Nicole," he said. "I know that. So does Headquarters."

"I'm impressed."

"What I don't understand is why you were down there."

I poured a bit of whiskey, neat, into a chipped coffee mug and offered it to Rodriguez, who took a pass. I swirled the brown liquid around and then set the mug down.

"Like I told the police, Nicole and I were going out for breakfast. Check her phone records. She called me an hour or so before I found her."

"I don't need to check the records," Rodriguez said. "Nicole called me directly after. Told me she was going to meet with you. Didn't say what it was about, but she sure didn't mention breakfast."

I expected Rodriguez to come by. Sooner or later. He seemed too smart not to. It wasn't even a bad thing. Nicole was dead. Just as dead as Gibbons. Just as dead as Gibbons' landlady. Maybe Rodriguez could help.

"What's the working theory downtown?" I said.

Rodriguez folded back into his chair.

"Wrong-place, wrong-time bullshit. Nicole was working late, decided to take the El home. Nicole was working late, decided to go out for a smoke."

"She doesn't smoke, and her car was in the parking lot."

"Like I said, all bullshit. But really, where else can they go?"

"Someone had access to the crime lab."

"Already checked. Nicole's was the only key card used last night. So unless her killer came in with her, Nicole had to have been attacked outside."

"Doesn't play, Rodriguez. At six in the morning Nicole had no reason to leave the building. I talked to her. She was expecting me and should have been down in the lobby."

"Which brings me back to my question. What did you have her working on?"

It was better than even money that I had somehow signed my friend's death warrant with my DNA request. If I could take it back, I would. If I could take her spot on the coroner's gurney, I'd do that, too. Instead, I would try to make her death matter.

"She was running some tests for me."

"On the old rape you told her about? She shared some of the details."

"Yeah, I figured she would. I gave her a piece of evidence. A shirt from the victim."

"Where'd you get that?"

"For right now, let's just say I acquired it."

Rodriguez nodded. I continued.

"When she called this morning, she told me she had gotten a profile. Told me it had come back as a match in CODIS. She said it tied in to some results you had gotten from the attack on that kid."

"Jennifer Cole?" Rodriguez said.

"Yeah."

"Nicole said that?"

I nodded. Rodriguez clasped his hands on top of his head and looked up at the ceiling.

"What're you thinking?" I said.

"I'm thinking she made a connection."

"One that got her killed," I said. "What happened with Jennifer?"

"Leave that for now. We need to figure out what Nicole got off your girl's shirt. Where is it?"

"Nicole kept it in the lab," I said.

"Shit. Her workstation was clean."

"What about her computer?"

"Nothing there but her assigned cases."

"Whoever killed her got inside," I said. "Took everything with them."

"Maybe not. Let me use your computer."

Rodriguez slid behind the desk and fired up my Mac.

"Nicole didn't trust her boss," the detective said. "Thought he was working with the DA to bury cases that deserved to be investigated."

"Sounds like Nicole."

"Yeah. Anyway, she wanted to build a case. Created her own private backup system."

Rodriguez pulled a thin black object from his jacket pocket and slid it into a slot on the side of my computer.

"I pulled this off her key chain at the scene. It's a memory stick. The question for us is, did she have time to run a backup?"

"Have you taken a look?"

"No. She trusted you. Figured I'd wait."

I offered a small toast with my mug.

"Thanks, Detective. You didn't have to do that."

"Yes, I did. If we get a lead, this goes off the books. You and me. Once we find him, whoever killed Nicole isn't getting a trial. You understand?"

I understood and told him as much. The detective gave me a short nod and dropped his eyes.

"Good."

CHAPTER 37

Vince clicked on a blinking icon, and Nicole's memory stick opened up. I was immediately lost. Fortunately, Rodriguez seemed to know his way around.

"The latest file on here was updated this morning. That means she probably ran a backup to whatever she did for you."

"Can you find it?"

Vince opened up what looked like a spreadsheet and began to read.

"This is it," he said. "Elaine Remington. Is that your client?"

I nodded.

"See these bar graphs in green?"

I nodded again.

"That's the DNA profile from her shirt."

Vince clicked and scrolled a bit more.

"I'm not entirely sure, but I think this is the matching profile."

Vince pointed to another set of graphs, these in red.

"Looks like she might have a match at twelve different loci."

"That good?" I said.

Vince looked up from the computer.

"That's very strong. You got a pen?"

I pushed one across the desk. Rodriguez began to make notes.

"Best I can figure, this is the case number from the matching profile. Can we get online here?"

"What do you want to do?"

"Jump into our police database," Vince said. "See if I can track this case number."

I nodded to my Mac.

"Be better if we can't be traced."

Rodriguez shrugged.

"You're probably right."

"Intelligentsia is down the street," I said. "They have a PowerBook we can rent and a DSL line."

Vince pulled the memory stick and we headed out. It was close to noon, and the shop was quiet. I got a coffee, black. Rodriguez got an espresso and logged on to the Chicago PD server.

I waited and sipped. Vince clicked and scrolled. Fifteen minutes later he sat back, looked at me, again at the computer screen, then closed it down.

"What is it?" I said.

Vince glanced around the almost empty coffee shop. Maybe there was a villain hidden in the Arturo Fuente whole-roasted coffee beans, on sale at $8.99 a pound, but I didn't think so.

"Talk to me, Vince."

The detective pulled the PowerBook open again and swung it around so I could follow along.

"What did Nicole tell you about the match?"

"She said it matched a profile in CODIS."

"That's it?"

"Yeah."

"Okay. Best I can tell, your sample matches semen found on at least two female vics in the John William Grime murders."

I flashed back to Ray Goshen and his broom closet full of horror.

"Grime? As in the serial killer?"

Rodriguez nodded.

"Not possible," I said. "Grime was on death row when Elaine Remington was attacked."

"I didn't say it matched Grime himself," Rodriguez said. "Let's back up a minute. In 1995 they pulled fifteen bodies from under Grime's house. All female. Most of them were clothed. Some were wrapped up in sheets. As you can imagine, a lot of physical evidence."

"They got a whole wing devoted to Grime over at the warehouse."

"Yeah well, last year Nicole's lab director decided to process some of the Grime stuff for DNA."

"The case was solved," I said.

Rodriguez held up a hand.

" 'A matter of Chicago criminal history,' the director argued. Anyway, everyone expected any genetic profile to be consistent with Grime."

"Didn't happen that way?" I said.

"They found Grime's DNA on most of the evidence. I mean, his semen was all over the stuff. But there was a second, unidentified profile."

"Semen?"

"On the clothing of two of the victims."

"Why didn't this make the news?"

Rodriguez took a breath.

"The lab was surprised, and at first there was a lot of conversation. Then people started to think it through. Grime's victims were mostly hookers. It would be normal for them to have other customers on the night Grime picked them up."

"The same unknown on two different victims?"

Vince shrugged.

"Maybe coincidence. Maybe not. Bottom line: the DA's office decided to let it lie."

"And now this."

"Yeah, now this. A rape two years after Grime went to jail turns up the same unknown profile. But that's not the only problem."

"Jennifer?"

"Yeah, Jennifer Cole. But it's not what you think."

All I could think of was the face of a twelve-year-old blurred by a piece of police car Plexi.

"I'm listening," I said.

"Earlier this week Nicole ran the semen we found in the alley off Belmont. It came back to the Grime file as well."

"The same unknown?"

"Actually, no. The semen we found in that alley was a perfect genetic match to Mr. Grime himself."

"Impossible."

"Not really. You ever hear of a guy named Norm Shannon?"

I shook my head.

"Guy in Milwaukee last year. Linked to three separate assaults through DNA. He's sitting in a cell waiting for trial when a fourth attack occurs. Shannon's semen is found inside the fourth victim. He files motions everywhere, attacking the credibility of DNA, saying how can it be, demanding his release."

"And?"

"Turns out Shannon masturbated into a package of mustard, mailed it to this woman from prison. She inserted it in herself and claimed she was raped. All for fifty dollars."

"Damn."

"Woman copped to the whole scam," Rodriguez said. "Didn't work, but hell, it was a nice try."

"And you're thinking that's what Grime did?"

"I'm thinking Grime had an accomplice in his original murders. One we never knew about. One Grime is still in contact with."

"And this guy is still active?"

"Looks like it. I think Grime somehow got this guy his semen and told him to drop it at one of his attacks. Who knows why. Just for fun. Anyway, that attack turned out to be Jennifer Cole."

"And now you think Elaine Remington's shirt can help ID this guy?"

"I think that is what Nicole was going to tell you at the lab."

We sat quietly for a moment, staring at the file Nicole had left us, the lead she had unwittingly died for. Vince clicked on another icon, and a newspaper photo came up, a group shot of men sitting around a mahogany table. The caption read GRIME PROSECUTION TEAM. Vince zoomed in on the photo.

"Appears Nicole was already pulling background on Grime."

"Yeah," I said, and scanned the blurry faces. A lot of them looked young. Never one to miss a microphone, Gerald O'Leary was front and center.

"E-mail that to me, will you?" I said.

I gave Rodriguez my address.

"When's the execution date?" I said.

Vince clicked through the file.

"Looks like he might go within the year."

"Where is he right now?"

"Death row at Menard. Down near Saint Louis. What're you thinking?"

"I'm thinking I need to talk to Grime."

Rodriguez thought that was pretty funny.

"He's been on death row for a decade," the detective said. "Never sat down with a cop. Never gave an interview to the press."

"He'll see me."

"Why?"

"Because he's a year from the needle and I'm the guy who's going to set him free."

Rodriguez shut down the computer and drained his espresso.

"Let's go," he said.

"Where?"

"If you're going to get inside a room with Grime, there's someone you need to talk to. I'll set it up."

CHAPTER 38

E ver sat down with a serial killer?"
The next day Rodriguez took me to a one-room apartment above a Jimmy John's in the Streeterville section
of Chicago. The apartment's sole occupant was long and thin, a
lot of bones and angles, with muttonchops and a gray handlebar
mustache. Sixty, maybe a bit more, he wore a Fat Tire T-shirt and
smoked a lot of dope. At least that is what the bag of weed on the
coffee table would have the private investigator in me believe.

"No, I haven't," I said.

Robert J. Trent III took a sip of his ginger tea and offered a
measured look into the abyss. I snuck a look at Rodriguez, who
held up a hand for patience. According to the detective, Trent
had bumped knees with more than a hundred serial killers. Even
better, he had actually gotten results, offering profiles and breaking major cases with the FBI and beyond. I never heard of the guy.
According to Rodriguez, that was by design. Trent was a free-
lance criminal profiler, a guy who never got the degrees or
worked the mainstream press, a guy who lived under the radar
because "that's where the killers were."

"Tricky business," Trent said. "Need to be strong-willed.

Don't let them get into your head. Because once they get in, they never get out."

"I don't expect to have any nightmares," I said.

"Few do. I know a homicide detective who spent a couple hours with Ted Bundy down in Florida. Cop went home. Seemed fine. Two weeks later he woke up in the middle of the night. Bundy was sitting at the bottom of his bed. Not doing anything. Just sitting there, grinning. Guy's wife had to call 911. Took three cops and a syringe full of Valium to calm this guy down. He quit the force six months later. Now he's divorced, sells stationery, and drinks a fifth of vodka before he shuts his eyes at night. Bottom line . . . these guys prey on the weak."

"What can you tell us about Grime specifically?" Rodriguez said.

"Never spoke with him. Am I to take it you're the one going in?"

Trent offered me a set of watery red eyes over a pair of half-moon, CVS-issue reading glasses.

"Working on it," I said.

Trent pushed the glasses up on his nose and hooked one knee over the other.

"Very good. Let me just review the facts here. At least as Detective Rodriguez presented them over the phone."

Trent gave Rodriguez a sideways look, as if using the phone was somehow beneath us all, then continued.

"As I understand things, Mr. Grime has somehow ferreted his DNA out of prison and into the eager hands of an accomplice. Hmm?"

Rodriguez and I nodded. Trent pressed his lips together, consulted his notes, and continued.

"You gentlemen believe Mr. Grime has had this accomplice insinuate said semen into the particulars of an attempted sexual assault, thereby, and on the surface at least improbably, implicating Mr. Grime himself."

More nods.

"Very good. You also suspect that said accomplice himself is and has been actively assaulting women over a period of years, perhaps at Mr. Grime's urging and behest."

Trent was on a roll now and didn't wait for our acknowledgment.

"Further, you suspect this accomplice was actually a participant in the original set of serial murders for which Mr. Grime himself is currently looking at multiple death sentences. Finally, you contend that you will be able to prove all of this with DNA."

"Not so sure about the last part," Rodriguez said. "We have the accomplice's DNA but no idea as to who it might be."

"Hence the conversation with Grime," Trent said.

"Hence," I replied.

"Does it add up for you?" Rodriguez said.

Trent took a sip of tea, unhooked then rehooked his legs, crooked an elbow, and laid the long palm of his hand flat under an even longer chin. Finally, he looked up our way and answered.

"Oh, it adds up, Detective. It adds up beautifully. Classic serial killer. Classic Grime."

"How so?" I said.

"John Grime is all about two things," Trent said. "Controlling the present and reliving the past. Both are powerful narcotics. If, as you suggest, he is capable of pulling the strings on an active rapist or killer, it offers the ultimate release."

"He relives his own crimes through the actions of his accomplice," I said.

"Even better, Mr. Kelly. Even better. In his mind he physically places himself at the scene by putting his own semen there. His signature, if you will."

"And he's in control," Rodriguez said.

Trent nodded and shifted back in his chair.

"Completely. Killing, raping by remote control. From a cell on death row. I abhor it, gentlemen, but you must admit, if even close to true, awfully impressive."

"Fuck impressive," I said. "How can we get him to talk? Give up the name of his accomplice?"

Trent shook his head.

"I don't know exactly what will work. But I can surely tell you what will not. Don't bother confronting Mr. Grime with facts he has gone to such lengths to arrange."

"Explain," I said.

Trent shrugged.

"His semen found at the latest assault. He knows it's there. In a very real sense, he put it there. He also knows that you know it's there and that he put it there. By acknowledging any of this, you give him more control, more enjoyment, less reason to do anything but shut up."

"Shit," Rodriguez said.

"Precisely," Trent offered.

"So what can we do?" I said.

"What do you want?"

"Like I said, the name of his accomplice."

Trent considered that for a moment and answered.

"I will tell you what I tell anyone who talks to a serial killer. Don't lie. Even the least artful of these serial types are better liars than any of us could ever dream of being. With Grime, you are talking state of the art. His IQ is off the charts. Not genius level, but close. He will have this thing thought through.

"Tell him the truth. Make it a hard truth. Something he doesn't want to hear. Gives you credibility. Gives you respect. Gives you at least a bit of strength. Then somehow convince him that giving up the name of his accomplice is in his best interest. Ultimately, Mr. Kelly, these guys are, for lack of a better word, selfish fucks. They will act in their own self-interest one hundred times out of one hundred. Therein lies their intrigue and their vulnerability. Use it, but don't expect too much."

"You don't think he'll talk?" I said.

"You never know," Trent said. "You never know."

The profiler picked up the bag of weed and some rolling papers. In less than a minute he had tapped out a professional-looking joint.

"Sorry, Detective, but you know. Glaucoma."

Trent fired up and smoked. Just a toke or two. Then he pinched off the joint, closed his eyes, and sat back. After a few seconds' repose, he continued.

"I will offer one more item for your consideration. Nothing more than a guess, but I believe Mr. Grime wants very much to help you identify his accomplice. If nothing else, it raises the stakes, pushes the rush."

"Helps his God complex," Rodriguez said.

"Exactly," Trent replied. "He decides when the fun is over, who gets caught, and when. As for the accomplice himself . . ."

"Yes?" I said.

"Impossible to say how he would react to Grime's betrayal. I will, however, say this. It seems more likely than not that he will continue to hunt and continue to attack women."

"Until he is caught," I said.

"No, Mr. Kelly. Until he is killed."

CHAPTER 39

As I drove home, I thought about what Trent had told us. Rodriguez stared out the window and didn't blink very much. I had put Nicole aside. At least for the moment. Rodriguez wasn't entirely there yet.

"Where am I dropping you?" I said.

"I parked on Addison, around the corner from your place."

I pulled up to his car and stopped. The wind was picking up off the lake. A plastic bag scurried across the street, then straight up, into the tangled branches of a tree. A few drops of rain spattered across my windshield, found their rhythm, and began to fall in a light, steady patter.

"I'm going in after Grime," I said and flicked on my wipers. "A letter and a request to visit."

"It's a long shot."

"But worth it. Besides, he'll never sit down with a cop."

Rodriguez climbed out of the car and stuck his head back in through the open door. A cold, wet draft blew his voice across the front seat.

"Just remember, Kelly. This is a private gig. So go low-key. Don't use any names. Don't give up a lot of detail. Inside or outside Menard. And be careful. Trent is right. Grime is good at what he does. And Grime is all about Grime."

I nodded.

"You all right, Rodriguez?"

"Not really. Not yet. But I will be."

"I know," I said. "Just going to take some time."

The detective slammed my car door shut. I rolled around the corner and down the block. I found a space in front and walked to my building, composing a love letter to a serial killer in my head. A gust of wind pushed me the final few feet toward my front door. She was sitting on the stoop. I almost stepped on her before she said a word.

"Michael."

I hadn't heard her voice in a year. It brought back feelings I thought were gone, or at least reduced to memory.

"Annie," I said.

Now she was up and close, arms around my neck, cheek touching mine. For a moment, everything was as it once was. Then it wasn't.

"I'm sorry about Nicole," she murmured.

It had only been a day, but already Nicole seemed dead a lifetime. I held Annie lightly, felt her let loose inside. She had known Nicole. Not as I did, but enough to make it real.

"It's all right," I said.

My words hung in the air, glorious in their artlessness, mocking their creator. I fumbled for my keys and opened the door.

"Let's go inside."

Five minutes later, we were sitting in two armchairs, looking out my windows, watching the weather. Patches of fog drifted in from the lake, squeezing down side streets and alleys, filling doorways, and curling around the gutters tucked under my roof.

Above the mist sat the heavy artillery. Layers of clouds, veined in purple and full of wind. They blew shop signs against their moorings and pedestrians across intersections. Then the sky split and the clouds emptied themselves in earnest. The October storm was as complete as it was sudden, spending itself against my window, streaming into a crack along the frame, and forming a pool near a cup of tea my old flame had laid on the sill.

"Never got that drip fixed, did you, Michael?"

Annie sniffed a bit, wiped up the forming pool of water with a napkin, and took a sip of tea.

"How are you?" she said.

"I'm okay."

"Sorry about outside. I read about Nicole in the papers, but it wasn't until I said her name. I don't know. Just lost it."

Then Annie lost it again, gentler this time. I moved beside her, spoke without thinking.

"She loved you, Annie. I know you guys hadn't talked much in the past year or so, but she loved you a lot. You should know that."

I felt her lean into me in acknowledgment.

"Something else, Annie. I was there when Nicole died."

She stiffened and looked up.

"That wasn't in the paper."

"I know, and it's not something we can really talk about. Just understand it was a mean death, Annie. And Nicole was brave. Very fucking brave."

The sadness I expected to feel inside wasn't there yet. Well, it was there, just not right up front. Instead there was a coldness, fierce pride for Nicole, and anger. I hadn't known about the anger until I spoke, but that's often the way it is. Annie didn't push it. Maybe she knew better.

"When is the funeral?" she said.

"Tuesday. At Graceland, one o'clock."

She nodded and wiped her nose. I stood up and moved to the windows. Gave both of us some space. After a minute or so, she spoke again.

"You look good."

"Yeah, right. I look like hell and you know it."

I turned around. Annie was curled in now, blond hair still damp from the rain, blue eyes perched over a cup of tea, searching mine for answers to questions she'd never asked.

"Fine, you look like hell," she said. "I look great."

The humor was quiet, soothing, easy to fall into. I sat back down in my chair and waited. The hard part was over. I had a feeling the impossible was only about to begin.

"I'm sorry about how it ended," she said.

"I know."

"It was the best way."

"I know."

"I'm not a coward."

"I know."

"Do you?"

I thought about that day. I had left Annie in the kitchen. She said she was going to make some lunch and read. She had been distant. I had been distant. We both knew it wasn't working and didn't want to talk about it. So it sat there. The relationship. Like a great, grinning eight-hundred-pound gorilla. In the corner of each and every room in our two-bedroom flat. Peeling away the skin of our collective life. Grinning and eating. Piece by piece. Getting bigger. Getting harder to ignore every day.

That particular morning, however, had been better. We talked about her work. I made a joke. She laughed. We even talked about what we might do for Christmas, a conversation that made the considerable assumption there was another Christmas together in our future. I remember she reached out and held me close before I went out the door. Thought that was a good sign. I was only half-right.

I ran seven hard miles along the lake. Felt loose and fast. Fell into an easy rhythm. Then I walked for a bit, enjoyed the scenery and the sweat. Just like always. It was a little over two hours by the time I returned to the apartment.

I came in through the back door. The kitchen was dark, the counter wiped clean. I remember walking to the sink and feeling the sponge. Still wet. A single bead of water hung off the faucet and then fell. I wanted to yell her name but stopped myself. Instead, I walked into the living room. Like the kitchen, it was dark. I could hear a clock ticking on a table next to the sofa. We had bought it at a barn sale in Wisconsin because it looked old and cool. Now it just sounded loud.

Beyond the living room was our bedroom and a closet. Open and half-empty. Near the front door, a table. On it a solitary pool of soft light warmed the sharp, white creases of a single envelope. I walked over and picked it up. My name was scratched across the front. In a comfortable, familiar scrawl that hurt to look at. I ticked the envelope open and found myself back in the kitchen, reading in the late-afternoon darkness. The words ran together as my eyes tore over the pages, picking out the operative phrases. It was beautiful. It was elegant. It was heartbreaking. It was seven pages. It was the speech. Annie was moving on. And I was not moving with her.

I hated her. Hated myself for hating her. Hated being in the apartment. Being in that moment. I'd get over it. Sure. But still, a year later, the ache doesn't forget.

"It's not that big of a deal," I said.

"I could have told you. Face-to-face."

"Why didn't you?"

"What do you think would have happened? If we had talked it out?"

I had thought about a lot of things in the past year. But never that.

"How many times had we broken up?" she said. "How many times in the last year had we agreed it was over? Eight, ten, once a month?"

I smiled. Sad, but a smile.

"At least," I said.

"Exactly. Neither one of us had the strength to do it face-to-face. Neither of us could have ever walked away. Not like that."

"But we had to."

"Yes."

"So that was the best way?"

"It wasn't the best way, Michael. It was the worst. But it was also the only way. Like I said, I'm sorry."

She wiped away a lonely tear, took a sip of tea, and looked back out at the storm. I noticed that she jiggled one foot against the ground and the cup shook lightly in her hand. Our relationship had taken its pound of flesh. I hoped it wasn't hungry for more.

"You did what you had to do, Annie. What you thought was right. I know that now. Pretty much always known that, I think."

She didn't respond. So we sat and listened to the wind. Two people, comforting a relationship that left town a long time ago. And wasn't coming back. After a while she got up quietly, found her coat, and headed to the door. I followed. Annie turned.

"You're a good person, Michael. That's why I loved you back then. That's why I love you right now. For a long time I thought that would be enough. For both of us. Turns out it wasn't enough for either."

"I know."

She tilted her head.

"You do?"

"I ran into you the other day. By accident. With the guy."

She blushed, more than I wanted, and pulled her coat tight.

"Wow. Didn't know that."

"Serious?"

She looked up at me. This time she told the truth. No matter how much it hurt.

"Yeah, Michael. Pretty serious."

"I'm happy for you."

I didn't know if I meant it until I said it. Then I knew it was right.

"I won't be at the funeral," she said. "Don't think I can take it. But I'll stop by the grave next week. Say my good-byes."

Annie hugged me. Then she left. I sat by the window and watched as the Hawk blew her down Lakewood and across Addison. In a small frame, on a table by the window, was a picture of myself and Nicole, snapped at a Cubs game last summer. Saturday afternoon in the bleachers. I picked up the photo and lingered, if only for a moment, in a newfound sense of freedom, joined at the hip with freedom's ugly cousin: an all-encompassing sense of isolation otherwise known as loneliness.

CHAPTER 40

Nicole was buried two days later. On a Tuesday afternoon. She had two sisters. I stood between them at the grave and held their hands. Rodriguez stood behind me, dark glasses shading a face of stone. I didn't see Annie. I didn't need to look.

Rachel Swenson offered a reading at the service. Bennett Davis was in the back of the crowd. Tight-lipped, he gave me a nod at the edge of Nicole's grave, dropped a rose into the hole, and drifted away. Bennett would be okay. I'd check up on him in a day or so.

Nicole's death was a run-of-the-mill tragedy, nothing more than a one-day story in Chicago. Young black woman, forensic scientist, dedicated her life to catching killers, done in by the same. Nice angle, but ultimately, just another random act of violence. Or so it went. Rodriguez kept my name out of the public record and I appreciated it.

"You haven't returned my calls."

I was walking away from the service. Alone. Diane came up from behind. She was dressed in black and looked every bit the part.

"Sorry," I said. "It's been tough."

"I know. She was my friend, too."

I held her close. Diane cried for more than a moment. I waited and felt the first bit of peace inside. It surprised me.

"You want to come over?" I said.

She pulled away, almost embarrassed, and moved back within herself.

"I can't. I've got to do the six o'clock."

"How about after? We can get some dinner."

Now she was far away. Or at least seemed that way.

"Let's see how it goes. I'll give you a call."

I nodded and turned to go. Diane reached out and touched me at the elbow.

"Kelly."

I paused but didn't look back.

"You okay?" she said.

"I'm okay."

Her fingers slipped off the sleeve of my coat.

"Good. I'll talk to you later."

I heard her move away and continued walking. Phillip's grave was at the very back of the cemetery, in a section neither the groundskeeper, nor anyone else, visited very often. I didn't have any flowers to leave, not even a cigarette to lay on top of my brother's headstone. He would have liked that.

Instead, I stood there and remembered. Flickering moments of childhood memory, ground into dust by the gears of fate and time. Phillip had been dead too long for me to really miss him. But I could still be angry, still wonder why. My brother and Nicole lived at the heart of what was once my youth. Now they'd be buried together. If nothing else, it was convenient.

After a minute or so had passed, I made the sign of the cross, ran my fingers along his name carved in the rock, and left. As I walked back to my car, I stole a glance through the trees. The backhoe was at work. Pouring dirt on my friend's coffin, sending her on her way through eternity.

CHAPTER 41

Ileft the cemetery and drove to the Century City Mall at Diversey and Clark. I pulled into a no-parking zone, put on my flashers, and got out. It was midafternoon and the mall was pretty empty. There was a bass line playing inside my head, a hiss of static underneath, pulsing just below the skin. I pushed a button and waited for the elevator. Just as the doors opened, a guy and his girlfriend brushed past me and into the car. The guy was wearing a cut-off T-shirt and a Red Sox hat on backward. He punched a button and the doors began to close. I was still outside. The girl was laughing. The guy gave me a little finger-wave through the six inches of space left between the doors. I stuck my foot into the gap, reached through, and began to pry. I could hear the guy stabbing at the buttons, but it wasn't working.

"You don't like to wait."

My voice felt low, dangerously in control.

"Whatever. We don't have all fucking day."

It was the girl. She was dressed in hipster jeans with a cut-off tank top. She was overweight and out of shape. I watched her belly fold over her jeans and palpitate as she screeched. Then I looked over to the guy. He was muscled up, a soft sort of weight-room muscle. The kind that looked good until you took it out for a little exercise. He was looking at me, wondering what I was going to do. He had a little sneer running across his upper lip. Not because he was tough. Not because he was capable. Simply because he didn't know any better.

"Take your shot," I said. The kid's eyes jumped a bit.

"Excuse me, dude?"

"I said, Take your shot."

I moved closer so he could understand that this was going to happen. The thrill of violence ran across my shoulders, fired down my arms, and coiled in my fists. Maybe he'd back down. I didn't think so. At that moment, I sincerely hoped not.

"You want to go?" he said, and looked over at the girl, who was all eyes now.

I didn't say anything, just waited. Like most guys who don't know how to fight, he started out predictable and only got worse. A long slow right, looping in from the side, losing steam and then crashing into the side of my head. I moved just enough to take the punch, yet blunt its power. It only took an inch's worth of movement. The trick was to know which inch and when.

I waited a beat. The kid looked at me, looked at his fist, and back to me again. Then it was over. A right hand caught him on the jaw and sent him back against the wall. He wanted to go down but I had him by the shirt. Not yet. I fired two more rights. Straight shots. Short and lethal. The first snapped his nose. The second closed his right eye. Then I let him go, and he slumped to the floor. It was over in less than five seconds. The girl was frozen in one corner of the elevator. Ready to run if I made a move her way. I got out, punched the button to close the doors, and took the stairs.

The movie theater was on the third floor. I bought a Coke, made my way in, and found a seat in the back. I could hear a bit of commotion outside. Sounded like security. Then it settled back down. I wasn't sure what film I had bought a ticket for, but it didn't matter. The knuckle above my ring finger was sore, so I finished the Coke and shoved my hand in the ice. Then I sat there for a while and stared at the screen. Tom Cruise was saying something to a Hollywood-looking girl, but I couldn't really follow. It didn't matter, either. In the darkness of the theater, I was safe. Just me, Tom, and a cupful of ice. Then my best friend, Nicole, came down the aisle and sat beside me. Wrapped an arm around my shoulders, touched my face, and told me how it was going to be okay. How I'd get along just fine. How I'd find someone else to trust, someone else to love, someone else to grow up with. How someday I'd forget it was my fault she was in the ground at the age of thirty-three.

I dropped the cup to the floor, bent forward, and ran my hands through my hair. Nicole. I thought about her in the darkness. In the theater. I didn't want to think about Nicole. I couldn't think about her. Ever again. That was over. This was beginning. That's what I told myself. But it doesn't work that way. At least not for me. So I let her in. Then I cried. Deep and quiet. In a way I hadn't thought possible. I cried until I couldn't anymore. The movie played on. I shook, I raged, I heaved. All barely above a whisper. And then there was no more. I waited, wondered. Whatever it was, however, was gone. I found a napkin on the floor of the theater and wiped my eyes. Tom was about to get blown up, shot, and kissed. All at the same time. I wished him well and left the theater.

The mall was quiet. No sign of the kid or his girl. I wanted to give him some money, offer to pay for medical expenses, something. Instead, I took the elevator down. It was empty, save for a spot of blood against the wall in one corner. I walked back down Diversey and found my car. No ticket. My lucky day. I got in and drove back to my apartment. Nicole was in the ground. Gone. And there was work to be done.

CHAPTER 42

Even a decade later, the street-mime killer was never far from a headline. The latest article I Googled on John William Grime was dated a week ago. A local businessman had bought some of his prison sketches and held a public bonfire. A week before that there was a piece in the *Chicago Tribune* about the house on Hutchinson. The split-level under which Grime had buried fifteen young women was being sold to a developer. A couple of dozen people dressed as mimes sat silently on the sidewalk as the house was bulldozed. Each held a picture of one of Grime's victims. According to the reporter, plans called for a Kentucky Fried Chicken to replace the house. Everyone got a charge out of that, since Grime himself was once a KFC cook. That was only slightly before he murdered sixteen-year-old Tamara Kennedy, his first known victim.

I had fixed myself a cup of tea and was digging through the accounts of Grime's arrest and trial when the phone rang. It was Diane.

"What are you doing?"

I checked my watch. It was twenty past six.

"Why aren't you on the air?"

"I am. It's a commercial break. Turn us on and I'll lick my lips for you."

"Funny. You coming over?"

"You want me there?"

"Yes."

"How was your afternoon?"

"Fine."

A pause.

"I'll be over after the show."

"Great. I got a question for you. Didn't you guys do a retrospective on John William Grime last year?"

"John Donovan did it. Ten-year anniversary of the arrest. I think we brought a lot of the families together."

"If you can, bring that tape over and anything else you can dig up."

"Grime?"

I could hear a music cue in the background and her director's voice.

"I'll explain when you get here."

I hung up and clicked on the TV. After the commercial break they went to a studio shot, and then there was Diane, up close, telling Chicagoland about Beluga whales at the Shedd Aquarium. There was no smile on her face and not even a hint of lasciviousness about the lips. In fact, she looked a bit distracted. I clicked off the set and returned to the serial killer.

A *Time* magazine piece from 1996 had photos from the crime scene itself, including the excavation. Best I could tell, Grime had stacked the bodies two deep in three long trenches. He accessed the graves through the floor of his bedroom closet. Fashioned a pulley system, tied the feet of his victim to the pulley, and lowered away headfirst. Not a lot of room, but the bodies were there, so I read on.

Grime hunted on the city's strolls. Usually at night. He drowned or strangled most of his victims and raped all but three. Fifteen-year-old Eileen Hayes was found at the bottom of one of the graves. Her fingers were dug into the back of the corpse beside her. The medical examiner speculated Hayes was still alive when Grime buried her. According to the ME, Eileen Hayes could not have lasted more than a few minutes after regaining consciousness.

I stretched, walked to the window, and wondered how long would be short enough to be awake in your own grave. Across the street a CTA bus disgorged its passengers into a sudden, soft rain. A space cleared, and Diane stepped through it. She popped open an umbrella and cast her eyes toward my window. A minute after that there was a knock at the door.

"Hey, babe."

She moved easily into my body. A couple of good moments later, we parted.

"How you doing?" she said.

"I'm doing fine."

"Good. You hungry?"

"Not really," I said. "But we should eat."

I pulled a variety of take-out menus from a kitchen drawer.

"What do you feel like?" I said.

"Whatever."

Diane had her back to me and drifted her fingers across an old bookcase I kept by the front door. Inside it were the collected works of Plato. I pulled a menu off the pile and dialed.

"What are you getting?" she said.

"Chinese."

"I hate Chinese."

Diane had one of the volumes open now and was reading. I hung up the phone and picked up another menu.

"Is this Greek?" she said.

"Ancient Greek. Fourth century B.C."

"Looks hard."

"Not if you lived in Greece."

Diane turned with a smirk.

"You mean in the fourth century B.C."

"Exactly," I said. "You like pizza?"

"Who doesn't?"

"This is East Coast pizza. Thin crust and round."

"Sounds great. You got beer?"

I pointed in the general direction of the refrigerator and ordered. Diane got us a couple of beers, green glass and cold. She sat down in the same chair Annie had sat in, tipped the bottle back, and then wiped her upper lip.

"How and why?"

"What?"

She had put down Plato and held up a copy of Aeschylus' *Agamemnon.*

"How and why?"

I moved back into my mind and shrugged.

"Something I got into early in life. Studied in high school, college."

"I was a history major in college," Diane said. "I don't have my apartment stuffed with American history books."

"Maybe you should."

"Interesting," she said.

"You think so?"

I grabbed the volume of Aeschylus and opened it.

"What do you know about this guy?" I said.

"Aeschylus?"

"Aeschylus."

She shrugged.

"What everyone else knows. Didn't he kill himself? Drink some hemlock?"

"That was Socrates."

I copied out a line for Diane to read.

Ἔστιν Θάλασσα-τίς δέ νιν κατασβέσει;

"This is ancient Greek," I said.

"Cool."

"It's from Aeschylus' *Agamemnon*, part of a trilogy of plays called *The Oresteia*. This line translates 'There is the sea, now who will drain it dry?' Clytemnestra says it to Agamemnon just before she sets him up to be killed."

"Messing around, was Agamemnon?"

"Not really. But the point is, when you say this line in the original Greek, it comes out like a hiss. A lot of soft *sss*'s. Aeschylus wanted Clytemnestra to actually sound like the snake she was. Here, try this line."

I copied out another line of Greek text.

γνῶθι σ' αυτόν

"This was on the wall of the oracle at Delphi," I said. "It means 'Know thyself.' According to Plato, this was the key to true wisdom, true happiness."

"Know thyself," Diane said. "Sounds great."

"You think so?"

"Sure. Until you learn too much."

"Speaking from experience?" I said.

"Common sense. Ask enough questions of yourself, you might find out some things you don't like."

I didn't tell Diane how close she had struck to Sophocles' Oedipus. Figured I'd save that chestnut for another day.

"Anyway," I said, "that's what I get out of it. A way to look at life, a way to live life. Something that stays with you. So I like it. Now let's talk about Grime."

Diane returned *Agamemnon* to the bookshelf and turned on my VCR.

"Bulldog is our expert on Grime," she said. "You realize he covered the actual trial."

"Of course."

John "Bulldog" Donovan was a throwback, not to mention a legend. A guy who wore a soft hat, carried a notebook, and licked his pencil before he wrote.

"Bulldog's the best reporter in the city," I continued. "Gets it right the first time."

Diane popped in a tape. Donovan's deep baritone rolled over footage of the house on Hutchinson and then the only shot anyone ever got of Grime, twenty seconds of footage as police led the serial killer into the station for booking. He looked pudgy, sort of dazed.

"What do you think?" I said.

Diane tilted her head to one side.

"Looks like a million other guys. Guess that's the trick, huh?"

"Serial Killer 101," I said. "Gotta look like the guy next door."

"In Grime's case, the loser next door."

I paused the tape on a photo of Grime, his face turned away from the lens and half-hidden in his hands.

"Did you know he performed a mime for every one of his victims?"

Diane shook her head. I continued.

"He'd cover his face and body in white pancake and do his mime. You'd be handcuffed in his tub. Screaming until you couldn't breathe. Promising anything for another moment to live. And meaning every word. He'd finish his show, scrape the makeup off, and look at you. Not evil. Not mad. Just look. Then he'd slip your shoulders and head under the water. Slow. You'd hold your breath for a minute or so. Then you'd release, go down easy. To the bottom of the tub and into your grave. Meanwhile, he'd just watch. That's the Grime way."

Diane got up, switched off the TV, and pulled her chair close.

"I got it. Bad guy. Good thing he's on death row. Now why are we talking about him?"

She was leaning forward, mouth slightly open, hard white teeth smeared with delicate bits of red lipstick. For the first time I noticed an overbite. Delicate, but an overbite nevertheless. Made her look like a very pretty wolf.

"I tracked down a piece of evidence from the rape Gibbons was looking at."

"Elaine Remington's?"

"Don't ask me how. Just chalk it up to luck."

"What do you have?"

"The victim's shirt."

"Lost bit of evidence?"

"Something like that. We ran some tests, found some semen, and got a profile. No ID yet."

"Have you told Elaine?"

"No."

Diane leaned back and considered. Then she picked up her beer and took a sip.

"She might appreciate the progress report."

"I'm going to give it a couple of days," I said. "See if I can come up with a name."

"And where does our friend the serial killer come in?"

"Getting there."

I pulled out Nicole's report.

"Nicole was running the profile through the state's DNA data-bank on the morning she was killed."

Diane put down her beer and picked up the report.

"Nicole worked on this?"

"Yeah. This is where it gets tricky."

Diane flipped through the pages, searching for a clue, finding nothing but science.

"You'd have a better shot with Plato," I said.

"Funny guy. Where's the tricky?"

"I'll tell you, but it's got some news value."

"How much news value?"

"That's for you to decide. What I need is for you to hold the story. Not forever. Just until I tell you."

"You changing our deal?"

"No. This is part of the deal. You just need to trust me."

Diane put the report down and offered up a measured sigh.

"And you need to trust me. Fill me in and I'll hold up my end."

I took a final look around and jumped.

"Last year the state's crime lab found a second source of semen in the Grime murders."

Diane pulled out a notebook and started writing. That made me nervous, but I continued.

"They decided it was a coincidence," I said.

" 'They' being the DA?"

I nodded.

"It makes sense," I said. "A lot of Grime's victims were prostitutes, so you might expect to find other sources of semen. Problem is, the same DNA profile was found on two different victims."

"Big coincidence."

"That's not the end of it. That profile is also a match to the one pulled off my client's shirt."

"Elaine's shirt?"

"Yeah."

"So whoever raped your client is tied in to the Grime murders."

"You should be writing headlines," I said.

"Wow."

I wasn't ready to tell Diane about Grime's own semen showing up at a crime scene while the killer himself sat on death row. The reporter had more than enough to chew on.

"You know Gerald O'Leary made headlines with Grime," Diane said.

"So I've heard."

"Have you talked to Bennett Davis about this?"

"No," I said. "A little too close to home. For right now, we do Bennett a favor and leave him out."

"Fine."

"There's another thing," I said. "When they checked Nicole's lab, everything she was working on was gone. The shirt, her reports, everything. I got the match off a set of backup files she kept."

"So you think her murder was tied in to this, too?"

"I do."

Diane's eyes touched mine and steadied.

"It's not your fault," she said.

"How do you figure?"

"You couldn't have known."

"That's right. I couldn't have known, didn't know a goddamn thing, which is why I should have left her out."

"She was a big girl, Kelly. She knew what she wanted to do in life. At that moment in time, she wanted to help you."

I didn't buy any of that and told Diane as much. Instead of backing off, she drew us in deeper.

"I know a little bit about Nicole. Maybe a little bit more than you think."

I felt a pulse beat at my temple.

"What do you mean?" I said.

"I mean she told me about her rape."

"Let me ask you something. Did you get it on tape?"

"She was twelve years old, Kelly. She needed to talk about it to someone."

"Did you get it on tape?"

"Yes."

"Fucking great. Play it back at one of your luncheons. Make for a fun afternoon."

I broke away and reached for my bottle of beer. Diane brushed her fingers against the back of my hand and lingered.

"She also told me about you, Michael. Off camera."

I pulled away again, tried to shrug off the topic. A woman once told me that was my way with the big things. Move around it. Pretend it doesn't exist, and it will go away. Some topics, however, just don't seem to cooperate.

"What did she tell you?" I said.

My voice sounded thin and strange. The voice of someone I was neither familiar, nor entirely comfortable with.

"She talked about the rail yards, about a man. Showed up in your neighborhood one day. A white man, big, with shoulders."

Diane's words jump-started the images that slept somewhere inside. The movie reel danced, flickered, and began to turn. Silent all these years, the man was back, grinning at the boy, now grown. Mocking the passage of time. As if that had changed anything.

"The rail yards are at Grand and Central," I said.

Inside the boy was still kicking and screaming. But I moved forward. No real choice in the matter.

"In the middle of my old neighborhood. Some older kids had boosted a Good Humor truck and dumped it there. Free ice cream, you know. Nirvana for a pedophile. Anyway, that's where he took her."

I shook my head, but the movie continued to play.

"The back of his skull was shaved. Heavy forehead, pale white skin, small eyes like black raisins. Face was pitted, covered on one side with a birthmark. Sounds scary, huh?"

Diane nodded.

"Thing was, he had a bag full of string licorice. Remember that stuff? I loved the red kind. So did Nicole. That was how he took her, I think. Trolled around the ice-cream truck and then used the licorice."

"You found them?"

"I was a couple of years older. Fourteen, maybe. I guess I knew the basics of sex, but I had never seen it. Didn't think it would be like that."

"It isn't, Michael."

"At the end of the rail yards is a place we used to call 'the swamp.' Pretty much what it was. Ran right under the tracks. He had her sitting on a rock, head down, his hand in her hair, forcing her mouth onto him. I remember seeing him turn first toward me, then her face followed. She was crying, but there was a freight train rolling overhead so there was no sound. Well, there was plenty of sound, just nothing from her."

I took a pull on the beer, but it had no taste. The movie played, the train rolled. No sound but plenty of pictures. Diane inched closer, knees touching mine, took up both my hands, and held them close. I didn't pull away anymore.

"I wasn't a big kid," I continued, "but I was probably the toughest in a tough neighborhood. Wouldn't have mattered. The guy was huge, would have killed me. Still, when I saw him, saw Nicole, the world went black. It used to happen when I was a kid. Things would get fuzzy, sort of a hot mist. Then just black. After that, it was like I was outside myself. Watching. Waiting to see what might happen.

"I guess I got lucky, grabbed at an old piece of board. Had a big old nail on the end. Caught him with it just above the temple. Man fell like a wall of bricks. Knees first, chest, then his head. With a slap on the ground. I was on top of him. Actually, both of us were. Me and Nicole. Beat him until we couldn't lift our arms."

I finished off the beer. The buzzer rang at the front door. Diane got up, paid the pizza guy, and set out plates. Then she sat down, took my hands in hers again, and waited.

"I think he was dead," I said. "Pretty sure. I think the nail did it. It was early spring, a Friday afternoon after school, and we left him there. I remember his tongue just peeking out between his lips. Ran like hell. Left him in the swamp. Goddamn freight train was still running overhead."

I picked up a piece of pizza and took a bite. Tasted like nothing, too.

"What about after?" Diane said.

"There was no after," I said. "That night we had a huge rainstorm. Mudslides, flooding. Monsoon-type shit."

I stopped for a moment and felt the rain again, black and cold, dropping straight down from the sky, hammering on the roof, tearing at my bedroom window. I stayed in there, alone, thinking someone, somewhere was angry. And I wondered at whom.

"We couldn't even get near the swamp for a week and a half," I said. "When we did, Nicole and I, the water was still and deep. The entire ledge where we left him was washed out. If he was still there, he was under a lot of water and a lot of mud. If he was alive . . . well, neither one of us ever saw him again."

"So you really don't know?"

"If I killed him? I always figured I did. Unless and until I see that face again, that's how I look at it."

I shrugged.

"Some people can kill. Others can't. I found out early on that I belong in the first group. I'm okay with that."

"How about Nicole?"

I shook my head.

"Hard to say. The years went by. We'd talk about it every now and then. But we mostly left it alone. Seemed easier that way."

"Usually is. And now?"

"Now I need to talk to John Grime."

"You think he has an answer for you?"

"Depends on what the question is. Right now, I think it's worth a try."

Diane urged me softly to my feet. I let her. She led me into the bedroom, closed the blinds, and put my world on hold. We didn't have sex. Instead, we made love. For the first time. When we were done, I thought the tears were mine. Until I realized they were hers.

CHAPTER 43

Illinois executes its killers inside a grim pile of brick just outside Chicago called Stateville prison. Death row itself, however, is located four hundred miles away, inside an even grimmer pile of brick called Menard. I flew into St. Louis, hired a car, and drove back across the state line. Diane knew the warden down at Menard and made the first phone call. He had no problem with my request to visit Grime, but only if the killer indicated, in writing, he wanted to see me. According to the warden, Grime had not taken a visitor who wasn't an attorney in more than five years. Still, I scratched out a note, sealed it up, and sent it down to the prison. A week later my phone rang. Grime gave the okay. So here I was.

"Empty your pockets into the tray."

The voice bled through a wooden speaker on the wall. A plastic tray was shoved through a metal slot set in a piece of opaque Plexi. I dumped my pockets into the tray and slid it back through. A few minutes later the disembodied voice returned.

"Pass through for shakedown."

A lock turned to my left, and a door opened. I walked into a larger room with three correctional officers: two females and one male, sitting in three cubicles and not smiling. One of the females pointed to a door on my right.

"In there. Take your pants off and wait."

I walked into the room and waited. Kept my pants on. After a few minutes, a correctional officer with a shaved bullet for a head muscled through. He didn't have rubber gloves on, and I felt immediately better.

"You're supposed to have your pants off."

"And why would that be?"

Bullet-head smiled.

"Mostly we do it just to see if people will comply. Gets boring out here. Let me just pat you down and we can go in."

Five minutes later I was in a small holding room, a visitor's badge clipped to my chest, waiting.

All prisons are basically the same. Some more so than others. Especially if they are old. Menard had housed more than a hundred years' worth of human suffering. Anguish and fear, sweat, piss, and bedsprings sharpened into steel shanks. Empty shower stalls and guards who couldn't hear the screams. Gang rape and prison bedsheets fashioned into a noose for a convenient suicide.

I heard the shuffle of footsteps and muffled voices. The turn of a key in one lock, then another. Finally, the footsteps were outside and a door opened. Bullet-head came in first. He had two officers with him. Each carried a pump-action shotgun. Bullet-head did the talking.

"All right, Kelly. Here's the deal. The prisoner is in a cell across the hall. He is cuffed, hands and feet, with a belly chain. If you want, we can take off the handcuffs."

I nodded. Bullet-head mumbled into a walkie-talkie clipped to his shoulder.

"Okay," he continued. "You can shake his hand if you want

but that's it. No other physical contact. If you want to give him anything, give it to me now and I'll clear it with the warden."

"I got nothing for him."

"Good. Just talk and keep your distance. Everything will be fine."

I nodded again.

"He's got cigarettes and a bottle of water in there. He brought down a shitload of paperwork and some of his paintings. Any idea about that?"

"No."

"If you don't mind me asking, what's this all about?"

"You going to be in there while we talk?"

"My two friends here will be on either side of the prisoner. I'll be right behind you."

"Then you'll hear it all anyway."

"Fair enough. Don't make a scene and get him riled up, or my orders are to cut off the interview. Got it?"

"Got it."

"Good. Let's go."

They were still taking the cuffs off as I came in. Grime was sitting in a folding metal chair, at a table stacked with material from a decade's worth of appeals. More files lay on the floor at his feet. One of the guards unraveled the belly chain and stepped away.

"See this?"

Grime pulled a thick brown binder off the table. It had orange, green, and yellow tabs running down its side.

"This is information I pulled on all the victims. Private investigators I paid for. Good money to find out what they could about all these kids."

Grime pulled open a tab to reveal the face of a young girl. I didn't catch the name, but she was smiling.

"Complete workups on all of them, who they were, who they knew, how they got to Chicago. Most of these kids weren't saints, you know."

Grime dropped the binder to the floor and looked at me full on for the first time. He was like any other old guy gone to seed, except worse. Around sixty-five, white hair slicked back in a bad John Dillinger and thinning, with a serious case of dandruff. His skin was the color of wet gravel and his face hung off his cheekbones. His eyes were shoehorned into swollen pockets of flesh, and his mouth dripped down toward his chin. A decade on death row had not been good to Grime. Then again, it wasn't supposed to be.

"Why all the investigation?" I said.

"To prove who killed them."

I sat down in a chair opposite. The men with the guns were on either side, just as Bullet-head had promised. And Grime talked, just as he had promised.

"I brought some of my sketches down."

Grime pulled a canvas off the table.

"This is a self-portrait of me working on Michigan Avenue. I call it *Michigan Avenue Mime.*"

Grime grinned a row of teeth, crooked and mossy, but they were all there.

"Want to see one of my routines?"

Before I could say no, Grime had drawn both of his hands close together over his head. He looked up through spread fingers, turned his palms flat, and fought against an invisible ceiling dropping from above. Then he slipped his hands to either side and pushed against the heaviness of his imaginary walls. Finally, Grime dropped his palms in front of his face, peered through his fingers at me, and mimed fear. I wondered if this was the last thing his victims saw in their short bit of life.

"Not bad, huh?" the killer said. "I had real talent. You want to see another sketch?"

He pulled a second self-portrait off the table. This time it was Grime the Mime entertaining a group of kids.

"This is me at Brody's Ice Cream Emporium. Get it?"

Grime coughed up a laugh and took a look around. I didn't get it. Neither did anyone else. It was a tough room, but Grime kept on.

"Brody's. The company with fifteen favorite flavors. I worked as their mime. Fifteen flavors. Fifteen bodies. Get it?"

I smiled.

"Got it."

"This is one of my Disney paintings."

Grime pulled out a painting of the Seven Dwarfs. It was winter, and the misshapen Dwarfs were sitting around a campfire, shovels tossed aside, trying to stay warm. Grime provided running commentary.

"Walt Disney was a mentor of mine. I love the Dwarfs. Sleepy, Sneezy, Happy, Doc. Every year I do a different season. This is *The Dwarfs in Winter*."

"You do these in your cell?"

"Yeah. I do forty or fifty of these every year. Next up is summer."

"Same scene?"

"Always the woods."

"Where's Snow White?"

Grime smiled again. Everything except his eyes.

"Not there, is she? Why are you here?"

Grime put the painting away and took a sip of water.

"I mean, I read your letter. New information about my case. You knew that would get my interest."

I nodded.

"So how can you help me?" he said.

"I don't think you're innocent, John."

Grime's face remained flat.

"I don't really give a shit what you think, mister. How can you help my case?"

"I think you had an accomplice. Tell me about it, and maybe I can help."

Grime took another hit on the water and leaned back in his chair. His belly strained against the buttons of his shirt. Prison-issue blue.

"You know I serve Mass in here? Ask the chaplain. Altar boy."

Another pause.

"You have a lawyer, John?"

"A fucking fleet of them."

"Ask them. An accomplice changes your case. Changes the evidence. Maybe gets you a new trial. Where you sit, that's a good thing."

"What makes you think I didn't do them all myself?"

"Like I said, tell me about it, and maybe I can help."

"No, fuck wad. You tell me about it. Or get the fuck out of my jail."

I leaned forward. Grime didn't move.

"I'm your best chance, John. Believe it or don't, but I can prove you had help. Now tell me about it."

"Why should I give it to you?"

"Why not?"

"Maybe I think it'll keep me alive."

"Want me to show you a calendar with your execution date on it? I'm figuring sometime next December. Enjoy."

"You don't get it, do you?"

"Tell me," I said.

"This is so much bigger than the murders now. I'm so much bigger."

Grime blinked once and looked at me like a high school kid might look at a frog just before he dissects it. Kind of funny, but mostly curious.

"You know how many people die each day?" he said.

"No, I don't."

"Hundred fifty thousand a day. Ten thousand since you sat down here. Look it up."

"I'm not following you, John."

"You're not following me. No one follows me. That's the point. Shit, for every person alive right now, there are billions who are already dead. Billions. So where the fuck do you get off saying these fifteen are so special?"

Grime used his foot to flip open the brown binder again. It fell flat to a picture of a girl named Donna Tracey. About seventeen years old, with long, stringy hair and bad skin. Looked like a mug shot.

"Just part of the herd," Grime said. "Millions of them, scraping along, sucking down their Big Macs, listening to their tunes, flipping through the idiot box. That's the life, mister. Get out of the house, drink up some warm beer, then wrestle with a wannabe car mechanic in a backseat somewhere. Like they invented sex."

Grime closed the binder with his foot.

"Get knocked up at what? Fifteen, sixteen? For what? To procreate? Propagate the species? Fuck that. Just another generation of mediocrity. Spitting out their mediocre kids. Then trudging along to a grave. These fifteen just got there a little earlier."

"And no one really gives a damn about any of them. Right, John?"

Grime craned his neck and took a look around the room. No one had moved. Everyone was listening. The killer loved it, which was okay. As long as he kept talking, I was in the game.

"You look like a smart guy," Grime said. "Let me ask you something. You know the name of your great-grandfather? Great-grandmother? How about we go back another generation, great-great-grandfather? That's less than a hundred years ago, but most people have no fucking idea. Their own flesh and blood. So fucking sacred. Once you're in the ground, you're gone. Within fifty years. Like you never existed."

"But not that way for you, huh?"

"Probably not, mister. Probably not. So you say these assholes are going to kill me and you have a way out. I say, so what. Kill me. I'll live forever anyway."

Grime looked past me. To Bullet-head.

"I'm done here."

With that he stood up and held out his hands. The officers redid his cuffs. In front of his body. Then they began to pack up his files.

"Sorry, Kelly. Maybe you have something. Maybe you don't. Just not enough in it for me."

"You already have what you want?"

"Looks like it."

I stood up and moved closer. Trying to get in the killer's space, change the dynamic.

"What if you could walk away from this?" I said. "Even a little bit. Don't you think the legend would only grow? And if you were ever released, how big would that story be?"

Grime paused as they secured the hallways outside. He looked for all the world like a broken-down old man, one who liked to have sex with little girls and squeeze their necks until they were dead. By his own estimation, one of this generation's immortals. Tell the truth, I figured he wasn't that far off. Then the serial killer leaned forward and, for the first time since I entered the room, surprised me.

"Tell you what," he said. "You do your own legwork. See if you can make the case. Otherwise, I talk and it comes right back here. Sits in my lap."

"Fair enough. But I need something."

A guard grabbed Grime by the elbow and began to tug.

"Time to go," Bullet-head said.

"I'll think about it," Grime said. "But understand, you start down this road, you might end up under a house, too."

He smiled when he said it. I think Grime enjoyed the notion. Then he left the room. Bullet-head stayed behind.

"Who picks up his stuff?" I said.

The guard shrugged.

"Are you kidding me? The guys fight to get to carry this stuff up to his cell. One of those paintings goes into someone's locker. Sell it on eBay for twenty grand."

"No kidding?"

"No kidding."

We walked together through a couple of locked doors and back down an open breezeway. The yard was to my left, a scattering of inmates smoking cigarettes and lifting iron in the cold.

"You get what you need?" Bullet-head said.

"Not yet."

"Yeah, well, Grime is an asshole."

"Not well liked in here?"

"Guy like that. Rep like that. He pays to stay alive."

"Really?"

"Sure. Carton of smokes a month or we find him in the shower with a shank in his neck."

We came to the end of the breezeway. Bullet-head turned a key and opened another door. An officer waited on the other side.

"Here is where I get off. Good luck, Kelly. Hope you learned something."

We shook hands. I walked down another long passageway, through three more doors, and back to the shakedown room. A female correctional officer passed over my keys, money, and wallet without a word. I filled my pockets and was about to leave when a phone buzzed. The officer whispered a few words into the receiver, looked up at me, whispered a few more, and hung up.

"Mr. Kelly," she said.

"Yeah."

"Wait just a moment."

I sat back down. Two minutes later Bullet-head pushed back into the room.

"Kelly. Glad we caught you. Your boy wanted to give you something. Already cleared it with the warden."

Bullet-head handed me a piece of paper.

"Just a note. Yeah, we took a look at it. Doesn't mean anything to me, but there it is."

I unfolded the note from Grime, just a single line of type.

CST . . . 9998.

Bullet-head watched me closely.

"Mean anything to you?"

I shrugged.

"Nothing. Not yet, anyway."

CHAPTER 44

I actually knew what Grime's note meant the moment I saw it. It was the same method cops used to file away news clippings in a homicide book. *CST* stood for *Chicago Sun-Times*. I Googled their archives, but they went back only two years online. I could have called a *Sun-Times* reporter and asked for a favor, but one journalist in my life seemed like more than enough. I punched in Diane's cell. She picked up on the first ring.

"Where are you?" she said.

"Nice to talk to you, too. I'm at my office, Googling with no apparent effect."

"When did you get back from Menard?"

"Couple of hours ago," I said.

"I left you a message."

I looked at the blinking light on my machine. Not for the first time.

"I know."

"Michael, you need to return your messages."

"I know."

"I was waiting to hear how it went with Grime. And don't tell me you know."

"Okay."

"How did it go?"

"Actually, I don't know," I said. "In fact, that's what I'm working on. I need access to the *Sun-Times* clip morgue. You guys can do that, right?"

"How far back?"

I took a glance at Grime's note.

"September 1998."

"What day?"

"Let's just keep it at September until I get down there."

"You don't have to come down. I can access the clips from your computer. Is this going to be good?"

"I don't know yet."

"I'm leaving now. Be there in a half hour. Did he creep you out?"

"Grime?"

"Who else?"

"See you in thirty."

I had just hung up with Diane when Rodriguez punched in.

"We got test results back from Miriam Hope's bedsheets," he said.

"And?"

"The same guy who helped Grime in 1995, raped Elaine Remington in 1997, and cried in Miriam's bed three weeks ago."

"Some guy."

"Yeah. For my money he's also grabbing twelve-year-olds and leaving Grime's semen behind. Just for kicks. What did John himself have to say?"

I told him about Grime and the note he gave me.

"What do you think?" Rodriguez said.

"I don't know. Diane Lindsay is coming over. We're going to go through the clip file."

"Can she keep her mouth shut for a bit?"

"She will."

Rodriguez didn't like it but held his fire.

"Fine. If she helps us ID this guy, we give her the exclusive. Biggest story any of us will see."

"You got that right," I said.

"Keep me posted. And remember, Kelly. Me, you, and Lindsay. That's it until we find this guy."

I hung up the phone and looked past a week's worth of mail, to a single package sitting on my desk. A missive from the desert. Most likely a waste of time. But there it was. Waiting to be opened.

CHAPTER 45

The FedEx package from Phoenix had lain there for three days. As promised, Reynolds had included the entire Gleason murder book along with a note that read, "Where the fuck is my file?" The detective knew me not at all and yet very well. I packaged up a copy of Remington's street file and posted it to Phoenix. Then I began to wander through the Gleason homicide.

The first thing I pulled out were a set of autopsy photos. Carol Gleason looked up at me from the examining table, eyes flying open in surprise, a small neat hole drilled through her breastbone. In death, she looked a lot like John Gibbons, and that bothered me. I was about to dig into the forensics report when my buzzer rang. Five minutes later Diane was set up on my Mac, ready to sleuth.

"Okay, I need the date," she said.

Diane turned her face my way and held out her hands. I handed over Grime's scrawl.

"I told him I thought he had an accomplice. He basically told me to take a hike. Then, as I was about to leave, he sent this down."

"Sent it down?"

"From his cell. With one of the guards."

Diane laid the note flat on my table and leaned in close.

"You can look as close as you want," I said. "It doesn't say any more than what it says."

Diane continued to study the note as she talked.

"So he gives you this after he talks to you and after he returns to his cell?"

"Yes."

"Which means he had some time to think about what you said and maybe decided to play ball."

"Could be," I said. "Or he might have been interested from the start and needed to get back to his cell to get the date. Or he might just be a fucking lunatic with nothing better to do on death row than run me around for shits and giggles."

Diane punched in September 9, 1998, and looked up from the computer.

"Maybe," she said. "Let's see what we get."

The first article she pulled up celebrated Mark McGwire hitting number sixty-two against the Cubs. The picture was a close-up of McGwire and Sammy Sosa in a bear hug. They both looked huge. They both looked happy. Neither condition would last.

"What a difference eight years makes," I said.

Diane closed up the file and moved on without a word. We began to go through clips. Political turmoil for Mayor Wilson. Noise problems at O'Hare. Roger Ebert's insightful commentary on *There's Something About Mary*.

"Maybe Grime wants us to channel Cameron Diaz," I suggested.

"Fuck off, Kelly. What are we missing?"

She clicked on another article, a few inches of column print from page twenty-three.

"Hold on a second," I said. "This looks interesting."

The headline read: MAN ARRESTED; HOLDS HOSTAGE IN BASE-MENT. The body of the text described how police followed up on a tip. Found a young girl tied up and held prisoner for a day and a half in a Chicago basement. The house belonged to a man named Daniel Pollard. Police arrested him and were considering charges.

"You think this is it?" Diane said.

"I think Grime attacked young women. I think he tied them up, and I think he buried them in his basement. Where was the girl found?"

"Fifty-two fifteen West Warner. That's on the Northwest Side."

"Dump it into MapQuest."

Diane was already on it. A map of Chicago streets jumped up on the screen. Warner dead-ended into thirty-six acres of open space called Portage Park.

"Less than a mile from Grime's old house," I said.

Diane flipped opened her cell and began to dial.

"Hang on a minute. That name looks . . . John, hi, it's Diane. Yeah, listen. I'm doing some research on the Grime case. I know, a long time ago."

Diane scratched out the name *John Donovan* on a piece of paper and showed it to me. I thought about making a fresh pot of coffee but settled for instant and plugged in the kettle. Diane continued to talk.

"So anyway, I came across the name Daniel Pollard. That sound familiar to you? Really?"

Diane raised an eyebrow and started to take notes. The water began to boil, and I washed out a couple of mugs.

"I had a feeling he was connected," said Diane. "Is this all in the court transcript? Really?"

More notes. I tried to read over her shoulder, but it was in some sort of reporter shorthand. Instead I put a cup of coffee at Diane's elbow and settled back with mine. Diane's foot tapped out a steady rhythm on the floor. Her pen flowed across the page. The reporter was excited. I printed out the photo Rodriguez had e-mailed me of Grime's prosecution team and took out a magnifying glass. Five minutes later I was still looking at the photo when Diane finished up with Donovan.

"Yeah, John. Thanks. No, it's just some background right now. But really helpful. I'll let you know if I decide to do anything. Thanks again, John."

She flipped the phone shut and leaned forward.

"Goddamn, I'm good."

"If you do say so yourself."

"The name Daniel Pollard. I thought I saw it somewhere before."

"And?"

"It was in an old magazine piece about Grime."

Now I leaned forward.

"How so?"

"You remember Grime wound up changing his plea to insanity just before the trial started."

"Yeah. Didn't work out too well for him."

"Right. Because of the plea, most of the testimony at trial focused on his mental state and not so much on what actually happened inside the house. There was, however, some pretrial stuff. Before the plea was changed."

"Pollard was part of that?" I said.

"Apparently. There was one kid, a minor, who gave a sealed deposition. He supposedly testified about seeing some of the missing girls around Grime's house. I guess he was pretty specific."

"And you think this kid was Pollard?"

"In this magazine article I read, they interviewed some of the local kids who knew Grime. Pollard was one of them."

"What does Donovan say?"

"He said Pollard was the kid everyone felt had given the statement. He was seventeen at the time."

"Would the deposition still be sealed?"

"Oh, yeah. There's another thing. Donovan says the rumor was that the DA's office at the time had cut a deal with the kid."

"A deal?"

"Full immunity for his testimony."

"Immunity from what?"

"Don't know. Like I said, it was only a rumor. At the time the press was so fixated on Grime the whole thing just sort of got buried. No pun intended."

I pulled up the *Sun-Times* article on Pollard and scanned it quickly.

"What do you want to bet this case was never filed," I said.

"I can find out tomorrow," Diane replied. "What we need now is a current address."

"I know a guy at the DMV," I said. "If Pollard drives in Illinois, we'll get his address. Come on. I'll make the call in the car."

"Where are we headed?"

I pointed to the *Sun-Times* article.

"Grime fed us an address as well as a name. Let's go back out to the old neighborhood and see what's around."

CHAPTER 46

There was yellow police tape around a hole where Grime's house used to sit. A couple of college kids stood nearby, taking pictures of each other in front of the site with their cell phones. Brave bastards. Probably going to download it to all their buddies back at the dorm.

"Not much left," Diane said.

"Just the memories. Let's drive over to Pollard's house."

It was less than a mile, maybe a ten-minute walk. A Chicago bungalow, two stories of brick, slotted into a row of the same. Working-class digs built when the city called its mayor Boss and never tried to hide it. I parked a half block down the street and turned off the car.

"Hang on here," I said. Diane didn't respond.

I pulled out a flashlight and walked up to the house. It was still early evening, and lights were just coming on up and down the block. Fifty-two fifteen West Warner, however, felt empty, its blinds drawn tight. There was a single buzzer with no name and a glass door that looked into an interior foyer. I took a chance and leaned on the bell. No answer.

I flicked my flashlight across the foyer but couldn't make out a name on the mailbox inside. Then my light caught a scattering of mail spread across the floor. Good old Chicago post office. Sometimes letters make it into the box. Sometimes they don't. Two were addressed to "Occupant." The third wasn't. I could make out only the first two letters of the last name: *PO.* Daniel Pollard, it appeared, had never moved from the house in Grime's neighborhood. I took a walk around back and found an alley leading to a small yard, cemented over, and a wooden garage, empty. I flicked off my flash and returned to the car.

"I think he still lives here."

"Ten years later?"

"Apparently. Must like the neighborhood. Anyway, he gets his mail here. That's good enough for me."

"What're you going to do?"

I was about to respond when a green Pontiac appeared in my rearview mirror. I had my lights off and sat quiet as the car pulled into the driveway of 5215 and disappeared into the back.

"That him?" Diane said.

"You should really think about being a detective."

"Funny guy."

After a minute or so, lights came on inside the house. I started up the car, drove down the block, and around the corner to the nearest bus stop.

"All right, Diane, this is where we part company."

"Really?"

"Yeah, really. I'm going to follow this guy for a while and might need to get out of the car. It's a lot easier when I'm by myself."

"I know how to make myself scarce, Kelly."

I reached over and popped open the passenger door.

"No time to argue, Diane. The longer I stay here, the longer the house remains uncovered. If he gets in his car and drives off, well . . ."

I shrugged my shoulders and waited. Diane didn't like it but didn't have much choice. She got out of the car without a word.

"See ya," I said.

Diane slammed the door and headed to the bus stop. I slugged the car into drive and headed back to the house on Warner.

CHAPTER 47

It was two more hours before I got my first look at Daniel Pollard. He poked his head out the front door at just past nine-thirty. Under the flicker of a Chicago streetlamp, Pollard looked smaller than I expected. He winced at the wind as he turned the corner on his house and shrank into the night. A moment later, I heard a garage door creak open. The Pontiac pulled out and cruised past me.

I gave him a half block's worth of room and followed. He stopped at a Jack in the Box, went through the drive-in, and ate alone in the parking lot. An hour after that we were cruising Main Line Road, a nasty stretch of pavement in a town on the edge of Chicago called Calumet City. As a cop, I had worked the area for prostitutes. Not to arrest them. Just for information.

On the street hookers represented the bottom of the food chain, usually desperate for cash and willing to sell whatever they knew. Three out of five girls on the corner were HIV-positive, the majority dead, one way or another, within a year or two of hitting the stroll. You might think that would deter prospective johns. You would be wrong. I asked a customer once, a doctor and father of five, if he was concerned about HIV.

"Oral sex only," he said. "Besides, I have these."

He smiled and pulled a bunch of condoms out of his pocket. I made sure they called the doc's wife when they booked him.

Pollard stopped at a convenience store. I pulled over and waited. A woman walked out in front of my car and opened up her coat. She was naked underneath. Subtlety was never a major selling point in Cal City. She was still standing there when Pollard exited the store. I pulled around her and followed the Pontiac. He was driving slow enough to get a look at the action, but Pollard wasn't shopping for a woman. At least not yet.

He moved out of the strip and cruised into a darker, more industrial neighborhood. The cars were less frequent here, and I slipped farther back. After a couple of miles Pollard pulled into what looked like a mostly empty trucking yard. I switched off my lights and followed. Two hundred yards in, I could still see his headlights bouncing along the road in front of me. Then the lights seemed to slow and steady. I stopped my car and slipped out.

Two minutes later I was creeping along the side of an abandoned flatbed, and snuck a look around the corner. Pollard's car sat in the middle of a dirt path, still running, doors open, lights illuminating a large blue dumpster. Best I could tell, the car was empty. I was about to move forward for a closer look when a head poked out of the dumpster. It was Pollard, clutching a pillowcase stuffed full of what I suspected was someone else's garbage. He climbed to the lip of the dumpster and, after some hesitation, jumped to the ground. Then he scuttled back to his car, unloaded whatever was in the bag into his backseat, and returned to the dumpster. Climbing up the side looked difficult, but Pollard managed and dove headfirst into the depths. I sat back for a moment, thought about going home, then thought better of it. Instead I lit a cigarette and waited.

Pollard dove the dumpster and then three more like it. At one point I snuck close and took a quick look inside his car. I saw what I expected to see. Three plastic bags, one burst at the seams and spilling out old clothes; a spool of gray wire; a rusted-out car battery; broken pieces of old toys; a bent street sign that read KEDZIE AVENUE. And that was just half of the backseat.

It was pushing two-thirty before my friend had gotten his fill of other people's garbage. Pollard cruised the stroll one more time before calling it a night. The Pontiac seemed to linger over the girls a bit longer this time around but ultimately moved on. Pollard was back at the house on Warner by a little after three in the morning.

CHAPTER 48

I was tired and wanted to go home. There was one thing, however, that needed to be checked out. I left Pollard tucked away in bed and headed back to Cal City.

She was half-hidden in an alley, nothing but the glow of a cigarette marking her presence. I waited a beat. She moved into the street. Now she was slightly more than a silhouette. Tight, firm, cut against the night. She wore blue jeans and a short black leather coat. Like any working girl she carried nothing save a small black purse. Inside would be money, smokes, and her stash of condoms. I never would have given her a second look except for the blond hair, not a cheap dye job but the real thing. She wasn't there the first time Pollard cruised by. On the return trip he'd given her a good look. I thought she might have motioned his way, but Pollard didn't bite. Now she stared again. This time, my way. I pulled the car around and rolled down a window.

"Hey."

She seemed unsure, for just a moment. Then Elaine Remington ground the burner under her heel and swiveled over.

"My very private investigator. Stalking your own clients now?"

"You interest me, Elaine."

She laughed and laid one hand across her cheek. The move looked flat and phony. I couldn't tell if she was nervous or just high.

"I'm flattered."

"What are you doing out here?" I said.

"What does anyone do in this part of town at four in the morning?"

"You're working?"

The phony look coalesced into one of pure sexuality.

"Some call it work, Mr. Kelly. I call it therapy."

She rested her arms on the car door and leaned forward, her head tipping toward mine, her scent close behind. I kept my hands on the wheel and my eyes above sea level.

"Really?" I said.

"Really. Anyway, I do have a dark alley here and not a soul to share it with."

Now I leaned forward and inhaled. She smelled sweet, almost ripe. I wasn't sure if she lowered her eyelids, but I detected a trace of a smile, a hint of triumph as our lips touched. She slid her lower lip under mine just as I moved for the purse hanging loose in her hand. The fun was over. Probably a good thing.

"What the hell, Kelly."

I had her bag open. A pack of cigarettes, lipstick, a few dollars, and no condoms.

"Working, huh? Bullshit."

I dumped the contents onto my front seat. At the bottom was a gun, black and heavy. Probably the same gun Elaine had pointed my way the first time I met her.

"Give me that fucking purse."

"Get in the car, Elaine."

She tapped her toe against the pavement for the better part of ten seconds, then found her way to the passenger seat.

"Such a hard-ass, Kelly. Jesus."

Elaine pushed her stuff back into the bag. Then she reached up, pulled down the visor, and began to play with her lipstick in the mirror.

"So you want to tell me what the hell you're doing down here?"

"Take me for a drink, and I'll tell you the whole, sad story."

"No thanks."

She sighed, shrugged, and moistened her lips with her tongue.

"What is there to say? I'm pushing thirty but I still look good. So I like to get dressed up and hang out down here. Do it once or twice a month."

Elaine licked her lips one more time, flipped the visor back, and adjusted what I guessed was some sort of exploding bra.

"It's an escape, role-play, turn-on. Call it whatever you want. But sometimes I do it. Not do it like a pro. I mean, I'm not a fucking hooker, if that's what you're asking."

I kept my eyes on the road and let her talk.

"Really though, Kelly. What's the big deal? Twenty-five dollars for a mouth, ten for a hand. Shit goes on in every single bar in the city. Buy me dinner or just give me the money up front. Same fucking difference."

"Lot of difference."

"You think so?"

"Down here the mouth might belong to a thirteen-year-old, and the date might be looking to rip your throat out," I said. "But you know all about that. Is that what you're trying to do? You want to get back there?"

I didn't expect a response and didn't get any. Instead she propped her feet up on my dashboard and sulked, but only for a bit.

"You're cute when you get mad, Kelly."

I ignored her.

"Have you found out who attacked me?"

"Working on it."

I didn't want to tell her about the DNA match between her shirt and the Grime file. Or about the possible connection to Pollard. Not yet anyway. I wasn't sure why, but there it was.

"Is that what you were out on now?" she said. "My case?"

"Listen, Elaine. Your evidence file was destroyed a couple of years back. Whatever I find probably doesn't matter. The DA would never touch it."

"You just don't get it, do you?"

"I don't get hardly anything when it comes to you, Elaine. So why don't you tell me about it."

She looked out an empty window and into herself. I can't say exactly what she saw. Loss. Regret. Unrealized anger. Maybe all three.

"At the end of the day," she said, "nothing gets undone, does it? I mean whatever happened, happened. No district attorney, no court is gonna change that. So really, I just want to know. A name, a face. Someone, I guess, to hate. Is that so wrong? Most people probably think it's pretty sick."

I didn't say anything, just let it go. She seemed good with that. After a while she lit up another cigarette, rolled down the window, and blew smoke out of it. I broke the silence and got back to business.

"You have any paperwork from the assault?"

"What sort of paperwork?"

"Hospital admissions form, police reports, anything."

"Nothing. I woke up in the hospital."

"Police never came to visit you?"

"Nobody."

"Didn't that seem strange to you?"

"I was half-alive when they released me. Just wanted to get home. Back to Sedan. Didn't really care about the rest."

"Not back then."

"Nope. Just wanted to go home and hide."

Elaine took a deep drag, flicked her butt out the window, and rolled it up.

"I guess your feelings changed," I said.

"Apparently. Take a left here."

I took the turn. Ten minutes later we pulled in front of a late-night bar on Diversey called the Bel-Air Lounge. Sixty years ago it was a hot spot, a place where Humphrey Bogart would go to get lost, get drunk, and get laid. Now it was a place where a man with a bad hair-weave played Billy Joel on the piano all night. Divorced men and women snuggled around, throwing money in the jar just like the song said, getting drunk late, thinking about all the things they never had and pretended they missed. Eventually the bar would close. The lights would go out and they would melt away, sometimes together for a coupling, quick and ugly, then, inevitably, each to his or her own.

"It's not that bad," Elaine said. "The guy will stay open as long as I want. Sound good?"

She was on again, a live current, jittery, dangerous, exciting.

"No thanks," I said.

"What's the matter, Kelly. You don't like?"

She moved across the front seat, closer now, and tilted her head up at me.

"Or maybe you're screwing the redhead?"

"You know you're fucked."

She laughed.

"You are screwing the redhead. Wow."

She moved away again and picked up her purse.

"All right, Kelly. That's interesting. Thanks for the talk. It really settled me. I'll see you around."

Elaine Remington got out of the car, walked across the empty divide of Diversey Avenue, and into the lounge. An old man at the bar gave her a leer you can only get away with at five a.m. in Chicago. She cozied right up and ordered a drink. The old-timer slid his stool a bit closer as I slid the car into drive and headed home, to my long lost and mercifully empty bed.

CHAPTER 49

So what did you find?"

It was Diane. It was just past ten in the morning. It was entirely too early to be talking about Daniel Pollard.

"He likes to go dumpster diving," I said.

"Come again?"

"That's what he did. Cruised a stroll in Cal City for a while, then hit the dumpsters. Pulled up a bunch of garbage and stuck it in the backseat of his car."

Silence at the other end of the line. Understandable. Finally, she spoke.

"And then what?"

"Back to the stroll for a little more girl watching. In bed before sunrise."

"Weird."

"Yeah. Want to hear another weird thing? One of the women he was ogling turned out to be my client."

"Client as in Elaine Remington?"

"I pulled her off a curb. Claims she likes to go down there every now and then. Plays dress-up."

More silence. Longer this time. A lot longer.

"Is that what she told you?" Diane said.

"Yeah. I'm going to put a call in to Rachel Swenson today. See if I can set up some time with one of her counselors."

"You think Elaine will go for that?"

"I think she's dangerous. At least to herself."

"Maybe finding the person who raped her will help."

"Not sure that's going to do it. But we can try."

"What are you thinking?"

"Covert DNA," I said.

"From Pollard?"

"I think it answers all our questions. I'm going to call Rodriguez today and set it up. You want the exclusive?"

"You know it."

"Rodriguez will have to sign off. Swing by my office. Two o'clock this afternoon."

I got off the phone and made the same arrangements with Rodriguez. Then I made a pot of coffee and pulled out Elaine's street file. I got a piece of paper and began to make some notes. At my elbow was Reynolds' working file on the Carol Gleason shooting. I read through it for about an hour, laid it beside the street file, and thought for a while. Then I picked up the phone and dialed.

"Masters."

"It's Kelly."

A weary sigh.

"What do you want?"

"Nice to talk to you again, Detective. Listen, I need a favor."

"Of course you do."

"You remember the old file on Tony Salvucci?"

"The cop shooting? I'm sure it's around."

"I need to see a copy."

"Told you I can't do it."

"Why?"

"Because you're not a cop. Because I don't know what you're up to. Because there's nothing in it for me. Pick a reason, Kelly."

I felt the conversation about to end and switched tactics.

"How about this. I swing by there with some information. You run with it. If anything pans out, I step away. You take the credit."

"And if I don't like it?"

"You walk away. This conversation never happened."

"What are we talking about?"

"Long shot, but potentially? A career changer."

There was a pause. I could feel the veteran cop calculating the risk. He didn't like it, but I knew he would bite. Too much upside not to.

"Be here in thirty minutes. Ask for me, and don't talk to anyone else."

"Sure."

"See you then."

Masters hung up. I looked through my notes on Gleason, placed a call to Phoenix, and talked to Detective Reynolds for about ten minutes. Then I put the phone down and picked up the photo of Grime's prosecution team. I had circled a face in the back. The image was blurred with time, but still very much there. I dropped the picture back on my desk and headed out to see Masters.

CHAPTER 50

That afternoon Diane arrived at my office first. We sat without saying much. Rodriguez showed up five minutes later. Diane's presence wasn't a surprise. Still, the detective wasn't happy.

"Before we get started," he said, "let's talk about some ground rules. For the press part of this."

I had not broached the subject with Diane. Figured Rodriguez would set the boundaries here. Diane apparently felt the same way.

"What are your concerns, Detective?" she said.

Rodriguez looked at me, then back at Diane.

"Before we begin, everything here is off the record. You all right with that?"

Diane nodded. Rodriguez walked off, looked out my window, and exhaled. Soft and sad. When he spoke, it was with his back turned to both of us.

"I loved Nicole. You know that?"

I wasn't sure which one of us he was talking to but Diane answered.

"Yes, Detective. Actually, so did I."

"Love being a detective, too," Rodriguez said. "Only thing I ever wanted to do."

He moved back into the room and sat down in a chair, head down, knees almost touching Diane's.

"You think Daniel Pollard killed Nicole," she said. "So do I. DNA, however, won't make the case against him, will it?"

I sat down in the third chair and leaned into the conversation.

"If he matches on Elaine's rape, then we got him as an accomplice on Grime," I said. "And won't that be a fucking zoo. We also more than likely get him on some current assaults. But probably not for Nicole. No DNA there."

Diane kept her eyes focused on Rodriguez.

"And it won't be a death case," she said. "No matter what."

Rodriguez shook his head from side to side. Just once.

"Probably not."

"So if you find him," Diane said, "you want to kill him."

The detective looked up. Slowly, inevitably.

"If the DNA comes back a match to Pollard, I roll on the arrest. Alone. Whatever happens, happens."

Diane reached out and touched his knee.

"Can you live with it?"

Rodriguez nodded.

"Fair enough," she said. "If that's how it happens, no one will ever be the wiser. At least not from me. Story is big enough as it is. He was killed resisting arrest. Now, how do you plan on getting his DNA?"

CHAPTER 51

T hink this guy knows he's being followed?" Rodriguez said.

It was just past eight o'clock at night. We were in my car, cruising north on Western Avenue. Pollard had just left a Capt'n Nemo's, where he'd consumed a roast beef sub, chips, and a diet iced tea. At the end of the meal he'd smoked a cigarette and watched the traffic move by. Then he'd picked up the used butt, his sandwich wrappings, and the empty iced-tea bottle. Had taken the whole thing back to his scratched-up green Pontiac and dumped it into the backseat.

"I think he's cautious," I said.

"He's our guy."

The detective was getting antsy. We had been tracking Pollard for four days. Each was pretty much the same. A ten-minute drive to work at a local car wash. Lunch at the McDonald's. Once again, Pollard would pick up all his trash and head back to work. At night he would leave his house just after eight. Then it was a careful dinner, followed by a slow cruise down one of the city's prostitution strolls. Pollard would stop and watch but never buy anything. I was waiting for another dumpster dive. If nothing else, it would break the routine.

"Why don't we creep his house?" I said.

On one level, it made sense. If this guy was never going to trial, how we got his DNA didn't really matter. On the other hand, I wasn't sure Rodriguez had the stomach for killing Pollard. In that case, a legally obtained sample of his DNA would be essential for court.

"Let's try to keep it legal," Rodriguez said. "For now."

I shrugged. Pollard found his way south and jumped on the expressway.

"He's headed south," Rodriguez said and looked over. "Gotta be Cal City."

We drove another five miles. Pollard got off the highway two exits before Calumet City and cruised through another industrial park. It was dark now. No hint of a moon.

"This isn't right," Rodriguez said.

"Maybe it's the dumpster tonight," I said.

The tail was harder here. No cars on the road. Nowhere to hide. I pulled back another hundred yards. Ahead, Pollard's blinker indicated a left. I followed and almost ran right up on the Pontiac. Our suspect was outside of the car, sitting on his back fender. Smoking a cigarette. Enjoying the night.

"I assume you guys are cops."

Pollard was talking before we even got out of the car.

"Picked up on you yesterday," he said. "How long you been following?"

I held up four fingers.

"Four days, huh? You guys are pretty good."

Rodriguez moved slightly behind and to Pollard's left. He undid the clasp on his .40 caliber and kept his hand there. Pollard kept talking.

"You know, the feds used to send guys out. For a week, first week of April. Never knew why. They'd follow me around, take pictures, video. One year I brought them out a pizza on the last day. You guys like pizza?"

Pollard's face was cast in shadow by the arc of an overhead streetlight. He squinted a bit and angled his head to look at me. Rodriguez was just out of his line of sight. That bothered Pollard.

"By the way, my name is Daniel Pollard. Sorry, but I don't shake hands."

He laughed, a little too high, a little too long.

"Epithelial cells from the skin. All us bad guys watch *CSI*, you know."

I brushed eyes with Rodriguez, who gave the slightest of nods. I slid down on the bumper. Pollard took another drag on his cigarette. I noticed his fingers were brown with nicotine.

"Don't want anyone to have a look at your DNA, Daniel? Why would that be?"

"First name. Very good. Establish a bond with the suspect. You have a warrant?"

"You know we don't."

"Then piss off."

Another laugh. The hand holding the butt was in a steady state of quiver.

Rodriguez came in from the side, pulled Pollard off the car, and pressed the gun under his throat.

"Maybe we're the sort of cops that don't need a warrant." Rodriguez spoke softly. "Maybe we don't even need any DNA."

Pollard tried to get a look behind him, but Rodriguez kept the gun tight at his neck. Pollard's eyes rolled back toward me. I avoided him and thought about Nicole.

"Go ahead," Pollard said. "Do us all a favor. Then they can own you for a while."

The gun shivered just a bit. If I waited, if I didn't say a word, Rodriguez might do it. I thought that, believed it. Then I spoke.

"Who are 'they'?" I said. "Who owns you?"

Pollard blinked, as if seeing me for the first time.

"Let me guess," Pollard said. "He showed you his paintings, right? Then he showed you the *Sun-Times* clipping. Wrapped it up all nice and neat, did he? Well, they should have figured on it. That's not my fault."

"You still talk to Grime?" Rodriguez said.

"He's there every time I turn out the light," Pollard said. "How about you?"

The detective dropped his gun and released Pollard.

"Let's go," he said and walked away.

Pollard sat back on the hood of the Pontiac. He was still there as I put the car into gear and drove into the night.

"We don't know it all yet," Rodriguez said.

"No shit, Detective. We don't hardly know half of it. That's what I thought we were trying to find out."

"Pull over here," Rodriguez said.

I pulled well off the road and shut off my headlights. The car ticked softly as we waited.

"This looks like the only road out." The detective's voice felt tight, a current of uncertainty rolling just underneath.

"Let him come by," he continued, "then we pick up the tail again."

"Why?" I said.

"He talked about 'them.' Who do you think he was talking about?"

I thought I knew who Pollard was talking about. Rodriguez was smart. I figured he had an idea as well.

"Whoever killed Nicole somehow got into the crime lab," I said. "If it was Pollard, he had to have help. Had to."

"From inside the police department?"

"That's one possibility."

"There are others," Rodriguez said.

Just then a set of headlights flickered behind us. Pollard slowed, gave us a wave as he cruised by.

"Know what I'm thinking?" I said.

"What?"

"We need a new car."

"Yeah."

"Then what?" I said.

"We creep his house," Rodriguez said.

"For DNA?"

"Fuck the DNA. He did it. We need to find out who else is inside his head."

CHAPTER 52

Two hours later, we had traded my car for Rodriguez's black SUV. Not as anonymous as a '93 Olds, but then again, we weren't working a tail anymore. Now we were simply breaking and entering.

"You ready?" I said. Rodriguez nodded.

We were sitting across from Portage Park, around the corner from Pollard's house. His driveway was empty, lights off. Once Pollard was out, he usually stayed out. I figured we had a good hour or two to look around. The detective looked edgy.

"Take your gun," I said. "Leave the badge. We'll go in through the back door. Shouldn't take me more than thirty seconds. Once inside, we make sure the house is empty. Work each room together, back to front."

I gave Rodriguez a final look.

"Crossing a line here, Detective."

"I know."

"I can do this alone," I said.

"Let's go."

We moved along the side of the house and up to the back door. It was made of cheap wood with an even cheaper lock. Twenty seconds later we were in. Light filtered in from the street and cast shadows on a small and spotless kitchen. Rodriguez led the way, gun drawn, barrel up. The living room was also empty, no television, no couch. Just a single leather recliner in the middle of the room, facing the front windows, and a wooden chair beside it. I moved up to Rodriguez's ear.

"Not big on furnishings, is he?"

The detective shrugged and pointed to a short hallway leading off the living room. Three doors fed off the hallway. Two were open, the rooms beyond were dark. The third door was closed, a thin strip of light showing from underneath. We stacked on either side of the door. I went through first, gun up, breathing evenly, moving left and scanning to my right. Rodriguez was behind me, moving right, providing an overlapping field of fire.

Daniel Pollard was sitting up in a bed, shirt off, eyes open, two bullet holes in his chest. To his left was a night table. On it was an unfinished line of coke, a package of condoms, a bottle of whiskey, and some glasses. I could taste a whiff of cigarette smoke. Otherwise, the room looked empty. Rodriguez felt for a pulse.

"Dead."

I nodded.

"Let's check the rest of the house."

Outside the bedroom, the flat hardly seemed lived in. I wondered what Pollard did with all the garbage he collected. I also wondered what we might find under the house. We returned to the bedroom. There was a basketball in one of the closets, and I thought about Jennifer Cole. Rodriguez sat down on the bed and looked at the corpse.

"Goddamn," he said.

The detective wanted answers, had looked forward to them. I pulled out a DNA kit and swabbed blood off a leaking bullet hole.

"Run this. Tell you some of what you need to know."

Rodriguez stuffed the sample into a jacket pocket.

"What do you think happened?" he said.

I looked down at the nightstand.

"Looks like he had one party too many."

"Tried to take another girl," Rodriguez said.

"Maybe. She surprised him."

"That's for sure. I have to call this in."

"How are you going to explain finding him?" I said.

"Will be a lot easier if you're not with me. Take a few minutes to look around. Then you have to split."

"Okay. But do me a favor. Tell your guys to keep it off the scanner. No press until tomorrow."

"Diane?" Rodriguez said.

"I promised her an exclusive."

"Fair enough."

Rodriguez returned to the body. I took a look at the nightstand. The bottle was half-full, the shot glasses beside it still wet with whiskey. There were six cigarettes in the ashtray. Two of them were Lucky Strikes. The other four had filters, two with smudges of lipstick. I looked over at Rodriguez. He had pulled out a small camera and was beginning to snap photos. I slipped one of the smudged butts into a plastic bag and then into my pocket.

"I'm going to take another look in the living room," I said.

"Sure."

I walked down the hall, sat in the recliner, and looked out over Warner Street. A row of houses made of cheap red brick. Identically poor. Identically depressing.

I kicked the recliner back and let my hand trail to the ground. A piece of carpet, the "588-2300 Empire" stuff, crumbled underneath my fingers. I got to my hands and knees and flicked on a small flashlight. It was a burn mark, probably from a cigar. I used my vast experience with burn marks to figure this out. That and the fact that the brown butt was still there, less than a foot away. I scooped it up and into another plastic bag. Put it in my pocket beside the cigarette butt and figured it was well past time to get out of Dodge. I had committed at least five or six felonies that evening, only half of which Rodriguez actually knew about.

"Okay, Detective. I'm gone."

"Hold on a second."

Rodriguez came out of the bedroom. He had a shoe box in his hand.

"What is it?"

"Letters. Up on a closet shelf. Just sitting there."

The letters were stacked neatly. Identical in appearance. I took a look at the top envelope. The preprinted return address read "Lockbox 711, Menard, Illinois."

"Grime," I said.

Rodriguez nodded.

"Advice on how to pick victims. When and where. How to tie the best knots. What to do with bodies. Shit, here is a primer on DNA from 1998. Grime tells Pollard to start using condoms."

"How do you think he got the letters out?" I said.

"How did he get his semen out? Who the fuck knows? But this is gonna be a major-league shitstorm."

"Better run Pollard's DNA. Quick."

"First thing tomorrow."

"Know what else?"

"Huh?"

"I'd take a look under this house if I were you."

Rodriguez dropped his eyes to the floor, then back at me.

"Yeah."

"Call me tomorrow."

"Yeah."

I slipped out the back door and down the street. I walked three blocks and hailed a cab. The first cruiser flew up behind us a couple of blocks later. My cabbie pulled to the side and grumbled.

"Fucking cops. Always in a hurry for nothing."

I grunted in assent, closed my eyes, and let the world fall away, if only until I got home.

CHAPTER 53

Walk along Chicago's lakefront, past the North Avenue Bridge and then across a couple of baseball fields. In a hollow just south of the Lincoln Park Zoo you will find a small lagoon, a walking path, and a shade of trees. I got there at a little after three in the afternoon, staked out a comfortable bench, and pulled out Elaine's street file one more time. I had scrawled Pollard's name across the top. Below it were five more names. All of them dead. John Gibbons was first; followed by a second cop, Tony Salvucci; the ER nurse Carol Gleason; an EMT named Joe Jeffries; and Gibbons' immediate boss, Dave Belmont. I was running through it a couple more times when my cell phone buzzed. It was Masters.

"You know the file you sent over to me?"

"Hello to you, Sergeant."

"Yeah. You know that file?"

I circled Carol Gleason's name.

"The one from Phoenix?"

"Yeah, Gleason. Is that going to cause me problems?"

"You tell me."

"I ran the tests you wanted."

2 6 6

"Against the Gibbons shooting?"

"And Salvucci."

"Right."

"The ballistics are a match," Masters said. "Same gun, nine millimeter, that killed Gibbons was used on Salvucci two years earlier and the Phoenix woman two years before that."

"There's one more you're going to need to run."

"Already did it. Same nine was used on the EMT, Joe Jeffries, in 2000."

"In San Francisco?"

"Yeah. What else you got in that old file?"

"Just Dave Belmont," I said. "He died of a heart attack."

"I might check the autopsy on that one," Masters said. "So, tell me you know the whereabouts of our gun?"

"I think I do."

"And would it be attached to the hand of our shooter?"

"I might need a little time on that."

Silence. Then Masters' voice came back over the line.

"Let me ask you this. You think there might be anyone else in danger here?"

I watched as a black Town Car pulled to the curb and Bennett Davis stepped out. Alone.

"I don't think so," I said.

"You got a week. After that, I bring you in and start squeezing. And I do mean squeezing. You got me, Kelly?"

"Yeah. Remember what I said. Keep a lid on this until I come in."

"Have you heard anything from me yet?"

"No."

"All right then. Get the fuck moving on whatever it is you do."

Masters hung up just as Bennett Davis approached, hand extended.

"Michael. Thanks for meeting me on such short notice."

I shook Bennett's hand. He sat down beside me.

"How are you doing?" he said.

"Fine, Bennett. How about you?"

"Been better, Michael. Been better. The Nicole thing."

"Doesn't really go away, does it?"

Bennett shrugged as the weight of so much grief settled about his shoulders.

"Not really. There is something, however, I need to talk to you about."

"I'm listening," I said.

"We've known each other a long time, right?"

I nodded.

"Here's the thing. I think I might have a problem."

"What kind of problem?" I said.

"Vince Rodriguez worked a homicide two nights ago. A man named Daniel Pollard. Shot twice in the chest. Ballistics came back this morning. The gun they used was the same one that killed Gibbons. A nine."

I took a beat and then responded.

"And you want what from me?"

Bennett rubbed his chin and ran his tongue over his lower lip, like he was thirsty but not sure for what.

"I know you're working that case, Michael. I think you might know where I could find the gun."

"You think so?"

"Whoever killed this guy Pollard also killed Gibbons. We can prove that now."

"I know all about your case, Bennett. In fact, I was there when Rodriguez found Daniel Pollard's body."

Bennett Davis peeled back his lips and pushed out a smile. If I hadn't known it already, I did now. My friend was dirty. The only question left for me: Was he also dangerous?

"Maybe we should go back downtown and get on the record," Bennett suggested.

"Maybe. But hear me out first."

I pulled a plastic bag from my pocket. Inside it was the cigar butt I had taken from under Pollard's recliner.

"You see this? It's a Macanudo."

I gestured to the row of cigars stacked inside the assistant DA's overcoat.

"Your brand, Bennett. Yesterday I took a piece of this down to Gentech. Ever hear of them?"

Bennett shook his head.

"I hadn't either. Rachel Swenson recommended them. A private DNA lab out of Joliet. Can work fast if they have to. They isolated saliva and are certain they can get a DNA profile. Takes three days to get back preliminary results. I'm guessing it comes back to you."

Bennett Davis got up to go. I kept talking.

"Go on, Bennett. But you're going to hear the rest. Either here or in a press conference."

He stopped.

"Pollard was your mistake," I said. "The first and biggest one you ever made."

Davis sat down again, pulled out one of his cigars, and rolled it between his fingers. Otherwise, he just listened.

"You didn't appear in any of the press because you were just too green. But you worked the Grime case. Donovan remembers you."

I pulled out the photo of Grime's prosecution team.

"That's you in the background. How old were you? Twenty-six?"

"Twenty-five."

"Fucking prodigy. None of us ever knew."

"I hated that goddamn photo," Davis said. "Only one taken of all of us, you know."

"You cut the deal with Pollard. I had to plow through five boxes' worth of paperwork, but I found it. You gave Pollard the immunity deal for his testimony."

"He was key to the case," Davis said. "Closest thing we had to an eyewitness."

"What you didn't realize was, your eyewitness was actually Grime's accomplice."

Davis looked up and opened his mouth but I kept going.

"Don't bother, Bennett. Not here, anyway. The cigar will put you inside Pollard's house. But there's more."

I pulled out a sheaf of papers.

"These are records from the Department of Corrections."

I put them on the bench, but Davis ignored them.

"Probably didn't seem like a lot, but the visits add up over the years. Twenty-three separate contacts with Grime on death row. Haven't talked to him yet. Once we do, he'll give you up."

Bennett Davis smiled. A grin of the damned.

"When did Grime first blackmail you?" I said.

Davis struck a match. Let the sulphur burn off and then drew the flame up into his cigar. The smoke came out thick, smooth, and cool, casting a veil, if only for a moment, between us. Then the smoke was gone and Bennett Davis came clean.

"Fuck it, Kelly. You're just too goddamn good. No, I take that back. You're not good. Just lucky. Sure, Grime contacted me. It was a year after he was convicted. Had one hell of a time with it. Taunted me. Told me I was a stupid punk. Gave immunity to a serial killer. 'How would that play in Peoria?' Grime would

always say, and laugh like a motherfucker. Pollard was his pro-
tégé. His surrogate animal on the street. And there was nothing I
could do about it."

"When was the first time?"

"Remington was first. At least the first that I knew of."

"And you fixed it?"

Davis looked past me and nodded.

"Damn straight I fixed it. Shut up everyone who needed to be
shut up. Some of them I bought. The rest I just bluffed."

"Like Gibbons?"

"He knew nothing. After that it became easier. Most of the
victims were hookers. At least at first. Not exactly high-priority
stuff. Later on, as long as Pollard used a condom, didn't leave any
DNA behind, I was safe."

I thought about Nicole and her cold files. I thought about how
much she cared for her friend Bennett. I found myself hoping she
never knew the truth about him, even as the knife slid across her
throat.

"The years go by," Davis continued. "Just becomes part of
your life. Of course I'd heard rumors about the street file on
Remington. Maybe there was some lost evidence out there.
Some DNA. If so, it was the thing that could link Pollard to
Grime."

"And you to Pollard."

"Eventually, yeah. After I talked to you at the lockup, I figured
Gibbons was looking for the street file. Or might have already
found it."

I thought about Gibbons' landlady looking to make a
buck. One hundred thousand volts, busting open her heart at
the seams.

"So you sent Pollard to see the landlady," I said.

"Again, beyond my control. Pollard was simply supposed to see if she had the file and grab it."

"And that brings us to Nicole," I said. "You talked to her at the Drake. She told you about Elaine Remington's shirt."

"I couldn't let her get a look at that evidence."

"I know, Bennett. At first I thought you might have sent Pollard, but then I thought again. There was no other key card used that night, which meant Nicole herself let the killer into the lab. Had to be someone she knew. Had to be someone she trusted. Had to be you, Bennett."

A well-manicured woman came close by walking her bichon frise. She gave us both a proper Gold Coast smile and moved past. Davis dropped the cigar between his legs.

"It could have been different with us," he said. "But that was her decision. Long time ago. This thing here. I had no choice. None at all."

Davis looked up and spread his hands.

"To be honest, if I thought I could get away with it, I'd do it again. Not easy to live with, but hell, there it is."

I counted to ten and kept my hand away from the gun at my hip. Maybe that was what Bennett wanted. Law and order's express lane. He wasn't going to get it. Not from me. Not today.

"You know what I wonder about?" I said. "The endgame. Where would it have ended? How would you ever get out?"

My former friend just shrugged.

"Grime gets executed."

"And then?"

"And then Daniel Pollard disappears and the problem goes away."

"Maybe call in a guy like Joey Palermo for that?"

"You know about that, too. Interesting."

Bennett Davis smiled. The last one I ever saw.

"So what happens now?" he said.

"Walk with me," I said.

The two of us got up and walked.

"You have another cigar?"

Davis cut one for me and I lit up.

"You remember *The Godfather Part Two*, final scene?" I said.

"Yeah."

"Michael sends Tom Hagen to see Frankie Pentangeli in the pen."

"Yeah, Michael. I remember."

"Frankie asks Tom the same question. Tom tells Frankie what the Romans did when their plot against the emperor failed."

"They went into a hot bath and opened up their veins."

"That's exactly what they did, Bennett. Now, your family is never going to get taken care of and I don't think you deserve a hot bath. But an Italian friend of mine did give me a bit of advice I'll pass along."

Then I told Davis about Vinnie DeLuca and his cannolis and about eating a bullet in a bathroom stall.

"DNA comes back in three days, Bennett. Then the state takes over. And whoever else decides they need you dead."

"Fair enough," Davis said.

"More than you deserve."

Davis sat back down on a bench.

"Going to sit here awhile and think."

"Good-bye, Bennett."

I began to walk away. Twenty yards later Davis' voice plucked at my shoulder.

"One more thing, Michael."

I stopped but didn't turn.

"You never answered my question about the nine millimeter," he said. "Same gun used on Gibbons and Pollard. One thing I know for sure. It wasn't me."

I began walking again. Bennett Davis didn't deserve an answer. Of all the things he told me, however, the last rang truest of all.

CHAPTER 54

My plane landed in Tulsa at a little after seven o'clock in the morning. I had turned my cell off for the flight and powered it on as I drove across the Kansas state line.

The DNA on Daniel Pollard had been a rush job but worth it. A full match to Elaine Remington's rape, the Grime unknowns, and the tears left on Miriam Hope's bedsheets. Diane would break the story sometime tomorrow. There would be a press conference after that. Then it would go national, and it would be crazy. For a minute I thought about Bennett Davis. He'd either eat a bullet or be in cuffs by tomorrow night. I was rooting for the former. My cell phone buzzed. It was Rodriguez.

"Hey."

"You getting there?" he said.

"I think so."

"You sure we don't want to call in any help on this?"

"I got it. You worry about Davis."

"Speaking of which, we got the rest of the CODIS run back on Pollard."

"Let me guess," I said. "Nothing."

"How did you know?"

"Bennett told me Pollard took Grime's advice, started using a condom years ago."

"How many do you think he did?"

"Lots," I said.

"Just rape?" Rodriguez said.

I thought about Miriam Hope, talking to Daniel Pollard, trying to save her life, trying to buy a few more decades of loneliness.

"He knifed the old man in the apartment," I said. "I wouldn't be surprised if there were more."

"Yeah, the cold squad is going through its old homicides. See if they can find any more links."

"Has anyone talked to Grime yet?"

"Not yet. We'll pay him a visit this week."

"Okay. I should be back in Chicago tonight."

"No chances on this, Kelly. You want me to move here, you call."

I flipped my phone shut and passed a sign that read SEDAN, KANSAS, 22 MILES. I pulled over and took out the street file. Elaine's hospital admittance form had a name for next of kin but no address. My client herself had provided the town the night I picked her up in Cal City. Not a lot, but enough to give it a try.

I pulled in to Sedan a half hour later. It wasn't much of a town, a mile's worth of boarded-up storefronts and a load of dust. At the end of the strip was a five-story hotel that took up an entire block. It was boarded up, too. I cruised right through, didn't see a soul.

Down the road a bit, I pulled up behind a couple of cowboy hats. They were sitting in a pickup, waiting for the light to change. Problem was, there was no light. Just two country roads, intersecting in a field of mud. I got out of my car and walked forward.

"Looks nicer in the summer. When it's full of corn."

The driver spoke without turning his head. I realized their pickup was actually stopped, turned off. No key in the ignition.

"You guys just hang out here?" I said.

The passenger leaned across and grinned. He had the blackened remnants of teeth at either end of his smile and a carbuncle on his nose worthy of its own reality show. In one hand, he held a Starbucks mug. In the other, a pretty good-looking Danish.

"Coffee right here. Most mornings. You're welcome to join us."

I wondered just where the Sedan Starbucks might be located. I had a different agenda, however, and stuck to it. The locals knew exactly where I needed to go.

Five minutes later I pulled down a dirt road and stopped in front of a farmhouse that creaked in the wind. A barn stood off to one side. A few chickens scratched out the morning in between.

I slammed the car door shut. A horse whinnied. Whoever was inside heard me because a curtain twitched and then the front door opened. The man inside was on the shaded side of fifty-five. His face was long, lean, and tough. The eyes were brown, color of the fields he had spent a lifetime working. The man took me in at a glance and moved a toothpick from one side of his mouth to the other.

"Help you, sir?"

He spoke without suspicion but with authority. He didn't know me and didn't expect any trouble. If it came, though, he had no problem with that, either.

"Name is Michael Kelly. I'm a detective. From Chicago."

Something moved between us and the man inside the farmhouse flinched.

"My name is Sam Becker. I expect you know that."

I nodded. He opened the door.

"Well, come on in."

He walked back toward a solitary light, burning inside a lamp on a kitchen table. Beside the lamp were the remnants of a solitary breakfast. Strip steak with some eggs and coffee. Sam Becker cleared away the half-eaten meal, and I took a seat.

"Coffee?"

He poured me a cup and gave himself a refill. Becker motioned to the living room. I followed as he settled himself in a leather chair. I took the couch. There wasn't much between us but a low table. The walls were bare here. Much like the kitchen. In the corner of a bookshelf I caught a wink of gold in a panel of light. The line of a picture frame. Becker followed my eye and took down the photo.

"If you're from Chicago, I expect this is what you're here about. Almost ten years now. Hell of a long time."

He put the picture down and I picked it up. I figured the photo to be from a high school class picture. Sixteen, maybe seventeen. At any age she was blond and beautiful. At any age, however, she wasn't the woman I knew as Elaine Remington.

"This is Elaine, Sam? The girl who was attacked?"

Becker's face hardened around the eyes.

"She was murdered, mister. Attacked on the day before Christmas 1997. Died a few weeks later."

I kept my gaze steady and didn't wait to reply.

"I have to ask you something, Sam. Maybe it's going to get me thrown out of here. And maybe you'll want to take a shot at me. I respect that. But I got a job to do, and I'm going to have to ask. Did you ever see her body?"

"What the hell . . ."

I held out a hand.

"Let me explain. Most of the records in Chicago have disappeared. The ones we do have show a woman was attacked but not killed. I guess it's unclear exactly what did happen to her. That's why I'm asking."

Sam got up and went to a china cabinet along a far wall. He returned with a brown file folder, a bit tattered and bound up with string. He opened it up, and out fell the pieces of a young life. First I saw a couple of newspaper clips on the attack. Local stuff that had slipped under the radar of my research. Then the police reports I had already seen. Finally a coroner's report I had never seen. From a hospital in Chautaugua County, Kansas. Elaine Remington had died from multiple stab wounds to the chest and back. The date of death was three weeks after the attack. There was also a picture of the corpse. It was the girl in the photo, a Y-incision across her chest and down her belly.

"That's how you find out she's dead, Mr. Kelly. And that's why you keep it around. Just in case you start to not remember. You open up the folder and there it is."

I lit a cigarette and offered one to Becker. He accepted and we filled up our mugs. The file lay between us.

"Sam, I got a problem."

Sam wasn't dumb and had already figured that. So I told him about John Gibbons and the letter. I told him about my client, my own personal blonde named Elaine Remington. Then I told him about the nine millimeter that had killed, by my count, at least five people. Sam took it in and then stood up.

"Come with me."

The farmer walked stiffly up the stairs, down a dark hallway, and into what was once a young girl's bedroom. He pulled a year-book off the shelf. The spine read SEDAN HIGH, CLASS OF '94. Becker flipped through the book, back and forth, as if he were confused. I waited for him to settle. The farmer found the page he wanted and put the book down on the bed.

"That what you're looking for?"

The girl was a cheerleader and president of the Theater Club. Voted "Most Likely to Be a Drama Queen," she wanted most of all "to live among the lights." The girl was smiling and easily the best-looking face on her page. The girl was my client. The woman I knew as Elaine Remington.

"Her real name is Mary Beth. Two years younger than Elaine."

We were sitting on the bed now. The farmer and myself. The yearbook between us. I ran a finger across the picture. Sam told me the story.

"Remington was their mom's maiden name. She was found dead at the bottom of a well. Face beat in with a hammer, but everyone said she just took a bad step. Mary Beth was ten when her mom died. Now that might sound bad to you, Mr. Kelly, but that was actually the best part of this girl's life. When she turned twelve, her daddy took her. In the barn back there. Wanted to be the first one in. Before he rented her out to his friends, you see."

Sam stopped for a moment. Then he started up again.

"Mary Beth ran away. Came to Oklahoma. I was a bachelor. Thought I was hard to find but damned if my niece didn't track me down. Turns out her father came back for seconds one night. She was ready this time and fought like hell. He cut her with a knife. To this day she carries a scar right under her collarbone. Mary Beth returned the favor. Put a pitchfork through his neck. The old man bled out right there. Then Mary Beth patched herself up and ran to me.

"I fixed it with the sheriff and Mary Beth came back to Sedan. I came with her, did my best to be a father. Over time, I found out the old man had done the same thing to each of his girls when they turned twelve. Coming-of-age sort of thing."

Now Sam unwrapped a sad grin and shifted in his seat.

"Truth be told, as a dad, I was a better uncle. Elaine couldn't wait to cut loose. Can't blame her. Not a lot of good memories. She took off right after high school. Got herself as far as Chicago. Then she got herself dead. Mary Beth followed suit. Sounds like you know a lot more about her than I do. The oldest is the only one who ever kept in touch. Nothing more than a Christmas card, but it means something when you get old."

"The oldest?"

"Yeah, the third girl. First one to be taken by Daddy. She was the smartest. Probably the toughest. And that's saying a bit. Put herself through a local college. Got her degree and got out of Sedan. Determined to overcome. Never asked for a goddamn thing."

Becker pulled out another yearbook, this one from 1988.

"Here she is. Editor of the school newspaper."

I took a look at the oldest of the three sisters. Five minutes later I was on the road, headed back to the airport, both high school yearbooks on the passenger seat next to me.

CHAPTER 55

The loneliness came again, just past three in the morning. I had pushed against it. All the way back from Kansas and into the night. But it came anyway. Loneliness and I were familiar, if not entirely comfortable, traveling companions. I knew its tricks, the ebb and flow. The pains that crept up on you during the day, the moments of memory that paid their respects only at night.

As I got older, I got stronger. Not immune. Just able to weather the storm. Let loneliness run its course, take its pound of flesh, and be gone. I knew there was an end. I knew because I had already walked it. Loneliness knew it, too. And that gave me all the advantage.

Still, sometimes, occasionally, even at age thirty-five, I felt the bite a bit more than I should, more than I ever thought I would again.

This was one of those nights. And the problem was, I didn't know why. If it was Diane, I didn't know it straight off. If it wasn't Diane, then it was just a feeling without a target. And that was frightening. A mutation of the disease I had never encountered before. Perhaps one without a cure.

The phone rang on cue. I glanced at the caller ID. Wonderful invention that, sort of a dress rehearsal sometimes for life's little sorrows. I let it ring again, pretended to fumble a bit with the receiver, then picked it up.

"Hello."

She was quiet but awake. Like she had been sitting up somewhere. Maybe not with whiskey, but still awake.

"Sleeping, Michael?"

"Half and half," I said.

I wondered where she was. Her bedroom. A cell phone. The lobby downstairs. Then I picked it up. Steel on steel. An El train going by my window and coming out of the phone. All at once.

"I guess my cover is blown," she said.

"Where are you?"

"Three blocks from your house. A greasy spoon on Lincoln called the Golden Apple. You know it?"

I figured she wasn't inviting herself up. I figured it was probably for the best.

"Yeah, I know it. Give me five."

I threw on a pair of pants and a sweatshirt, grabbed my wallet, keys, and a Smith & Wesson revolver. After Kansas I was taking nothing for granted.

SHE WAS IN THE LAST BOOTH on the left. I ordered a coffee as I walked through the door. It was on the table by the time I got there. It was that kind of place.

"Where you been all day?" Diane said.

She was wearing jeans and a black sweater, with her hair pulled back, and eyeglasses with black frames. At first glance she seemed put together. Red lipstick, pale makeup. Flawless. When she smiled, however, I saw the first crack. A single line in her cheek, running up under her eye. After the first one, they became easy to spot. And just as hard to ignore.

"Just working some background," I said and ducked my eyes toward the table. She had a cup of tea and a copy of Aeschylus' *Agamemnon* lying flat by her elbow.

"The *Agamemnon*," I said.

"Figured I'd give it a try."

She said it with a pause. The testing kind, the kind you throw out in a relationship to see which way the wind is blowing. I tried to give nothing back, which, in and of itself, was probably everything.

"At three in the morning, that's some interesting reading," I said. "Part of a trilogy, you know."

"So you told me. *The Oresteia.*"

"What's your take?"

"I think it's all about revenge," she said. "How about you?"

I nodded and felt the blood thicken in my ears.

"Tisiphone, Megaera, and Alecto."

"Who are they?"

"Names of the Furies. They show up at the end of the second play. Three sisters who hunt down any perceived wrongdoers. They torture and kill without mercy."

Diane stirred her tea and took a tiny sip.

"Something wrong with that?" she said.

I picked up the *Agamemnon* and leafed through its pages.

"The Furies pursued their revenge through time. Through generations. Killed people with little or no connection to the crime. The Greeks portrayed them with snakes in their hair and blood dripping from their eyes. They were mad. All three of them."

"But they were effective?"

"You think so?"

"Why not? Eye for an eye and all that stuff."

I slid the *Agamemnon* back across the table.

"In the third play, the Furies are sated. They help to establish the Athenian court system. The blood feuds end, and the first court of law is established."

"Maybe I'll skip that part," she said. "Sounds a little boring."

"You like a good blood feud, huh?"

"Who doesn't? Besides, it's just a play."

Diane slid Aeschylus off the table and into a bag by her side. Then she smiled.

"Enough ancient history. Tell me about your sleuthing today. Background on who? For what?"

I went on for the next half hour, giving her every detail of my day, none of it about Kansas, all of it a tissue of lies. Diane nodded, sipped her tea, ordered, then ate some chocolate cake. She smiled at the end and didn't believe a word of it.

"Well, I better head home," she said.

"Big day?"

"I tape an interview with Rodriguez in the morning. They arrest Bennett Davis and we get our exclusive tomorrow night. Your name is still out of all this, right?"

I nodded.

"By the way," she said, "have you told your client about any of this?"

"Not yet."

"Her face is going to be out there sooner or later, you know."

"That's what you figure?"

"It won't come from my station. But absolutely, she'll eventually be out there."

I got up to go. Diane got up with me.

"I'll see Elaine tomorrow and catch her up," I said. "I also told Rodriguez I'd meet him at your newsroom after the interview. Tie up a few loose ends."

"Sounds great. We should wrap around noon."

She leaned in and kissed me. Red lips, long, strong, and hungry. Like she meant it. Or at least wanted to.

"Thanks for the story," she whispered. "You saved me and I won't forget it."

Then she turned and walked out of the diner. I went home and opened up a copy of the *Agamemnon*, found the line where Clytemnestra lures her husband into the bath and waits as he is knifed to death.

Ἔστιν Θάλασσα-τίς δέ νιν κατασβέσει;

I spoke the line aloud, rolling the syllables across my tongue as Aeschylus had intended. I wondered just how many Clytemnestras lurked in my life, where were the knives, and most important, who would wind up dead in whose tub.

CHAPTER 56

The next morning I woke up fast. I ran five miles along the lakefront, showered, dressed, and grabbed some coffee at Intelligentsia. By eleven I was headed downtown and on my cell.

"Yeah."

Detective Masters was his usual effusive self.

"Vince Rodriguez is going to be on the news tonight," I said. "Here's what you need to know."

I told him about Grime, Pollard, and Bennett Davis. I have always fancied myself something of a connoisseur when it came to the exotic curse. Masters, however, fashioned a string of expletives that would make a deaf man blush.

"You done?" I said.

"Yeah."

"So Vince does his thing today. He arrests Davis and lays out the Grime angle. Tomorrow belongs to you."

Then I told him about Kansas, how it fit together. It took a while. When I finished, there was nothing.

"Masters," I said. "You there?"

"When can I move?"

"I'm walking into Channel 6 right now. I'll call you when I'm finished."

My crossword girl was not at the front desk. Just as well. Not the best day for her. I met Rodriguez in a small office just off the main set. He had a cup of coffee and was trying to avoid talking to one of Diane's many producers.

"Give us a second," he said.

The producer looked daggers at me but left the room.

"Bennett Davis just called," Vince said. "He's going to turn himself in. Wants to make a deal. One o'clock. Down at head-quarters."

"Did he give you any of the details?"

"No, but he will. After a while, you can tell. This one has got no fight left. Besides, we got preliminary DNA back on the cigar."

"A match?"

Rodriguez nodded and continued.

"Looks like it. Davis also had a message for you. Said *The Godfather* plays a lot easier than real life. Said to tell you he just didn't have the stomach for it."

I thought about the reality of swallowing a bullet. Couldn't think of anything much worse. Then I thought about a life of hard time. For a former prosecutor. In a big-time lockup.

"He won't last long in prison, will he?"

Rodriguez shrugged.

"He'll be gang-raped first thing. Then it depends on what he can do for them on the inside. Or if he can pay. If I had to bet, I'd say he doesn't make it."

Diane stuck her head in the door. She looked tight around the eyes.

"Vince," I said. "Can you give us a minute here?"

"Sure," Rodriguez replied. "I have to head out anyway."

He turned to Diane.

"I didn't get a chance to tell you, but Bennett Davis is turning himself in downtown. Within the hour."

"We need to get a crew on it," Diane said. Rodriguez shook his head.

"Can't do it. Davis is coming in alone. I already agreed to no press. Tell you what. Once we have him in custody, I'll ask if he wants to talk to you. Maybe you get lucky again."

"Thanks," Diane said, and the detective left.

"You got plenty," I said. "More than plenty."

Diane moved closer, slid her arms around my shoulders, and laid her head flat against my chest.

"Yeah," she sighed. "I just get greedy. Want it all."

"I know."

"How you doing, baby? Seemed a little strange last night."

"A lot on my mind."

I pulled the yearbooks from Sedan out of a gym bag I'd brought with me and put them on the desk beside us.

"Sam Becker says hello."

She looked at the yearbooks and then up at me. I could see a small pulse beat in the hollow of her throat.

"So now you know," she said.

"Tell me about it."

"I'm sure Sam did."

"He told me what he knew. I figure there's more."

She walked across the room and closed the door. Then she sat down in front of the yearbooks, drew her palms together, and held her hands to her lips. For a moment she said nothing. She opened up to her sister's high school picture, then her own. Traced each with her finger. I had done the same thing a day earlier and not gotten any of the answers I wanted either.

" 'Know thyself.' Sounds simple, doesn't it?"

"Not really," I said.

"No. Not at all. I think I do love you, Kelly."

"Please."

"I almost told you last night. Almost told you everything."

Now there was a shiver in her voice, and that spooked me more than anything.

"Almost," I said. "I'm thinking you got lots of almosts for people. A lifetime full of them. Ultimately, however, there is just you. Nothing else."

The smile she turned out was a lonely thing, one that asked for no quarter and offered precious little in the way of regret.

"I love my sisters, Kelly. I love both of them."

I thought about Diane and her two sisters. Thought about their father and the day each girl turned twelve. Pieces of me ached for Diane. Maybe even a little for myself. Those were the pieces I had to ignore.

"How did it start?" I said.

"You know it all. It's right here."

She closed the yearbooks and pushed them back my way.

"It was June fourteenth, three years after Elaine was murdered. I was out of college, working as a reporter in Flint, Michigan. You remember I told you about Flint."

She tried to touch my hand but I stayed put. Diane shrugged and kept talking.

"Mary Beth called from San Francisco, told me she had killed a man. Then she told me why. I flew out there. There really wasn't much to do. Mary Beth had stalked him, met him at a bar, and gone back to a hotel room. She had shot him, made it look like a robbery, and walked away."

"Just like that?"

"Just like that. She was giddy about the whole thing."

"That was the first? The EMT?"

Diane nodded.

"Yes. She showed me her list of names."

"All the people who dropped the ball on Elaine's case?"

"Yes. All the people who didn't do their job. All the people who could give a fuck about our sister cut up and left for dead by some animal."

"And you covered for her?"

"I did what I had to do."

Diane raised her chin and looked at me. Maybe she was practicing for a jury. I couldn't be sure.

"Don't judge me, Kelly. Don't you fucking dare. Not after Nicole."

In three words, I glimpsed the final threads of her deceit. Woven through the fabric of so many lives. In a moment, I saw it all and wanted none of it.

"You targeted me from the beginning," I said. "You knew about me and Nicole, and you targeted me."

"Your finest hour, Kelly. That man raped your friend and you took him down. At fourteen years old, that took some guts."

"You figured I might be an easy touch for some vigilante justice," I said. "You sent me the street file. Not Mulberry. You and Mary Beth."

"Gibbons told Mary Beth you were the best detective he ever saw work. Gibbons was right. You were perfect, Kelly."

"Yeah. Perfect. Easy to manipulate, probably blackmail if it ever came to that. After Mary Beth killed Gibbons, I'd be the guy to help you find Elaine's rapist."

"Gibbons was the hook," Diane conceded. "Mary Beth wanted to kill him straight out, like the others. I knew we needed him. To get to you. So Mary Beth approached him as Elaine. He had only seen our sister once, when she was half-dead, and bought it straightaway. After that we just waited. Once Gibbons got you involved, Mary Beth gave him what he deserved."

I nodded and thought about my old partner. He'd fall for the damsel in distress. Ten times out of ten.

"And my prints at Gibbons' murder?"

"I slipped into your office a week before Mary Beth shot Gibbons. The door was open, Kelly. Not a good idea."

"You took a slug from the jar on my desk."

"I took a handful. Mary Beth dropped a casing at the scene. Just enough to get you tied in to the case a little deeper. Call it a backup plan."

"And that night on the strip," I said. "You put Mary Beth out there."

"I called her after you dropped me off. Told her Pollard was probably our guy. She wanted to do some homework. Hunt him a little bit, I guess you'd say."

Diane held her hands out, chin up.

"Bottom line, Kelly, it all worked. You took us to Pollard. If I could have shot him myself, I would have. Hell, for a while I thought Rodriguez was going to do it. As it is, you should feel damn good."

For Diane Lindsay, life was as simple as that. Death, even easier.

"And now?" I said. "Where is she?"

Diane's face stiffened into the look of a true believer. I got a bad feeling and wondered if I should have moved on Mary Beth sooner.

"She's going to be arrested," I said. "The gun matches up. The timeline will match up. It's done. Masters already has the warrant. Where is she?"

Diane shifted her gaze, looked out the window as she spoke.

"She has one more to do."

I grabbed her by the shoulder and pulled her around.

"Who?"

Diane closed her eyes and smiled.

"You know who's left, Kelly. Don't ruin it by pretending you don't."

On some level she might have even been right. Another thing I didn't need to think about. I flipped open my phone and punched in Rodriguez.

"Grab Davis," I said. "Now."

CHAPTER 57

The police took Diane Lindsay out of Channel 6 News in cuffs. Like wolves who eat their young, Diane's camera crew and producers hovered around every moment of the arrest, capturing their former colleague's humiliation for the late show. Maybe they'd get a raise.

I didn't get a final word with Diane like they do in the movies. Didn't really want one. Whatever there had been between us was gone. Left for dead in an ugly tangle, somewhere on the road from Kansas to Chicago. Instead, I got in my car and headed toward the Loop.

"Did she tell you where they were going?"

It was Rodriguez on the phone. He had crashed Davis' office after my call and found nothing. The assistant DA had somehow slipped out of the County Building.

"She told me nothing," I said. "Except Mary Beth was going to take him."

"I'm surprised she didn't shoot him on the spot."

"Yeah."

I was driving south on Michigan Avenue, crossed over the river, and into the Loop.

"I'm two minutes out," I said. "Where are you?"

"We're cordoning off three blocks all around and searching County, floor by floor."

"I'll be right there. Tell your guys to let me through."

I hung up and cruised south past Randolph. I was about to turn right when I caught a flash of blond walking up the steps into Millennium Park. I knew that flash of blond, and I especially knew the soon-to-be-dead attorney walking close beside her.

I double-parked in front of the Cultural Center. A meter maid was yelling at me a half-block away. Then I pulled my gun, and she started yelling louder. I thought that was a good thing and crossed over Michigan into Millennium.

As I got to the top of the steps I saw Mary Beth. She was weaving her way through a sparse midday crowd, around the outdoor skating rink, and up toward a sculpture Chicagoans call the "Bean." Its official name is *Cloudgate,* but it looks like a big aluminum bean and reflects everything around it in a 360-degree, sort of fish-eye effect. As I approached, a man and woman came out one side of the Bean. He wore overalls, a Carhartt jacket, and Packers hat. She wore a Green Bay jacket open to a sweatshirt that said FUCK WITH ME AND YOU FUCK WITH THE WHOLE TRAILER PARK.

I waited until the Packer fans had safely made their way to a hot dog stand. Then I walked into the Bean, gun stuffed into my pocket. Mary Beth and Davis were standing to one side. I stood opposite them. In between us was the kindergarten class, twenty-five strong, from Presentation Grammar School. Mary Beth caught my eye in the reflection from the roof of the Bean. The fish-eye effect made it hard to judge exactly how far away she was. It seemed like miles. I was beginning to work my way through the kids when a hand tugged at my sleeve.

"Excuse me, sir."

It was a woman, early thirties. Presentation's kindergarten teacher, no doubt.

"Could you take a picture for us?"

I shoved the gun deeper into my pocket, smiled, and grabbed the camera. Mary Beth pushed Bennett Davis toward the outer edge of the Bean. I noticed a dark smear of blood where Davis had leaned up against the aluminum. Then they were gone. I snapped the picture and moved after them.

Mary Beth headed past a yellow-slickered security guard riding one of those Segway people movers and looking awfully important. Then she ducked left into the Pritzker Pavilion, the Millennium's outdoor music venue. I followed her to the deserted stage and stopped about ten feet away. Mary Beth dumped Bennett Davis against a riser and stepped back.

"So you figured it all out, Mr. Detective. Bravo."

Mary Beth was talking to me but kept her eyes and gun trained on Davis. He had been shot once in the side and looked over at me, scared. He mouthed some words but nothing came out. I had my gun out now and drew down.

"Drop the gun, Mary Beth. This is over."

"Not yet, sir. Not just yet."

Davis crouched against the riser, covered the side of his head, and tried to make himself smaller. At a range of five feet, it wasn't working.

"Diane's in custody, Mary Beth. Whatever you get, she gets. If nothing else, do your sister a favor and drop the gun."

"Already killed five, Kelly. How much better is it going to get for Diane?"

"I don't know. But you pull the trigger here and it's a death case."

"Really?"

"Really."

Mary Beth lowered her weapon an inch or so and looked over. As she was looking at me, she fired once into Davis' chest.

"Oops," she said.

Bennett Davis crumpled to the ground. I moved forward. Davis was still alive, wheezing blood through his mouth. I reached for Mary Beth's gun. She fired again just as I got to her. The second shot did its job.

Mary Beth collapsed at a right angle to Davis. The round took off most of the back of her head. Her face, however, was still perfect. Lips full, mouth parted, and just a hint of a smile. Just like Frankie Pentangeli in *The Godfather Part II*, Mary Beth had done what she thought was the right thing. Too bad there was no family left to look after.

I closed my former client's eyes just as a hand clawed at my ankle. It was Davis. From the sound of things he had been shot in a lung and was drowning in his own blood. Not a pleasant way to go. His hand gripped my calf, and he raised his head to make eye contact. In his case, a final sort of eye contact. I thought of a Saturday morning and Nicole, under the Chicago El tracks. I removed his hand and walked out from under the pavilion. I wasn't sure exactly what Bennett Davis deserved, but this was probably as good as it was going to get.

I found my way over to the concession stand, stepped inside, and ordered a red-hot drug through the garden. The Packer fans stood nearby, eating a double order of cheese fries. Each.

"So is Favre all done?" I said.

They smiled and started in. I listened and nodded. In the distance I could hear sirens. That would be Rodriguez, followed probably by Masters. They'd get here soon enough.

CHAPTER 58

It was the day before Thanksgiving. The city was quiet. The holiday season beckoned.

I picked up Rodriguez downtown. We headed west on Madison. It had been more than a week since we last spoke. He had a lot to take care of. I had even more to avoid.

"Getting any better?" I said.

The media storm was finally settling. *Dateline* and *60 Minutes* had taken their shots, done their profiles. As had *The New York Times*, *Newsweek*, CNN, and the BBC.

Most of the coverage centered on Grime, Pollard, and Bennett Davis. Some of it focused on two sisters from Kansas and a third they needed to avenge. *Time* magazine ran a piece on the hidden costs of sexual assault. I actually read that one.

None of the coverage mentioned me. For that, I had Rodriguez and Masters to thank.

"Only two media requests this morning," Rodriguez said. "This afternoon I'm on live with Australia. They love Grime Down Under. By the way, your buddy Masters says to go fuck yourself."

"Tell him I said hello back."

"Yeah. Eventually we're going to have to get a statement from you. Probably take a couple of days."

"After the holidays?"

"Sure. By the way, she asked to see you."

Diane Lindsay had been in custody for nine days and tried to kill herself three times. The first was in a holding area after she discovered her sister had shot herself. Used a shard of Plexiglas to open up one of her wrists. Lost two pints of blood and took twenty-three stitches. The two times after that were in the hospital. Pills.

My brother had taught me all I needed to know. About prisons. About suicide. About how appealing death could sometimes seem.

"Think I'll take a pass," I said.

Rodriguez shifted in the seat beside me, pulled his gun off his belt, and laid it on the floor next to his feet.

"Probably a good idea. They got her pretty doped up. Pull in and let's get coffee."

We stopped at a Dunkin' Donuts and loaded up. Back in the car, I continued west, back to my childhood. Rodriguez sipped at his coffee and did a little reminiscing of his own.

"Let me ask you something, Kelly."

"Go for it."

"What put you onto the sisters? I mean, why did you ever think of taking it back to Kansas?"

I shrugged. Like any cold case, the answer was in the evidence box. You just had to know where to look.

"All those people in the street file," I said. "All dead. All, save Belmont, shot with a nine. Just didn't seem right. Then I remembered that first morning Mary Beth showed up at my house. With a nine. Another coincidence."

"That makes two."

"Yes, indeed. I talked to a detective out of Phoenix. Guy named Reynolds. He ran down a hotel receipt for me. From 2002."

"The year the ER nurse was shot?"

"A Ms. Remington, no first name, paid cash for her room, two miles and one day removed from the Gleason murder. That's when I knew I had to go to Kansas."

"How about Diane?"

"Didn't see that coming," I said. "Not even a bit."

We let it sit for a minute. Listened to my tires rumble over Chicago asphalt.

"Funniest thing about the whole case," I said. "Diane gave me the street file. Gave me the lead that hung her and her sister."

"Stupid," Rodriguez said.

I nodded and thought maybe not. Maybe it was the sort of ending she needed.

We drove west on Grand, took a right on Central, drove a bit farther, and parked. Most of the neighborhood was gone, replaced by strip malls and weeds. The rail yards, however, were still there. As were the train tracks beyond.

"This where you grew up?" Rodriguez said.

"About a mile east of here. This is the spot, though."

We walked around to the back of the car and popped the trunk.

"By the way," Rodriguez said, "your boy Grime is a little nervous these days."

"How so?"

"Seems the protection money that kept him alive has dried up."

"It came from Bennett?"

"Probably. The boys at Menard make it sixty-forty Grime

never sees the needle. Side bets are coming in on how he gets it. I got ten down on a shank to the stomach."

Rodriguez smiled, the one you earn from all the nights of closing eyelids and zipping up body bags. From calling parents and listening to the pain.

"Anyway, that piece of shit is done," Rodriguez said. He pulled a shovel out of the trunk and handed it to me.

"Been meaning to ask you something," I said.

"Go ahead."

I leaned on my shovel. Rodriguez gave me a look as he pulled out the other spade.

"Think you would have done it?" I said.

"Done what?"

"Pollard."

"Taken him out?"

"That's it."

The detective slammed the trunk shut and put his foot up on a fender.

"Don't know, Kelly. I mean, I would have liked to, but things never really got that far."

"Bullshit."

"Excuse me?"

"Bullshit. The night in the industrial park. You could have done it. You thought about it. Thought about it hard."

"You think so?"

"Yeah, but I knew you wouldn't pull the plug. Not in your nature."

I moved off the car, stepped over a chain strung across the road, and started to walk across the rail yards. Rodriguez was a beat behind.

"Nicole told me a little bit about this," he said. "How you're always talking about people's nature, their way of being. She said you got it from Cicero or something."

"Changing the subject, Detective."

"Maybe I am. Maybe I'm not. You're right. I thought about it. Came close."

I looked over.

"But you stopped," I said.

"There's a line there, you know. Once you step across . . ."

"You live with it."

"Guess I couldn't do that. Still, there's a part of me that wanted it, still wants it. Still thinks about it."

"That's okay," I said.

"My nature?"

"Yeah."

The detective shrugged and took a look around.

"You know where we are here?"

I thought back to that day twenty-one years ago. Fourteen years old, standing in the swamp. Seeing Nicole. Watching her rape. My first look at a live sexual act. Feeling the first hint of darkness. Surrendering to it.

"Some things have changed," I said. "But I got an idea."

I headed out across some old tracks and through the back of the yards, to an alley I had cruised three times in the past week. Best I could figure, this was the front end of the old swamp. Twenty yards behind it was the south end of the tracks. I remembered those. In between sat a depressed bit of ground, littered with beer bottles, condoms, and a couple of bums sleeping it off. The back end of the swamp. The end where Nicole was assaulted, where I might very well have killed a man.

"You realize we aren't too likely to find anything," Rodriguez said.

I hefted my shovel, picked out a spot, and started to dig.

"I know," I said.

"But you have to try."

"I guess so."

"Let me ask you something," Rodriguez said. "What if we do find something?"

I stopped. There wasn't much of a hole yet, but I could feel the pulse in my temple, the first flush of blood through my arms and shoulders. It was work. It made me feel better.

"We call Homicide," I said.

"Yeah?"

"Yeah."

Rodriguez put a foot to his shovel and turned over a layer of dirt that was more like dust. A fragment of ancient text ran through my head:

Μία ψυχὴ δύο σώμασιν

It was Aristotle's take on friendship:

"One soul living in two bodies."

I dug into the hard ground again and waited for the sweat. Either way, my friend Nicole and I would get our answers. Either way, it was going to be okay.

AUTHOR'S NOTE

This is my first novel. As such, it is as much the product of good fortune and the beneficence of others as it is anything I might have done. The following people contributed their time, talent, and heart to this novel. I cannot thank them enough.

Jerry Cleaver, Deborah Epstein, Laura Fleury, Anna Gardner, David Gernert, Garnett Kilberg-Cohen, Erinn Hartman, Bill Kurtis, Leslie Levine, Tania Lindsay, Diane Little, Maria Massey, Dan Mendez, Megan Murphy, Mary Frances O'Connor, Jordan Pavlin, Pegeen Quinn, Roel Robles, John Sviokla Jr., John Sviokla III, and Patrick Sviokla.

Special thanks to my mom and dad for sacrificing so much, and to my five sisters and brother for being the best people I know.

Most of the action in this novel takes place in Chicago. I have, whenever possible, tried to be faithful to the city's geography, buildings, and institutions. Where necessary, however, I have intentionally taken certain liberties to fit the needs of the story. My apologies in advance to those of you who live in the world's greatest city and know full well where all the imperfections lie.

Michael Harvey is a journalist, documentary producer, and writer, as well as the co-creator and executive producer of the television series *Cold Case Files*. Mr. Harvey's work has won many national and international awards, as well as an Academy Award nomination. Mr. Harvey earned a law degree from Duke University, a master's degree in journalism from Northwestern University, and a bachelor's degree in classical languages from Holy Cross College.